THE MOHANDAS

THE MOHANDAS

YARON LEVITE

ROMANO
WORLD

First Published in the UK and the USA in 2025
By Romano World LTD.

ISBN: 979-8-9992955-1-4

For more information contact: office@levite.co.il

Any who saves one soul, it is as if they saved an entire world.

Sanhedrin, Book 4

He who saves a life shall be as if he had given life to all mankind.

Quran—5:32

PART ONE

Chapter 1

Hashim

"It's a direct hit!"

A loud cheer filled the Gaza Elementary School courtyard, with a few *Allahu Akbar*s, Allah is Great, thrown in for good measure. An armed youth released a short burst of automatic fire into the air, and, much to his joy, a few more armed men joined in, firing happy potshots toward the bright-blue sky. Backs were slapped, and smiling faces were everywhere. The team sent by HQ had achieved its mission—within a few minutes, they had orchestrated a seemingly spontaneous street demonstration that had spilled into the dusty, orange-peel-strewn schoolyard. Over one hundred men in green headbands and black *keffiyeh* scarves had arrived to celebrate the latest freedom warrior to emerge from the ranks of the militia. This time, the new hero was one of those <u>almost</u> mythical creatures; a member of an elite, awe-inspiring group, those whom the people call Mohandas. Engineer.

Green Hamas flags flapped loudly in the breeze that drifted up from the nearby beach and into the schoolyard. The sizable crowd of men jostled forward in an effort to get closer to the spokesman who was standing on a scratched, green school table; rifle pointing at the sky on one shoulder, megaphone strapped to the other. His voice echoed and bounced off the gray cement walls of the surrounding blocks of flats.

"The Mohandas was guided by Allah himself to reinvent the Qassam rocket. The Mohandas, in his wisdom, has single-handedly created a weapon with greater accuracy than ever before. People of Gaza, once again the Zionists are reminded that we, not them, will be the masters of our lands. Soon we will be returning to our homes in Jaffa, in Haifa. Allah bless the people of Gaza, the Hamas party, and the Mohandas."

The crowd let out a great cheer.

Hashim Abu Tir smiled dazedly as hands grabbed him and lifted him onto dancing shoulders. His faux-leather jacket ripped at the sleeve, and he felt as if he would find himself flung off his bearers' shoulders at any moment, but he didn't mind. His green eyes shone radiantly with joy. Nothing could penetrate the strange numbness he felt from being the center of attention.

Beneath him he could see his father, who was laughing with proud tears in his eyes.

It felt unreal and wonderful.

In the back of his mind, he knew he had done nothing close to what the spokesman was announcing. He had not created a new weapon and was far from being a true Mohandas. At eighteen, he'd only just left high school behind and was still years from becoming a real engineer.

But Hamas was desperate to present a win to the people of the Gaza Strip, and his minor feat of amateur engineering was all they had to work with. So, as he sat on the shoulders of his fellow Gaza citizens, surrounded by hundreds of worshipping men, he allowed himself to ride the wave of adulation. Even if it made no sense.

Chapter 2

Hashim

Two months earlier Hashim had graduated from high school, and he was already missing his studies. Without the right connections and with no family ties to Hamas, all three Gaza universities had turned his application down. Weeks passed and he could find no opening for a job. The waitlist for construction work in Israel stretched into years. So he and his best friend, Ahmed, filled their days at the beach—kicking around a soccer ball and body-surfing, their skin tanning to a dark shade of brown. As they lay on the warm, golden sand, the two young men passed the time by dreaming grand plans for the future. Ahmed swore he'd make it big and move to Dubai. Hashim's eyes glowed as he described how he would become Palestine's first Nobel Prize-winning physicist.

Fall came, and Hashim could already sense the Mediterranean waters beginning to cool. One sunny afternoon, as he and Ahmed lay on their towels after a swim in the water, they were approached by a stranger who somehow knew their names.

"Do we know you, sir?" Ahmed asked, suspicious.

The stranger lowered his voice. "I am a recruiter for the movement."

Hashim's eyes widened as the man continued.

We have been watching you. You are both smart young men, high school graduates. You speak Arabic and also Hebrew. Come, run errands for Hamas. Help us decimate the Jews." The man looked at Hashim. "And you, Hashim—how would you like a chance to strike back at the animals who murdered your sister?"

Hashim looked at the man as if stung. There was nothing he wanted more than a chance to strike back at those who had killed his favorite person in the entire world. Na'ima.

Despite his friend Ahmed's protests, the next day Hashim found himself standing outside the small café the recruiter had named, his heart pounding with a mix of fear and anticipation. One short interview later, he was in—a foot soldier in a war he'd never dreamed he'd get to fight.

When Hashim's family learned of his new position, his usually courteous and soft-spoken father was fiercely against it. As the two sat on a set of red, embroidered cushions in the lounge, he lectured his son in an angry, yet subdued voice, making sure the neighbors couldn't hear. Hamas had ears everywhere.

"What in Allah's name did you think you were doing when you joined those murderers?" Hashim's father whispered furiously. "Do you really believe them, you donkey? And the missiles these animals are firing into Israel—for every one they fire, the Israelis fire ten. The movement is slowly killing us, and these are the people you want to work for?"

"They aren't animals." Hashim cried out indignantly, his voice rising a little louder than his father's. "They give us back our honor. And soon, in-sha-Allah, they will give us back our land. Our dignity."

"Dignity?" His father looked toward the door to ensure no one was listening. "Do you know that your mother had to wait for two hours today just to buy flour and rice? They allotted us one small bag of each for the whole week. Your precious Hamas is starving us all while they get fat on international aid."

Hashim shook his head vehemently as he leaned forward to his father. "They will pay me well, Father. We need the money, and we need more food. I can go to the black market and buy meat, or maybe a chicken. Anyway, it is the Israeli blockade that is making us all hungry."

"You are a fool." His father hissed. "There was no blockade until your insane friends began shooting their missiles."

Hashim stood up from the flat cushion, a replacement for the comfortable couch that had been sold a few days earlier. Towering over his seated father, for the first time in his life, he dared to raise his voice at him.

"I'm a fool? So whose bomb was it that murdered Na'ima? Was that Hamas's fault, too?"

Hashim watched the air escape his father's body, as if he had just punched him in the gut. When his father spoke again, his voice was strained.

"We have lost our daughter; I don't think I will survive losing our only son, too."

Standing over his father, tears collected in the corners of Hashim's eyes. He wanted to take a step forward, to apologize a million times, to sit back down and hug him. But instead he yanked his gaze away and left the room, leaving behind the unspoken realization that something in the house had changed forever.

* * *

Hashim was surprised at how swiftly he was called into action. Each day, he would hear of yet another military leader neutralized by Israeli Air Force drones, and he advanced swiftly up the organizational ladder. Within a few short weeks of his recruitment, he was running supplies and materials between the border smugglers and the underground missile factories that were scattered around Gaza City. Once the factories completed the missiles, it was Hashim's task to alert the *mujahideen*, those brave commando warriors who would then risk their lives to fire the rockets into Israel.

He was okay dealing with the Egyptian smugglers, fat-bellied businessmen who made their living scuttling under the border via long, haphazardly constructed tunnels. He loved meeting the commando soldiers—the brave few who openly dared to fire back at the Zionist war machine, their names praised in every home. But he hated every second in the missile factories. As he shared his experiences with Ahmed, he counted four reasons.

The first, he explained, was pretty obvious: being in an underground missile factory meant that missiles were being manufactured there. Homemade missiles with homemade explosives and homemade missile technicians. A terrible recipe for instant self-annihilation.

The second reason he hated the factories was that being so deep underground was a musty and claustrophobic experience. A thousand air shafts could not make him forget the tons of sand that weighed upon the paper-thin cement ceiling. He worried that at any moment the ceiling would come crashing down, burying him alive.

The third reason was the Israeli Air Force. High in the Gaza skies, remote-controlled drones patrolled the city, searching for those hard-to-find factories. And once found, Allah save any man or child in or around them.

But the fourth and main reason Hashim hated his runs to the factories was the technicians who designed and produced the missiles.

They made his skin crawl.

Twelve months from now, they would all be dead: buried alive, burned by accident, or blown up by the Israelis. Twelve months was the average lifespan of a missile maker, and they all knew it. Yet they went about their business, smiling, softly humming old Arab tunes.

Their nonchalance gave him nightmares. He tried to spend as much time as possible with the rocket commandos, and as little time as possible underground with the rocket makers.

During his initial runs, there was nothing in those labs that could spark anything but horror. He delivered the materials sent by HQ and hastily escaped the narrow cell without so much as a goodbye.

That was until the day he saw his first Qassam rocket.

Chapter 3

Hashim

It should have been a normal delivery run. The plan was to go in, deliver his package and leave within seconds.

Hashim slowly climbed down into the dark, sandy cavern. As his eyes grew accustomed to the darkness, the first thing he saw was an array of newly constructed rockets laid out neatly: a row of giant, six-foot-long, cigar-shaped tubes. Curious, he moved closer to have a look, noticing that the stabilizing fins of the rockets were simple metal squares; pieces of a stolen Israeli street sign that had been soldered on roughly. The rules of aerodynamics were still fresh in his mind from school physics lessons. Diagrams and equations seemed to materialize in the air, as though his old textbooks were open right in front of him. Hashim saw that by a simple streamlining of the fins and by filing down the thick, black soldering material, the rocket would become more efficient. It was so obvious to him that he couldn't help but blurt it out.

"I think you're not cutting the fins in the most aerodynamically efficient design."

The two rocket makers in the underground factory stopped their work and stared at him. Hashim didn't know their real names, but during the last few runs he had chosen nicknames for them: Toenails and Big-Eye. They were bent over a wooden workbench, their stained hands steady as they measured some kind of powder on an ancient-looking gem scale.

"The fins. They aren't efficient." Hashim repeated. "They're not streamlined."

The sudden stillness was deafening. Light from a single quartz lamp cast crazy shadows onto the yellowed cement walls of the chamber. Hashim could hear little bits of sand sliding through the cracks in the ceiling above and falling to the ground.

"Did you bring the potassium nitrate?" asked Toenails, ignoring Hashim's discovery.

Hashim pulled out a two-kilo bag of fertilizer from his bag and placed it on the table. The fertilizer had been smuggled into the strip that morning, and the contents, mixed with sugar, would fuel the rocket on its lethal trajectory.

The technicians looked at the bag wearily.

"Is this all of it?" asked Big-Eye, his overlarge left eye scanning Hashim creepily.

"You can't carry a heavier load?" added Toenails.

"Of course I can carry a heavier load!" said Hashim, bridling under the criticism, "But this is all that HQ has for you. This is all they gave me."

The two technicians shrugged their shoulders at each other as if to say, "What weaklings we recruit these days…"

"I can carry fifty bags like that one if I need to," added Hashim.

Toenails snorted.

Usually the meekest and quietest of boys, now Hashim got truly *majnoon*. He could feel his cheeks burning, eels slithered in the pit of his stomach, and—most annoying of all—he felt his eyes sting as tears began to form. It was a horribly embarrassing physical trait that Hashim could not control. He teared easily. He had been teased as a crybaby most of his life, and he knew what was coming.

But then he noticed the fins again and vented his frustration on the missiles.

"And I tell you—the fins you made are all wrong. They are square, and your messy soldering adds aerodynamic drag. There's no way you'll ever hit anything. They won't fly straight." Without thinking or asking permission, Hashim picked up a red crayon and ruler and slowly traced a simple design on one of the rockets.

The two technicians stared.

13

"There. That's how they should look. Then they'd fly properly." Hashim stared defiantly at the two technicians.

"Looks very professional..." said an impressed Toenails.

"*Aiwaaaaa...*" answered Big-Eye. "Indeed. Where did you learn this?"

"It is simple aerodynamics..." answered Hashim, his cheeks still flushed, "We did aerodynamics in tenth grade. It's basic material, I can't believe you didn't know this..."

"You can't believe we didn't know this?" Toenails advanced on Hashim, his thick, long toenails pointed at him like an array of missiles awaiting launch. "Who do you think you are? Do you think that if these rockets hit or miss, it's because of the fin shapes? Do you think it is all up to your physics? It is Allah who decides where the rocket will land. It is Allah who will exterminate the Zionists; it is Allah who will take us back to our homeland, and he will choose when and where his wrath will land."

"You conceited little droplet of dung!" added Big-Eye, just in case Hashim had missed the point.

Suddenly, the two technicians froze in front of him. It took a few more seconds before Hashim could hear the strange rustling sound from above. A rumbling that

14

grew louder and louder. *That's it*, he panicked. *The tunnel is collapsing. I'm going to die.*

But instead of the ceiling collapsing, two filthy boots appeared through the entrance hole above their heads, followed by the wearer, a short, dust-covered man who landed with a light jump onto the tunnel floor.

"*As-salaamu 'alaykum*!" The man squinted as his bright blue eyes adjusted to the light of the dull quartz lamp.

"And peace on you too, our hero!" answered the two technicians, their voices dripping with almost worshipful admiration. Hashim stared the short man and instantly recognized him as none other than the great Gaza warrior, Assad Ibn Samir, a.k.a. the Lion. Hashim could not believe his luck. One of Israel's most wanted terrorists, The Lion was a ruthless fighter and a massively popular local idol. His face stared out from posters plastered across Gaza City, larger than life. Seeing him up close in real life, Hashim realized those heroic images had never revealed just how surprisingly short the Lion was. Still, he couldn't stop staring at the man.

"Who is this?" asked the Lion, his clear blue eyes scanning Hashim.

"Delivery boy," answered Toenails.

The Lion flashed a movie-star grin at the three of them. "Are the rockets ready? We need to launch immediately."

"The rockets are ready," confirmed Big-Eye, his smile revealing a collection of brown, nicotine-stained teeth.

The Lion walked up to the workbench and studied the completed rockets. "What are these markings?" he asked, pointing at Hashim's work.

"The 'Mohandas' here has decided that the fins aren't efficient enough," chuckled Toenails. "So, he decided to design us a new rocket." Big-Eye sniggered along with him.

Hashim felt his face burning with embarrassment. He realized that Palestinian technicians had been constructing missiles like these for over a decade; they must know what they were doing. He had just embarrassed himself in front of none other than the great Lion.

The Lion looked closer at Hashim's fin design. He gently lifted one of the thirty-pound rockets and studied it from various angles. After a few seconds, he put the rocket back on the table.

"He's right. This design does look better. Closer in shape to the Russian Grads." Toenails and Big-Eye stared at the Lion, who turned to Hashim.

"Where did you learn engineering?"

"Me? I didn't. I'm not really a Mohandas; I graduated from high school five months ago. I chose physics as my main subject. That's all…"

"Let me ask you something. What do you say we should do with the fins? What would a real Mohandas do?"

Hashim thought for a few seconds before answering.

"What you should do is redesign half of the fins of the rockets, keeping the others square as a control. For a test case. Sort of…" Hashim felt his face redden again. He was sure the Lion was taunting him.

"Excellent!" The Lion beamed at him. "Then we could see which design is better by launching them side by side." He turned to the technicians. "We'll test this young man's hypothesis. But we don't have time. Cut one rocket like he tells you to. We leave in thirty minutes, so get moving!"

"We?" asked Hashim in a whisper.

"Sure, Mohandas, don't you want to test your case?"

Chapter 4

Hashim

Hashim sat in the shell of a burned-out trailer home as they waited for the Israeli drone to complete its patrol and fly back to base. He remembered this place from his childhood. His father used to do business with the Israelis who once lived here, before they had pulled out of Gaza. The place had once been the prosperous Israeli settlement of Dugit. But the Israelis had razed the whole settlement to the ground as they withdrew. A pile of torn clothes lay in the corner of the burned mobile home, fragments of newspaper littered the floor, and a single dusty sneaker hung from the steel prongs just above his head, shoelaces swaying in the light breeze. It was an uncomfortable hiding place, but Hashim was too excited to care. He wondered if the other three team members could hear his heart beating in his rib cage.

The unmanned drone buzzed above the small team's heads, filling the air with an annoying, frightening buzz that was hated by the whole strip.

Folks in the Gaza Strip had given these crafts the onomatopoeic nickname *Zannana*, i.e. nagging wife. Their humming kept Hashim inside his home, wrecked plans for outings with his friends, canceled family events. He knew that although the plane couldn't be spotted in the dark, pre-dawn sky, it could see everything, everywhere. It could see through walls and around corners. It could splash a laser marker for the missile units, waiting just a few hundred meters away over the border. The droning hum spelled death—especially if you were lying in a stretch of yellow, powdery sand, about to launch a missile in the early hours of the morning.

The rocket team waited in silence, not daring to move, smoke, or talk until HQ transmitted the all-clear via text message. Then they would have less than five minutes to deploy, launch, and vanish.

The Lion's second-in-command held the mission-critical cellphone. The phone was a brand-new burner and would be discarded right after mission execution. It rang at exactly 5:15 AM, five minutes after the hum had faded away to the north.

Mr. Second-in-Command smiled at the Lion. "All clear, let's go!"

The team members lifted their black *keffiyehs* to cover their faces and began their run into the open field. Hashim stumbled after them in the darkness, desperately holding on to one of the five missiles they were about to launch.

His breath turned into sticky vapor behind the *keffiyeh,* and sweat streamed down his face as he strained to keep up with the commandos. Sand poured into his sockless moccasins, and more than once the heavy missile he carried grazed the ground with a sickening scrape. He prayed to Allah as he ran, asking him to prevent humiliation. He would prefer dying; he would prefer going up in a ball of smoke rather than humiliating himself in front of the commandos.

"Set up," the Lion whispered. Hashim watched as the team spread crude metal tracks on tripods and aimed them eastward. Once the launchers were ready, they swiftly mounted the missiles onto the tracks. Five missiles, one with Hashim's design. He tried his best not to stand in the way of the Lion, who paced up and down the array, expertly feeling for the simple, homemade electrical connections on each missile, checking for faults that could delay or even abort the launch. One man screwed in the small warheads. Another member of the team was the *imam,* a robed priest whose sole responsibility was to bless the rockets and request heavenly guidance on their hopefully lethal trajectory. In less than two minutes, they had set up the rockets and connected them to an old car battery. The sky in the east was already radiating yellow on gray as the sun prepared to rise. Looking around him, Hashim began to see shapes in the darkness, black-on-black silhouettes of gaunt trees and burned houses. He felt exposed. Any moment now, and they would be spotted.

"Mohandas."

Hashim spun around.

"Yes?"

The Lion was holding the end of an electric wire in his hands.

"Here. I give you the honor."

Hashim had no idea what he was expected to do.

The Lion chuckled. "Come here and connect this cable to the battery."

He took the dust-covered wire from the Lion and, with an embarrassingly shaking hand, connected it to the negative pole of the car battery. Nothing happened. Hashim feared that the launch was a failure, but after a few excruciatingly long seconds, to his intense relief, all five missiles began belching thick white smoke, revving up for their moment of glory. Then, with a hazy whoosh, they were all airborne.

One missile took off in jerky spirals, let out a small ball of smoke, stalled in slow motion, and then slid back toward the ground, landing with a metallic clang a few hundred yards away. Three missiles shot into the morning air, traveling in crazy twists and turns, like a bunch of demented balloons set free.

But one missile flew straight and true, heading for Israel.

Hashim's missile.

* * *

"Mohandas! Mohandas! Mohandas!"

Hashim was embarrassed to hear the cries of the Hamas PR units as their trucks crawled through the streets of Gaza City, loudspeakers strapped to their roofs. It was unbelievable that they were rallying crowds for a victory demonstration that was caused by him. His victory.

News of the successful launch spread fast. Hundreds of Hamas fighters had answered the call, their faces covered with black balaclavas and green headbands. He was paraded down the main street, held high above his joyous comrades.

"Mohandas! Mohandas! Mohandas!" The excited militiamen chanted as armed officials shot joyfully toward the sky.

Hashim's father wiped the tears that streamed from his eyes with a roll of paper. As he watched his eldest son being celebrated by the throng, his opposition to Hamas had melted away.

"*Ya ibni*, my boy, I always knew that you would be special. I always said to your mother that you would stand apart and rise above the world. I was right. You are a hero, *ya ibni*. Look—hundreds have come to celebrate you. If only your sister were here."

Hashim was surprised to hear his father speak with such pride and respect. Speechless, he could only smile back.

The noise was deafening. Hashim's father waved, the crowd sang, holy men fought for attention by chanting as loudly as they could, and one smartphone camera clicked away, shooting high-definition snaps that within hours would star in a PowerPoint presentation titled *The New Mohandas*, screened before officers of the Israeli Defense Force, Gaza Division intelligence.

Chapter 5

Roni

"The city of Sedera is a marvel of Israeli settlement. A jewel in the desert, a breathtaking oasis that invites one and all to enjoy the clean air, vibrant nightlife, and the friendly smiles of a warm community."

Or so the printed pamphlets stacked by the municipality door claimed. It was, of course, like all tourism pamphlets ever printed: total marketing nonsense.

No matter where you looked, there was nothing marvelous about the small settlement of Sedera. It was dusty, featureless, and the nightlife scene, optimistically labeled "vibrant" by the pamphlet, was, in fact, nonexistent.

But these facts did not seem to deter Mayor Sami Uliel as he dictated this vision to his eldest son, Roni, who sat at the family laptop in the study, translating his father's flowery Hebrew prose into English. Roni's mother, Nava, refilled their coffee mugs as Mayor

Uliel enthusiastically painted an optimistic portrait of the township's future. When Roni raised a surprised eyebrow at the mayor's eloquent description of Sedera's dilapidated factories as a "regional commercial zone celebrating high-tech excellence and local startup entrepreneurship," his father was quick to lecture him on the ways of the world.

"The ability to raise funds is a God-given gift, my boy. There are four busloads of New Day Crusaders coming to our area, and I want them—and their money—here." Sami tapped the desk for emphasis.

"New Day Crusaders?" Roni frowned.

"A right-wing American evangelist organization that wants to invest in Israel and help the Jewish state protect itself. Absolutely crazy. Every single one of them." Sami shook his head. "Here, look at this." Sami drew a folded pamphlet from his pocket and ironed it out on the scratched wooden worktable. The cover showed a group of men fitted in full knight's armor, swords sheathed in scabbards. It was an impressive group photo, spoiled only by the incongruous white golf shoes they wore. The group held flags printed with the image of a roaring lion under a blue star of David.

"These are real *meshugas* with a lot of money and a lot of power. And your pamphlets, Roni, are going to shift some of that money and power to us."

Roni took a slow sip from his mug as he thought about his father's words. "What will you do with the money?" He asked.

"I'm sure I'll find plenty of opportunities to invest wisely for the benefit of our fine community," answered Mayor Uliel. He turned to leave the room before his son could ask any other delicate questions.

"What opportunities? Where will the money go? You can't just take it for yourself."

Mayor Uliel stopped short by the door, took a long breath, and turned to his son.

"Roni, you are a *gever*, a grown man. There is a lesson here that I want you to learn. It is written in the Bible that "To everything there is a season, and a time to every purpose under the heaven." And the reason these Crusader people are coming on this day," Uliel smiled warmly at his boy, "is because it's time for us to make a killing."

* * *

The missile attack siren began its heart-stopping wail just as Roni arrived at the municipality building. He dropped the bundle of freshly printed pamphlets at the entrance and sprinted down the main corridor toward the small concrete bomb shelter that was situated just behind the mayor's office.

When the Palestinians had begun to fire rockets at Sedera, like most of the citizens he had felt an almost crippling fear. He was so scared that it took all the courage he had not to freeze but to run as fast as possible to the nearest bomb shelter.

As time passed and the Palestinian bombings grew more frequent, another feeling began to emerge. It was a feeling that grew stronger in his mind and heart until it replaced the fear. It was a feeling of vicious hatred for the people who lived on the other side of the border—a nation that caused him, his family, and his friends to live in fear during the days and to dread the nights. As a child, Roni had sung joyful songs of hope for a better future with their neighbors. Today, he felt nothing but contempt for the naïve voices that still clung to the illusion of peace.

The siren was still wailing as Roni opened the heavy, steel bomb-shelter door. A social worker and an assistant of his father's were already there, along with two mothers who had come to sign their children up for the next school year. The small group stood together in the impossibly small space and talked nervously while waiting for the all-clear.

"Good to see you, Roni. Weekend leave for *Shabbat*?" asked the tall, thin social worker.

"So, they let you out early this week," his father's assistant smiled.

"Tell your mother that I will return the pressure cooker today. I'll drop by this evening," said one mother, a worried woman clutching her work bag to her chest.

Roni smiled politely at the small group as he squeezed in, closed the door, and locked the handle. He tried dialing his girlfriend, Vicky, but there was no reception in the concrete-walled shelter. One year younger than Roni, she was probably sitting inside the fortified school hall with the rest of her class. He hoped she was okay. The frequent missile attacks were beginning to give her nightmares, and she needed her rest. In two months' time, she was supposed to take her final exams.

Roni put down his phone and looked around him. The scene felt surreal: A group of adults standing squashed into this little space, making small talk while missiles were speeding toward them.

"There! Did you hear?"

"That wasn't an explosion."

"I think it was. Must have landed far from here."

"I didn't hear anything."

"Can we go out now?"

"I don't know. Wait for the all-clear."

"I'm telling you, I heard something. Didn't you hear it?"

"Did you hear whose house was hit yesterday? It was poor old—"

And then the shelter shook as if a giant earthquake had erupted. For a few seconds, the small group was too shocked to speak. Then everyone spoke at once.

"*Shmah Yisrael*. Oh God. Please keep us safe."

"Are we hit? Are we hit?"

"It hit our building!"

"Oh, Father in Heaven, please protect us."

"It hit us?"

"Oh God! I'm scared!"

Roni opened the steel door and looked out. There was no sign of damage. He turned to the group in the shelter. "We're okay. The rocket must have landed close by, but we're okay."

No one was listening.

He ran down the corridor and looked out of the main entrance. A giant dust mushroom was still hovering above the Tulip kindergarten, just across the road. Roni stood and stared, transfixed by the destruction that lay in front of him. The all-clear siren sounded, and within minutes his father arrived, flanked by his aide and various municipal workers. Roni hastened to join the small entourage as they made their way into the main playground.

Then, they all stopped dead.

A homemade Qassam missile lay wedged into the concrete slab that was the kindergarten's playground. The small warhead had exploded upon impact, and although the amount of explosive inside it had not been enough to cause much destruction, the explosion itself had been loud enough to shatter every plate of glass in the adjacent building. The smell of burned rubber filled the air, and light, dusty smoke was rising from the impact zone. A million tiny shards of glass covered the seesaws and swings. As Roni stepped closer to the empty, metal tube, his shoes crushing broken glass, he noticed that the rocket fins were manufactured from a stolen Israeli road sign—the city name Be'er Sheva was printed on one of the fins. Roni's face reddened as fury coursed through his body.

They steal the metal from us, then use it to bomb our children. We should never have left Gaza. We should have stayed there and killed them one by one until there was nothing left but sand and rocks.

Within minutes, military and police officials began streaming into the small playground. A worried mother dressed in a black business suit entered the gates at a run, pushed her way through the ever-growing throng, and with a cry of relief picked up her loved one from the group of children who were waiting in the reinforced concrete shelter. Well-trained since the age of three, the children had all reached the bomb shelter in time. No one was injured, but every single child was crying in unabated terror. The teachers were crying too.

Still furious, Roni watched as the mother tried to calm her screaming child. The explosion had been so close and so loud that the mother had to shout her soothing words to the temporarily deaf five-year-old. Roni turned back to his father, who had just finished a phone call.

"The Crusaders have canceled."

"They're not coming?" Roni had to shout above the din.

His father spat viciously at the still-smoking rocket. "Coming? No, they are five minutes away, but they heard about the missile strike, and they've dropped us from the program. They're going to visit some stinking kibbutz instead. And those cowards call themselves Crusaders. Richard the Lionheart must be spinning in his grave." Sami stormed away from the site, muttering, "This is going to cost us millions."

Roni watched the crowd of sweaty policemen and soldiers who smiled at his father with admiration. The heat was unbearable, the atmosphere charged, the young children's screams earsplitting—but the rescue teams were all smiling. He could never understand why, but these men loved his father exactly for moments like this. They had no idea who Richard the Lionheart was, but they loved Uliel. He was one of them, even if he was quick-tempered and sometimes grossly politically incorrect. If only Roni could have inherited some of the charisma that his father seemed to radiate. Although Roni stood a full head taller, he felt as if he were forever hidden in his father's shadow.

He turned and crossed the road back to the municipality building. A dry wind flapped the pamphlets stacked by the door. He plucked one out of the bundle and read it, secretly proud of his work. It was the first time he had seen anything of his own printed out. And in English, too. Damn the Palestinians. No one else would ever read it; it would be many months before a new group of investors would consider visiting Sedera. Meanwhile, the pamphlets would sit at the entrance and gradually bleach in the sun until the white nylon string binding the bundle snapped and the hot easterly wind blew a storm of false promises away from Sedera, over the electronically fenced border, through the rubble-filled alleys of Gaza, and into the Mediterranean Sea.

Chapter 6

Roni

The weekend ended too soon and Sunday arrived—the start of a new working week in Israel. By seven a.m. Roni was ready, dressed in his olive-green uniform with his M16 rifle slung over his shoulder. It was time to head back to base. Thanks to his father's clout, Roni had been posted to the famous paratrooper brigade, Gaza Division.

"*Mazal tov*, my boy." Nava Uliel walked into the kitchen, beaming at her son. "One year ago today, you enlisted."

Roni's father, seated at the kitchen table, looked up from his phone. "Today? A full year? Why didn't anyone remind me?" He stood up and beamed at his son. "One whole year gone already. I can't believe it. I remember driving you to boot camp as if it were last month. I promise you that the next two years will fly, now that you're done with your basic training. This is where it starts getting interesting."

Even though division headquarters was just a short drive from home, Roni got to see his parents and friends very little. He hated Sunday mornings. It was hard to leave the warm comfort of home: the scent of coffee and scrambled eggs, his own room with the soft bed. He re-checked himself in the mirror hanging by the entrance door. His dress uniform was crisply ironed, face clean-shaven, boots polished to a shine. His black hair was cropped at regulation length, and his light-green eyes shone in sharp contrast to his dark, olive-colored skin. He slipped the red paratrooper beret through the loop on his shoulder epaulet, and even though it was unnecessary, he gave his silver para-wings a quick polish with his fingers. He loved the gleaming metal wings. Parachuting school had been two weeks of adrenaline-filled action, and it was disappointing to think that the parachuting had been mostly symbolic. He knew he would not get to parachute again during his service.

He kissed his mother goodbye, picked up the heavy kitbag, and set off with his father on the brief journey to his second home, Gaza Division HQ.

* * *

He had just arrived at Gaza HQ and joined his squad-mates in their quarters when a sharp chorus of notification sounds filled the room. Nine screens flashed in unison with an incoming text message.

> *Team 2: intel room, 0900 hours.*

The team exchanged quick glances, their usual banter replaced by a quiet hum of anticipation.

"What do you think this is?" one of Roni's squad-mates asked, leaning against a bunk.

"We've never been called to the intel room before," another said, voice low but eager.

Roni felt his pulse quicken. After all the training and waiting, were they finally being called to action? He didn't say it out loud, but he could see the same question in the eyes of his team.

By ten minutes to nine the entire squad had made their way to the intel room. The shutters in the room had been closed in an effort to block out the light. An undersized air conditioner was waging a losing battle against the summer heat, and Roni could feel patches of sweat spreading around his armpits, but in his excitement, he didn't mind. At precisely 09:00, the door opened. Harsh sunlight spilled into the room, momentarily blinding them as Lieutenant Roy, Roni's direct commander, strode in. His presence commanded the room into silence.

"Good morning. I have just received a message from command, so listen up. Gaza City. We're going in. Team 2 is about to see some action."

The words hung in the air like an electric charge. Roni felt a jolt of excitement, and it took a great effort to maintain a look of cool, professional detachment.

Lieutenant Roy connected a thumb drive to a dusty projector. An image of a young Palestinian appeared on the wall. "This is the new Mohandas. We've received intel that Hashim Abu Tir is the engineer responsible for the upgrade of the Qassam missiles. This man has brought the war ten clicks north, which means that an extra two-hundred-thousand Israelis can owe him the pleasure of having their homes officially within missile range. In the next few hours, we will personally thank him on their behalf ..." His punchline hit home, and the nine young soldiers enjoyed a hearty chuckle.

"We will be participating in an extraction operation. Now—even though commandos will do the extraction, and we are only covering the extraction, I want to remind you all that *we are covering the extraction*. Which means it is our job to make sure nothing happens to the boys going in. We keep the area clean—no civilians, no bad guys. Is that understood?"

The faulty air-conditioning unit whirred and wheezed semi-cold air into the room. One of the many maps tacked to the cork boards was flapping lazily in the wind. But Roni didn't notice. Even though Roy was less than two years older, he spoke with a tone of cynicism and war-weariness that was just so… cool. Roni especially liked the little dramatic touch of saying "extraction" three times in one sentence. He then noticed that Igor, the team's sharpshooter, was looking at him, squinting slightly.

"Is it just me, or are the Mohandas and Uliel long-lost twin brothers? I knew he reminded me of someone." For a moment, there was silence—and then the room erupted in laughter. The other team members' eyes flicked between Roni and the projected image. Roni chuckled with them, though he personally couldn't see any similarity to the grainy image on the wall.

"*Yalla*—time to go." Lieutenant Roy wrapped up the briefing. "Check and double-check your kits. Seal and soundproof water bottles, and make sure you don't have anything that makes a noise or reflects light. Transport should be here any minute."

Chapter 7

Hashim

Hashim's greatest surprise was the number of marriage proposals he began to receive. During the twenty-four hours following the successful rocket launch celebration, his parents had spent a full day interviewing fathers of marriage candidates. From wide-bellied, corrupt political officials to gaunt, broken men, the long procession of fathers waited in a patient line out the wooden door, each prospective parent clutching a photo of his own beautiful jewel. Hashim was excited beyond words. He had hardly spoken to a girl since he turned twelve, and here were all these grownups, eager for a chance to give him their daughters. He just had to say yes, and any of them could be his. If all went well, he could be doing *it* soon.

He quickly shook away the last thought. Allah does not permit dirty, deranged morals in his true believers. Immorality and promiscuity were the twisted ideals of the drugged, Zionist culture.

So how come he just couldn't stop thinking about *it*?

He opened a slit in the curtain of his second-story window and peered at the line of fathers leading to his house. Then his heart skipped a beat. Standing on a rooftop across the road, he could see a group of women, all looking straight back at him. The veils they wore could not hide the petite frames of the Al-Budair girls. Though they were fully robed, he could recognize every one of them. They were his childhood playmates, and they had all spent hours of fun together until Hamas's takeover of the strip. Once Hamas decreed women could no longer leave their homes without a male guardian, the carefree days they had shared came to an abrupt end.

"Mohandas!" Hashim jumped back as if stung by a bee. Then his face broke into a wide smile. It was the Lion, here in his door. The Lion grinned as he crossed the room toward the window and glanced out of the curtain slit. The Al-Budair girls were still there.

"You fox!" The Lion flashed his film-star smile at Hashim.

Then much to Hashim's surprise, the Lion turned and began rifling through his belongings, opening and closing cupboard doors. Although the Lion chatted as if all were well, there was an urgency to his movements.

"You have earned the honor of the people. Thanks to you, we have pushed the war a full twenty kilometers into enemy territory. You're a *batal*, a Gaza City hero! There's no reason you shouldn't enjoy the fruits of your victory." The Lion turned his attention to the contents of Hashim's desk.

"Victory?" stuttered a dazed Hashim. "I just helped with the rocket fins. You are the one who takes risks every day."

The Lion stopped his rummaging for a moment and smiled at Hashim.

"Do you comprehend how great Allah is? There is a plan for every one of us. I have spent the last four years fighting almost every day. And you—you spent just one hour on those fins, and look—all of Gaza's women are yours for the taking."

A few seconds passed before Hashim dared to speak.

"Do you have a woman? A wife?"

"A wife? Well, my father received many offers, but I have decided not to get married."

"Why?"

"Because my days are numbered. I am a warrior, and I will be collected by Almighty Allah soon. I would not like to go, knowing I had left behind a woman who is dependent on me."

"In-sha-Allah, that never happens," Hashim answered, as an icy shiver ran down his back. He just could not get used to people in Gaza chatting about their own demise as if it were a quick trip to the Deir al-Balah beach. The Lion turned back and began choosing clothes from Hashim's wardrobe, laying them in a neat stack on the bed.

"Why are you looking through my clothes? Are we going somewhere?"

The Lion seemed to find what he had been looking for. He picked up Hashim's school satchel and turned to face him.

"Mohandas, we need to talk."

"Yes?" Hashim's voice came out as a whisper.

"Your life is in danger. As far as the Israelis are concerned, you have now become a wanted terrorist. I have been instructed to help you pack and escort you to a safe house. We leave in five minutes."

Hashim's stomach did a quick flip-flop. He could taste vomit at the back of his throat. The skies had fallen.

"What?" Hashim whispered in disbelief.

"The Israelis are probably on their way to this house as we speak. You need to get out of here as quickly as possible. We have a compound thirty minutes away. It's not as comfortable as this room, but you'll be surrounded by the best of the best, Allah's true heroes."

"What should I take?" asked Hashim, his mind blank, his mouth dry.

"Here, I have prepared everything you will need. One set of clothes. Toothbrush. Towel. And anything you want to bring that can fit into this bag here."

"My schoolbag? It's so small..."

The Lion's voice sharpened, "Listen, Mohandas! I will not say this a second time. You are to pack this bag and leave your father's house with me in the next five minutes. The Israelis are on the way, and you and your family are in danger. Do you understand, or do I have to drag you out by your hair?"

The safe house was situated in one of the central neighborhoods of Gaza City: an old block of flats which had paint peeling off the walls in long strips, with primitive light fixtures connected illegally to the electricity pole outside. The Lion led Hashim up the stairs and into an apartment on the second-floor. A pot of cold rice sat on an electric cooker, next to a dirty Coke bottle, half filled with tap water. The Lion shepherded Hashim into a tiny room.

"You can stay here."

Hashim smiled and tried to speak, but his throat was dry. The room was tiny. Two bearded men who appeared to be in their late forties sat on mattresses covering the floor. One was reading a book of scriptures; the other was listening to a small, handheld radio transistor. Out of the tiny window, he could see the depressing view of the house across the road.

The Lion quickly introduced him to his new roommates.

"This is Abu Jihad. He is the mind behind the recent bombing of Ofakim, most wanted by the Israelis. And this is Abu Marzouk. He is the imam of the white mosque, also wanted by the Israelis. In-sha-Allah, he will return there to worship and to lead his congregation."

Hashim could feel tears stacking up, burning his eyes. Only an hour ago he was screening marriage candidates. The hero of Gaza, the famous Mohandas. And now he was trapped in a safe house that was worse than a prison cell.

"Don't worry," said the Lion. "You'll get used to being here. And I can promise you that Allah and the Movement have much work for you. We will take care of your family; they will never want for a thing. And you—make use of your time here. Learn. The people taking refuge in this building are Islam's greatest warriors. All of them are ready to die in the name of the most merciful Allah. Learn."

Learn? He wanted to learn. More than anything else. Physics. Aerodynamics. Optics. He would be happy in any field. He would make the rockets even more efficient. He would develop a better explosive. He would work out sophisticated trajectories. And one day, once the Zionists were defeated, he could become a scientist. A professor. The first Nobel Prize winner to come out of Palestine. But the helplessness that descended upon him drained all joy and gave him a moment of clarity: The road to Stockholm did not begin here. And then he could hold back no longer. The tears streamed freely down his face, carving clear trails across his dusty cheeks. The Lion gave him a soft kiss on the forehead.

"It is okay to cry, Mohandas. It is okay. It means you still have life in you. It means you still have hope."

With one last bear hug, the Lion exited, leaving him alone with the two bearded men who were now staring at him with undisguised disgust.

Chapter 8

Roni

Roni lay on the tar-covered roof. Steel prongs jutted out of the concrete wall, the house unfinished. Dawn would soon break. The moon had sunk in the west hours before, and a humming streetlamp was all that now lit the empty street. A baby started crying in an apartment across the road. Roni raised his head an inch and had a quick look. He could see a couple of his teammates on the rooftop just across and under him. They were peeping too.

"Get your head down," snarled Lieutenant Roy. Roni lowered his head into position, smiling sheepishly at his commanding officer. He leveled his eye with the optical night-vision sight on his rifle, peering into a green-hued view of the target house.

It had taken twelve hours for Gaza Division intelligence to pinpoint the location of the Mohandas. The day had dragged by with tedious briefings, then more briefings, long waiting periods and sudden, short bursts of activity. He had not slept in almost twenty-four hours, but here he was, more awake and energized than ever.

He felt a spare magazine burrowing into his stomach from one of his combat vest pockets. He shifted his weight, trying to get comfortable without making any noise. Igor—the crew's sharpshooter—had had his mother buy him a comfy pad to lie on.

Smug bastard.

Roni uncovered his watch and lit up the dials for a split second. 04:40:30. Two minutes more and the commandos would go in. His heart was racing. His mouth had a strange taste to it, metallic and sour. And he desperately needed to pee.

He looked through the night-vision scope again. The building was a regular Gaza City apartment building—a three-story, rectangular box punctured by small windows. A few gunshot holes pockmarked the ground-floor wall. There was no pavement, and only one car: a dilapidated Subaru. The only thing the block had in plenty was an endless sea of plastic bags that danced and whirled around in the breeze.

The narrow street smelled of smoke and dust and sewage and futility.

Into the silence of the night, a distant growl grew steadily. Before long, a battered Peugeot truck appeared at the intersection and laboured into the street. Roni could see four bearded men sitting in the cabin. Six more sat in the open back, all of them bearded and dressed in what seemed like shabby,

Gaza-style street clothes—black cloth trousers, white, buttoned shirts, and windbreakers. Around their necks, they wore *keffiyeh* scarves; the edges flowing in the wind.

Shit, thought Roni, willing the truck to continue down the street and out of the neighborhood. But the truck slowed down.

He glanced at Lieutenant Roy.

"It's them." Roy mouthed the words rather than whispering.

Roni glued his eyes back to the bright-green picture in his scope.

The six men in the back jumped off as the truck drove past the building. Now that he was looking for it, Roni noticed that every one of them held a close-quarters combat rifle. Within seconds, the commandos were out of sight and inside the building entrance. The truck faded away, the world melted, the city erased. There was only the building in front of him and a team of Israeli elite commandos who were about to come face to face with the wanted Mohandas. It was happening.

Chapter 9

Hashim

Hashim had not been able to sleep. The mosquitoes, the heat, the hostile roommates, the snoring, the longing for his family: these he could bear. But lying awake on the thin mattress, with no distractions and nothing to do, the memories flooded him.

Na'ima.

How he would give everything he had to bring his big sister back. He missed her so much. The house had felt so empty ever since that dreadful day when she had been in the wrong place at the wrong time. And now he was gone, too. His parents must be sick with worry.

What have I done?

It had all been so different when he was a child. His father did business with the Zionists, building houses and buildings for the Jewish settlements. They had been well-off compared to most of the Gazan population. His childhood had been filled with trips to the beach, expensive toys, and hours of fun with Na'ima.

And then the Zionists left.

He could not believe it. The Israeli government, without negotiations or peace talks, had withdrawn completely from Gaza, razing the Jewish settlements to the ground on the way out, as if they had never been there. The entire strip had rejoiced, and for the first time there was optimism in the streets about the future.

But within a year, Hamas had taken complete control of the Gaza Strip. His family's income instantly dropped to zero. There were very few construction projects in the Gaza Strip nowadays, and those few projects seemed to find their way to family members of government officials. Once an active and charismatic businessman, his father could not come to terms with unemployment. Family savings were nibbled away, and then old heirlooms began to disappear from the house. Hashim would sit and try to think of a way to help his family, to make his father proud. After all, he was eighteen, a grown man. He would lie in bed at night, dreaming about coming home with pockets full of money, money he would proudly present to his father. But where would he find money in a starving Gaza?

The mysterious man's offer at the beach had been the answer to all his needs. There would be a weekly stipend that would be enough to cover his family's basic needs; maybe he would connect with someone up high in Hamas and make a few construction tenders come his father's way. He imagined his neighbors discussing his new career with awe and respect. And if Allah truly is wonderful, maybe he would exact vengeance from those very people who had taken Na'ima from him.

And, Allah be praised, he *had* made his father proud. He had made his whole family proud. But now he felt that maybe the price he was paying was too high. Try as he might, he could not fall asleep, and by early morning he had sworn a solemn oath: come sunrise, he would leave this nightmare of a building and go home to his parents. And the Lion could go jump in the sea. The minute the sun came out, he would leave.

The Israelis beat him to it.

It started with heavy footsteps coming up the stairs. His two roommates were fast asleep, but he sat up on his mattress, curious as to who would be coming to the building so late. And so fast. He craned his neck to try to see who was approaching when, suddenly, a small cylinder rolled into the room, exploding in a blinding flash of light followed by a deafening bang.

His arms were pulled behind his back. A kick in the stomach. Rough hands frisking him. Plastic cuffs cutting into his skin. The sickening smell of gunpowder.

And then a ringing sound in his ears, a soft sound that got louder and louder as his ears began to hear again.

Someone pulled him by his hair into a standing position. A hood over his face.

I can't breathe. I can't breathe.

Dragged through the door and down the stairwell. A step missed. Stumble. Spiral out of balance. Crash into the back of someone ahead of him. Dragged back by his shirt. Punch in the back of the neck. A shock of pain doubling him forward. Rough hands pulling him straight again. And the terror. Pure terror.

Within ninety seconds of initial contact, Hashim and his two roommates were trussed up in the back of a truck, ready for delivery. Hashim could hardly breathe for the fear that had taken over his body. He knew what was about to happen. It was clear; sharp like a razor cutting through flesh.

"I am going to die."

Chapter 10

Roni

Across the street, Roni Uliel followed the drama through his night-vision scope.

This was better than TV, man. This was crazy shit. Crazy!

And even though his most important role during the whole extraction was to simply lie there and watch, waves of adrenaline coursed through his body, inducing a natural high he had never experienced before. The truck drove away with its human cargo, and minutes later peace descended on the area as if nothing had happened.

Lieutenant Roy clicked his radio five times into his team's headsets, and the excited rookies crept away from the area, their first mission in enemy territory a brilliant success. Roni couldn't wait to tell his dad about it.

Chapter 11

Assad

In a dark niche, two floors beneath the soldiers' stakeout, Assad punched the bare concrete wall. Raw, red spots spread over his knuckles, but he kept on punching, willing the pain to numb the terrible feeling of impotence rising within him.

In the four years since his recruitment, he had been living in a constant state of vigilance. He had eluded the special forces raids and unmanned aircraft. And the traitors. He had become a legend in his own time, the Lion, hailed as one of Gaza's greatest heroes. But those four years had extracted a heavy toll. Inertia and instinct for survival had been keeping him alive, but he was slowly dying inside. The only thing keeping him from succumbing to depression—the only thing that refocused him after experiencing terrible flashbacks—was his belief in Allah and, by extension, in his commanders and leaders.

But now this.

The kid had touched a raw nerve. There was something about that virginal, naïve child that spoke to him. Hashim had not been the usual recruit. He was intelligent. He could read. He had interests. His family had been respected; his sister a martyr to the cause. He was not the standard starving teenager recruit, ready to kill anyone in return for some food and a little self-respect. He had real promise.

But it was all over. Hashim would be sent to wither away in an Israeli prison without trial. He would get sick from the oily food; the older and rougher inmates would viciously molest him. His soul would fade away.

Assad was a devotedly religious man, and his desire had always been to die in combat against the sworn enemies of Islam. He wasn't sure he believed that seventy-two virgins would be waiting for him in seventy-two emerald-green houses, as the *hadith* promised, but he did believe that paradise awaited all who gave their lives to fight the holy cause. But lately he had begun to doubt his very own path, his own actions. And there were the nightmares. They were getting more frequent, more violent. He had come to dread sleep, and the deprivation tired him down to the core of his bones.

Once he was sure that the Israeli soldiers had left, he let himself out the back of the building. He stopped to look at the line of posters glued to the building walls by Hamas. Young men and women, suicide bombers, shooters, protesters. The faces of the dead heroes stared at him as he continued down the alley.

It was his turn now.

It was time to become a *shahid*. It was time to become a martyr.

PART TWO

Chapter 12

Hannah

Hannah David's heart was in the right place. She was a Good Person. Hannah was the daughter of two of the most intelligent beings alive. Her father, Professor S. Moshe David, was a ballistics expert and entrepreneur working with the Israeli Aircraft Industry. His designs and concepts were at the heart of some of the most advanced weaponry in the world. Her mother, Professor Fanny Nakel-David, was a painter, an accomplished pianist, and a Professor of Jewish Thought and Mediterranean Cultures at the Hebrew University in Jerusalem. Hannah's parents had always held high hopes for their only daughter. But the apple had not fallen near the tree. The apple had not fallen at all. It had stayed stuck in the branches, shriveling away with each year that passed. Surrounded by sophisticated, well-educated company and pushed to excel at anything that came her way, she had always let her folks down. They could not comprehend that their only child was, well... normal.

For as long as she could remember, she had felt like an outsider in her own home. At an early age, Hannah had discovered that the only way to measure up to her peers was to rebel. As a teenager she had done everything possible to dismay her parents, to break free from their expectations. She dropped out of school, became goth for a few years, and ultimately spent time with some of the most unsanitary collection of creatures to be found in Jerusalem. In her twenties, she had experienced a short romance with religion, looking for her place in the ultra-religious neighborhoods of Jerusalem and, when that didn't help, in the ultra-hip classes of the Kabbalah. Months went by, but eventually, she gave up on that, too. God would not speak to her.

But if you try, try, and try again, you will get there in the end. At the age of forty, she discovered her true calling: radical political activism.

Voluntary service was her bread, political activism her butter, and the ability to annoy and provoke? Her jam and honey. Still single at forty, even the most patient and desperate lovers had rejected her. Her partners preferred to leave rather than get involved in her endless political causes, even though she was quite attractive. Her straight nose, blond hair, and light-blue eyes were quite a fetching novelty in the mostly dark-haired Middle East. Many a suitor sidled up to her at the vegetarian cafés she frequented, only to sidle away after receiving a private recitation of Hannah's favorite rant: "Occupation corrupts, and a corrupt state in the hands of baboons has no right to preach to the world about security. And what future can we promise our children?"

At four a.m., the old radio alarm beside Hannah's bed switched itself on, just in time for the hourly news bulletin. Hannah opened her eyes to the sound of the dramatic introductory music, catapulting her straight from deep sleep into the murky swamp of Israeli politics and continuous military conflict. By four-fifteen she was ready. No makeup, no fancy clothes. She glanced at her reflection in the mirror. *Just another ordinary woman, about to set off on a far-from-ordinary task.*

She opened her post-it-covered refrigerator door. Last night she had been forced to throw away most of the food, as the large satchel had taken up all the space in the fridge. Gently, she loaded the heavy bag onto her shoulders and immediately shivered as the cold fabric pressed against her back. She closed the fridge, turned the lights off, and made for the door. Carefully, she inched down the stairwell of her apartment building, praying to reach the street without anything happening to the bag.

She knew that one false step, one unfortunate bump to the satchel, and it would all be over.

At four-forty, ten minutes late, she watched as a nondescript gray Mazda stopped in front of her apartment building with a short squeal of brakes.

"Did you have to make such a noise?" Hannah asked the driver.

"Sorry." Seventeen-year-old Johnny Melamed smiled at her. It was an attractive smile, but she could see through it. Being a member of the Melamed clan, one of the richest families in the world, Johnny had once confided in her that anyone and anything can be bought. Money, blackmail, or a well-timed fake smile—Johnny had gotten anything he had ever wanted. It did not work with her.

"You're late. Now let's go."

For Hannah, Johnny was everything she detested about the wealthy. When he came to pick her up for a meeting for the very first time in his Porsche Carrera, she took the bus. She had made him buy this rusty piece of junk for their mission.

They flew by the dark, massive walls of the old city, the enormous stones shining orange-gray in the streetlight. The air was crystal and pure; she could smell the heady scent of pine. "What a crazy place," Johnny shook his head as the golden Dome of the Rock peeped through the ancient arrow slits in the turreted wall, a floodlit oasis in a dark city.

"Couldn't the different religions choose different cities? Did they all have to choose ours? Think of it—like, the Jews get Jerusalem, Muslims get Mecca and, like, Baghdad, and the Christians can have London. Or Rome. Why did they all choose Jerusalem?"

But Hannah wasn't listening.

"Please don't drive over the speed limit. The rules of the road have been written in blood." Johnny eased the car down to fifty-five kilometers per hour. It was clear by the frown on his face that he was wondering why he still bothered with her.

They had met at the preparations for a demonstration arranged by the "Israelis for Palestine Brigade" organization. Funded by a large group of international backers, the Brigade held weekly demonstrations at several friction points along the Israeli-Palestinian border. She was proud to be one of the organization's well-equipped members, fearless in their marches. She would demonstrate with a printed sign in one hand, phones with which to film the military brutality in the other. Although the organization described itself as a collective of Israelis who support a free Palestine, most of the brigade comprised Israeli Arabs. Hannah wished more Jewish Israelis would join.

She had been teamed together with Johnny while preparing for a demonstration in the border town of

Bil'in. They started the day off by preparing placards and ended it by having their tear-gassed eyes soothed by the Brigade medic. In every activity following that initial meeting, much to her surprise, she discovered Johnny requested to be teamed up with her. It wasn't sexual; she knew she was far from being his usual type. He went for young girls who wore $200 T-shirts and outrageously ugly Gucci slippers. For today's action, she wore purple corduroy trousers and dirty, scuffed white sport-shoes and a T-shirt demanding a Free Palestine. The only hints of frivolous fashion were three faded friendship bracelets on her wrist and a military-style overcoat patched with colorful, iron-on art. So, why did he insist on working with her? Maybe it was because she was the only person on this planet that, much as he tried, he couldn't manipulate. She challenged him. Or maybe it was because they had something in common, a private understanding: they were both rebels. Rebels against their own families.

She caught him staring at her at the next light.

"The light is green."

The car picked up speed as they began to descend westward, leaving the hills of Jerusalem behind them.

"Hannah, are you sure that it's wise not to report this action to Yossi?" Johnny asked nervously, "He repeatedly told us to update him on every action we take, and he requested any major protest should be coordinated by the Brigade ops."

"Yossi is so busy worrying about what the public thinks that he would never have authorized our mission."

"You sure?"

"Yossi's a pussy."

By five-thirty, she could smell the Mediterranean Sea. To the east, the desert stretched into the haze—a mixture of yellow-gray sand and rocks, dotted with small, dark-green shrubs. She knew they were almost there. It was happening. Tonight, her parents would see her on TV, on the news. Suddenly, Johnny slowed the car down.

"How about we stop for coffee? There's a great all-night café at the next junction. It's got the best espresso in the desert. Waddya say, Hannah, I'll buy?"

She turned to him. "Are you beginning to have second thoughts? Is this some kind of attempt to delay?"

"Delay? It's just that, well…you know where we're going. I wouldn't mind stopping for just one last good cup of coffee."

She looked at her wristwatch. "No. We can't wait. If you hadn't come late, we would have had the extra time."

"*Yalla!*" Johnny banged his fist on the wheel, the spoiled child surfacing for a split second. But he pressed his foot back on the gas. And as the best-espresso-in-the-desert flashed past them, he theatrically blew it a fond farewell kiss.

Chapter 13

Roni

Roni sat on a large concrete block, staring at the ground. The official armistice line ran under the cement square, which meant that he had one foot in Gaza and the other in Israel.

It was rush hour on the Palestinian side of the crossing. He watched the hundreds of Palestinians who were lined up patiently behind the rusty barriers, hoping against all hope to be allowed to cross into Israel. Pregnant mothers, ailing fathers, old, young, sick, very sick, starving—a silent line of humans with defeat in their eyes and laminated ID cards in their hands. Crossing the border into Israel would mean excellent hospitals with a continuous flow of electricity, experienced doctors, and nutritious meals. For some of those waiting to pass, crossing the border meant the difference between life and death.

Hamas policemen strutted up and down the line, suspiciously examining every one of the waiting citizens, monitoring those not allowed into Israel, noting the names of those who did enter in little black books. Roni turned his gaze toward the fields around the crossing. He counted at least ten Qassam missile craters from previous, unsuccessful attacks. Must be hell to be on border-crossing duty, he thought. A flock of sheep was grazing among the ruins of the bombed-out industrial zone. The old shepherd was wearing a three-piece suit and knock-off yellow Crocs. It looked surreal at first light.

He turned to the north. Just one kilometer away, a row of tractors was leaving Kibbutz Erez on their way to the fields. If one side of the fence was surreal, the other side was the essence of normality. The well-kept hothouses gleamed in the dawn light. The fields were painted in soft greens and browns, and reds. The northerly wind brought with it aromas of soil and morning coffee. Suddenly, Roni felt hungry as never before. He slipped off the concrete block and walked to the staff kitchenette, hoping to find a piece of bread to swallow, maybe even a cucumber or a hard-boiled egg.

"Uliel!" Roni turned and saw Lieutenant Roy approaching him.

"Yes, sir?"

"The intel guys have finished with the subject. They're sending a team to pick him up for a more extended interview at Unit 504. The rest of the squad are packing to leave back to base. We'll be gone in ten minutes. You wait here with the prisoner and deliver him to 504. Then, take a bus back to base. Clear?"

"Yes, sir."

Roy's voice softened. "You can take a few hours off on the way and go visit your folks. Say hello to that girlfriend of yours. But be back at base no later than nineteen-hundred. Got it?"

"Yes, sir. Thanks, sir."

Lieutenant Roy gave Roni a manly slap on the back. "You did well today. We all did." Roy turned and walked away swiftly.

Roni smiled. He, too, felt that he had done well. At long last, he was paying the Palestinians back for all they had done to the people of Sedera. And this was just the start. By the time his mandatory three years were over, he'd make sure that they paid more. A lot more.

His belly growled hungrily. Still looking at the long lines of hopeless Palestinians, he slipped off the cement block and walked off toward the kitchenette, where yesterday's bread, a few hard-boiled eggs, and salt awaited. It was one of the most delicious meals he had ever eaten.

Chapter 14

Assad

Assad Ibn Samir, a.k.a. The Lion, had always harbored ambivalent feelings toward the Sheikh. On the one hand, he was undeniably one of the wisest and holiest men in Gaza. All worshipped him as a great Muslim leader, an influential and charismatic freedom fighter who, with Allah's help, could move mountains.

But on the other hand, the Lion wondered what the population would say if they were to visit the Sheikh's mansion in the upmarket suburb of Remal. The Sheikh enjoyed the company of three beautifully dressed wives. His children wore Italian and American brands at home. His fridge was stocked with what must have been the only original Coke bottles in the Strip. His black BMW X Series was spotless. The Sheikh lived a good life—that much was evident—but where was the money coming from? The people were starving, but the Sheikh gained weight every month.

The Lion banished those thoughts from his mind. The Sheikh had proven, time and again, that he was dedicated to the Palestinian cause. He had spent more than five years in Israeli prisons and personally executed three men caught cooperating with the Zionists. He walked at the head of every funeral and demonstration, shouting his head off with rage. And his lessons at prayer time! He could make your spirit soar. When he spoke, for a few minutes, you'd forget that you were bound to this wretched earth, for a few minutes you floated in the light of Allah. So perhaps he siphoned funds away from the people into his Swiss bank account. If that's how Allah wanted it, then that is how it should be.

It was four in the morning when the Lion reached the Sheikh's house. He knew the Sheikh would be awake this early. It was during this peaceful hour that he sat at his desk, preparing his sermon for the morning prayers.

"Assad! Peace be upon you, my brother!" The Sheikh kissed the Lion on the cheeks three times.

"And peace be upon you, great leader," the Lion responded. The Sheikh guided him into his reception area. The room was stark—a dented plastic table and white chairs. The walls were bare except for one stylized rendition of the *Sura Al-Fatiha*, the first chapter of the Qur'an. There was no pavement outside, and the windows faced the street. A single lightbulb dangled at the edge of its electric wires, illuminating the room with a harsh white light. It was a room designed to project modesty and simplicity, but the Lion had once been invited into the other part of the house. Behind this ugly room lay a wonderland.

"You sounded troubled when you called me." The Sheikh pointed to one of the plastic chairs.

The Lion trembled slightly as he took his seat.

"I think my time has come. I would like to have the honor of giving my life to Allah."

Assad knew that the Sheikh had received many such visits. He had been a witness to some of them. Most were from desperate teenagers, unable to cope with the poverty and despair. Some of them the Sheikh had turned back, some of them he gave a good talking-to, and *then* turned them back. But a lucky few were granted their wish. If you came to the Sheikh and your timing was good, the equipment was ready and a target had been decided upon, within hours your wish was granted and you would be dispatched with a rifle or an explosive jacket for a one-way ticket to paradise— hopefully taking an impressive number of Zionists with you.

The Sheikh let out a long, heavy sigh. Then he stood up and walked across the room. Unconsciously, he took off his white *taqiyya* prayer cap and stared at it.

"Why now?"

"Why now?" The Lion stared at the floor as he spoke. "I have done my share in the Holy War. I wish to join Allah in Paradise. I have a target that will send a strong message to the Zionists. But time is short. Can you help me?"

The Sheikh adjusted the white prayer cap back onto his head as he looked up at the Lion.

"What is your target?"

"You remember the young man they call Mohandas? The Israelis captured him from the safe house. He's in their hands, and I want to punish those Israeli pigs! I want to hit them where it hurts. But we need to move now. There is a good chance that some of the Israeli soldiers who participated in the operation will still be at the crossing. We must strike back rapidly."

A few seconds passed in silence as the Sheikh stared at the Lion. Finally, he spoke. "You are right. If we manage to avenge ourselves on the very soldiers who kidnapped this young boy, it will be a great blow by us that will send an important message."

"Please, Allah."

"But, Assad. It is not yet your time. We need you here. You are one of the most able warriors we have."

"Abu Almas, I cannot fight anymore. I am tired. I am becoming useless to the cause. And you must agree that I have earned my place in heaven."

"You have indeed, and your time will come," answered the Sheikh. He withdrew a cell phone from deep inside his white robe and made a quick call. When he finished, he turned back to the Lion.

"Assad—I cannot send you today. But I will not leave your Mohandas unavenged. In two minutes, my cousin's daughter will be here. I want you personally to rig her suit up and escort her to the crossing."

"A girl? But honorable leader, I—"

"May Allah help us all, and especially the Mohandas." The Sheikh made it understood that the conversation was over.

"*In-sha-Allah*," answered the Lion, as disappointment took hold of him. This was not how he had imagined this meeting would end.

The Sheikh left the room, returning a minute later with an explosive device. It was a wide, soft cotton belt in which a series of internal pockets had been sewn. Each pocket housed a cylinder filled with explosives and various shrapnel—screws, nuts, and tiny ball bearings.

The Lion eyed the belt with disgust. He was frustrated that what should have been his job would be done by a mere girl.

"What is the material?"

The Sheikh gave a wide smile. "C4."

The Lion raised his eyebrows, impressed. He had no idea how the Sheikh managed it. The Israeli lockdown made C4 nearly impossible to manufacture or smuggle in. Most bomb makers relied on Acetone Peroxide—a substance so unstable it had earned the nickname *Umm Al Aysh Shaytan*—Mother of Satan. But nothing was beyond the Sheikh. He had Coke bottles, a spotless X Series, and, somehow, C4.

Still, as the Sheikh laid out the explosive belt, a shadow passed over the Lion's face. It should have been his mission. His vest. His sacrifice. But now he had to watch as someone else walked the path he had chosen.

There was a soft knock on the door.

"Come in!"

The door opened, and a young girl entered the room. She was excited and out of breath. Her cheeks were flushed as she smiled a dazzling smile at the Lion. Breathlessly, she turned to the Sheikh.

"Good morning, Uncle. I have come to give my life to Allah."

Chapter 15

Hannah

Hannah could sense the desert air heating up. The sun had crossed above the horizon, a harsh yellow disc that caused the dunes to shimmer. Johnny Melamed pulled the old Mazda to the side of the road, two hundred yards away from the Erez crossing.

"Drive closer," she commanded. "We can't walk far with the bag."

Johnny exhaled and leaned back in his seat. "Hang on, let's get a read on the situation before we go in. Check out the guards. The security."

"We've already been here three times. In twenty minutes, they'll be changing shifts. Everything is exactly how we planned it, so let's not waste time."

Johnny sighed as he shifted into first gear and rolled down the last few yards. He parked neatly in the bay closest to the crossing, jumped out of the car, and popped the trunk. Gingerly, he lifted the heavy satchel.

"Careful!" Hannah snapped.

"I am being careful, you stupid bitch," Johnny muttered. She heard him, but in the importance of the moment, she let it slide.

Silently, they walked toward the crossing, taking cover behind a tall sand embankment. It was easy to hide on this side of the border. The Israeli border patrol guards had no reason to watch them. All eyes were focused on the Palestinian side.

"We have ten minutes before the next shift," she spoke in a low tone. "Time to unpack." Johnny took a deep breath as slowly he lowered the satchel, unzipped it, and pulled out a large, black garbage bag. Inside were the missiles.

They were ready.

Chapter 16

Roni

"Uliel!"

Lieutenant Roy called out from one of the precast sheds that surrounded the Erez crossing. Roni turned and watched his squad mates approach him, the prisoner in front of the group, screened from the Palestinian side of the crossing. Igor stayed a few yards back, covering their flank.

Roni had been sure that TV reporters would arrive to immortalize the capture. But there were none there. Lieutenant Roy explained that you'll never find a reporter awake at this hour—they're all sleeping off their hangovers. The team members had a good chuckle.

"Take the captive to the Hummer," Roy ordered, "it's waiting on the other side."

Roni grabbed the blindfolded Palestinian and began to walk toward the crossing when suddenly a black missile flew clumsily past him. He froze as a few meters behind him, his lieutenant's stomach became a mass of red blood.

"Roy!" Roni screamed. For a few long seconds, the group of young soldiers stared in horror as their lieutenant stood there, still upright, staring down at his own bloodied torso.

"What the hell?"

Hundreds of frozen faces stared at Roy from both sides of the crossing.

Roni was the first to come to his senses. He ran to Roy, laid him on the ground, and started peeling off his combat kit. Roy shouted to no one, his tone a mixture of surprise and fear: "I can't feel anything. I can't feel anything!" Another missile zipped past. Igor's face became a bloody mess. Seconds later, another soldier was hit.

"Everybody to the ground!" Roni yelled, and the spell was broken. Chaos erupted as Palestinian families screamed and stampeded back toward Gaza. Hamas policemen shouted, hitting the fleeing families with their batons in an effort to control the surge. Israeli border guards rushed out, barking orders no one obeyed. The giant metal barriers were raised, sealing the crossing off. A siren went off in the distance. Chaos reigned.

Then a strangled female cry cut through the madness. "Genociders! Nazis! Family destroyers!" A second, high-pitched voice joined in with, "Corrupt army! Kill the government! Stop the genocide!"

And then Roni was brushed aside by Lieutenant Roy, who suddenly and miraculously stood up. Roni watched with horror as his gory commander straightened his uniform, strode toward a pretty lady on the Israeli side of the crossing and, without warning, smashed her head against a wall. She collapsed, senseless. A young man lunged at Roy, beating him with his fists. Immediately, two of the soldiers had the boy in an armlock.

Roy turned, his mad eyes stark white against the red blood spattered on his face, "It's just cow's blood. Not mine. They're throwing cow blood. It's a goddamn demonstration." He picked up Hannah's satchel and emptied out the remaining contents. Five thin black bags fell onto the ground and burst apart, red liquid pooling onto the pavement.

Pinned under two soldiers, the young man was still kicking, shouting: "I'll get you for this! I'll make you regret you're alive! You fascist Nazi shit! You Nazi pig! You'll burn in hell for what you did! I'll kill you!"

Only then did Roni's mind snap back to his mission. The prisoner! He turned. The Mohandas was still standing where he had left him, a lone figure dressed in ill-fitting fatigues, legs and arms cuffed, eyes covered with a long strip of gun flannel.

Roni turned to his lieutenant. "Sir? Should I take the prisoner in?"

Lieutenant Roy looked at the blood that was running in rivulets down the pavement. Slowly, he answered. "He's all yours."

Roni grabbed the Palestinian and once again made for the Hummer, leaving his team members to help restore order.

Two swallows zigzagged across the crossing.

A young girl was walking toward the group of soldiers, unnoticed by the border guards, who were still staring at the bloody mess their crossing had become. She glided, undisturbed, a radiant figure in a flowing white robe. She walked against the stream of Palestinians who were still rushing, herd-like, away from the crossing, her feet daintily stepping through the puddles of blood. She looked at Roni and smiled the most beautiful smile he had ever seen. Surprised, he instinctively smiled back.

For a moment, time stopped. Then, to Roni's astonishment, she ran toward his squad-mates who were still grouped around the screaming protester. Before he could shout a warning, the world exploded in a flash of white light. And then it all went black.

Chapter 17

Roni

He could hear a television murmuring from another room, the soft drone of a news bulletin.

His eyes were closed, but the darkness wasn't soothing. It pulsed with an unbearable glare, as if a blinding light burned inside his skull. He flinched involuntarily. Every attempt to open his eyes sent a sharp pain shooting through his head.

Roni struggled to sit up—only to collapse back down. It felt as if a horse had kicked him in the chest—a horse with twenty hooves. He didn't know where he was, why he couldn't see, he couldn't remember anything. He felt in total vertigo—out of touch with reality, spinning sickeningly in an empty void.

What was happening?

And then, mercifully, a magical voice called out his name, "Roni? It's OK, I'm here."

The weight pressing on his chest lifted. "Dad?" Roni inhaled huge gulps of air.

"You're home, my boy. You're home." His father's voice was calm and stable. "I'm here with Dr. Yuri. Come, drink this."

A metal spoon touched his lips. Roni opened his mouth and swallowed the sweet spoonful. He wasn't sure if he was dreaming or awake, but his father's voice sent a sense of peace through his body. He drifted into a long, solid, healing sleep…

Chapter 18

Hashim

He could hear a television playing softly from another room. In Hebrew?

Hashim's eyes fluttered open. He was in a room cluttered with a jumble of various items: a bicycle, a washing machine, a folded baby cot, bags of clothes, camping gear.

The bed he lay on was comfortable; the sheets were clean and smelled wonderful. There was a half-open door behind him. Next to it, draped over a chair, were charred Israeli combat fatigues.

Where am I? Why am I here? Whose uniform is that?

He heard footsteps approaching the room and quickly closed his eyes.

The door creaked ajar. He could hear hushed voices—a man and a woman speaking in Hebrew. Having spent many days in Israel, back in the days when his father had been doing business with the Zionists, Hashim's Hebrew was good enough to understand everything that was being said.

"He's still fast asleep," the man murmured.

"Are you sure he's okay?" the woman whispered.

"He's fine. The doctor said so."

"I wonder who he is."

"I don't know. When I got to the crossing, Roni wouldn't let me leave him there. He held on to him, and I couldn't pry his hands away. The medic at the border said that he's a patrolnik. His uniform is border patrol, and he was mumbling in Arabic."

"Must be one of those Druze boys who serve at the crossing."

"Yes…"

"So how does Roni know him? If he's a Druze, then he's definitely not from Sedera."

"I don't know. We'll see when they wake up."

The voices faded as the footsteps retreated down the hall. Hashim's mind spun.

Sedera?

That's on the Israeli side of the border.

I'm in Israel? Why? And who is Roni?

Hashim tried to organize his thoughts, hoping to identify a clue to his present situation. Gaza. He remembered Gaza. He remembered the rocket fins. He remembered the Lion, the Qassam rocket launch, the celebrations, the wedding proposals…

And that's where it went dry. Try as he might, he couldn't connect his last memory—sitting with his extended family in the crowded lounge of his house— to this strange room. One thing he knew for sure: he was now in Sedera. Which meant that he was less than ten miles from home. But he might as well be ten thousand miles away.

He was on the wrong side of the fence.

Chapter 19

Roni

"What can you see, Roni?"

Roni flinched as the fuzzy gray light sent a wave of pain through his head. "It's like I have a blanket over my eyes. A thick, gray blanket."

Dr. Yuri lit a small flashlight that hung on his keyring and directed it at Roni's pupils.

"Can you see the light?"

"Barely," he winced. "It's like a big, fuzzy, gray circle. And it hurts."

The doctor twisted the light off. "It looks good. Tomorrow, I want you to come up to Be'er Sheva for some tests, but for now, try to rest as much as possible. I'll be back in the morning."

He heard the doctor rise and leave the room with his father. "*Ima*?" His voice wavered.

"I'm here." Roni's mother answered softly.

"What's happening? Why am I here? I can't remember anything. Why can't I see?"

Nava took a deep breath. "There was an incident at the crossing, just as you were on your way out of Gaza."

The door creaked open again, and Roni sensed his father returning.

"I don't remember anything."

Mayor Sami Uliel's voice was quiet. "There was a suicide bomber at the Erez crossing. You were close to the bomb when it went off."

A chill crawled up Roni's spine. "A suicide bomber...? When?"

"This morning."

His throat went dry. "Was anyone killed?"

It took Sami Uliel a few long seconds before he could answer.

"Eleven Israelis dead, one Palestinian."

"Anyone we know?"

"Almost all of them," his father answered.

A sharp wave of nausea rolled over him. "Who?"

Sami could not speak. His wife, Nava, answered.

"From what we know now, one was a civilian. The others were your squad."

"My squad? All of them?"

"I'm afraid so. And there's one other young soldier from another unit who was injured alongside you," answered Nava.

"No, it can't be. You've got it wrong. They are alive! They have to be." He shook his head in disbelief.

"Your father drove straight to the crossing when he heard."

"I saw it all, Roni," Sami murmured.

Roni's body sagged as grief took hold of his entire being. They were gone. Lieutenant Roy, Igor the sharpshooter. All of them. And with their bodies, they had shielded him from the human bomb that had detonated but a few feet away. He was the only living member of a ten-man squad, men who had become his brothers, every single one of them. For a full year, they had shared the tough but rewarding experience of basic combat training, specialist courses, and life on base. He had lived almost every waking minute in the past twelve months with his squad, slept side by side in the dirt and cold. They had transformed from a bunch of young, loud-mouthed high school graduates into a tight unit of soldiers. A family of fighters. And he was the only survivor.

"Why me?" he whispered.

His mother stroked his arm. "Honey…" But there was nothing she could say.

His mind was spinning with endless questions that all had horrific answers. So he did all he could to focus on one thought.

"The other survivor—who is he?"

"We don't know. But he's here. In the spare room," Nava said. "Still unconscious."

Roni stiffened. "Here? Why?"

"He was unconscious when I arrived," Sami answered. But you were holding onto him so tightly. You were screaming at us, '*Don't let him go.*' So, once the medics made sure he was fine to be moved, I told them I was taking him home with us."

"And they let you? Why isn't he at his own house? Why is he here?"

"You refused to leave without him," Sami explained. "So I told them he was coming with us."

"And the medics let you take him?"

His mother smiled. "Your father wouldn't take no for an answer. He bulldozed you both out of the ambulance and straight home."

"I don't trust any of those eighteen-year-old military medics." Sami snorted. "Within five minutes, I had you here with Dr. Yuri by your side. He's been here with the two of you since the morning."

"And what did Yuri say?" he asked cautiously.

"You're both going to be fine," his father assured him.

"But I can't see!"

"It's the blast wave. You have some internal bleeding inside your eyes." Sami's voice tensed slightly. "Dr. Yuri said that the blood will drain out slowly, and your eyesight will return. You just have to take it easy and let your body recover."

"How long will it take?"

"You're young; it shouldn't take more than a day, maybe two. Yuri said that most chances by tomorrow, your eyesight should be almost back to normal."

"And what about the other soldier?"

Sami exhaled and got up. "I'll go see if he's awake."

A moment later, he was back.

"Nava, he's gone!"

"Where?" asked Nava, surprised.

Then the three heard the front door silently clicking shut. Sami ran out of the room.

"Wait! Where are you going?" he heard his father from a distance.

There was a short pause before a strange voice replied, "Home."

"Like that?! Come in, change your torn clothes, have something to eat. I'll drive you home in my car."

A few long seconds of silence passed.

"I won't take no for an answer," his father continued. "Come on in. How were you planning to get home? In that ragged uniform? With nothing in your pockets","

Roni strained to hear, but the soldier didn't reply.

Who was he?

Chapter 20

Prime Minister Rahav

Israeli Prime Minister Ya'akov "Yaki" Rahav was a man with an addiction. A terrible need that ruled his entire being and, as such, steered the nation's destiny with a merciless grip.

Rahav was addicted to polls.

Everyone—MPs, aides, ministers, rabbis, catering crews—knew that you should keep your distance every morning at seven-thirty. That was *pollster hour*. At that exact time every morning, the CEO of the poll service entered the Prime Minister's residence through a side door, memory stick in hand. For half an hour, the head of state was not to be interrupted. There were at least twenty polls taken every day, paid for by the Israeli public, all crafted for and viewed by one man. The poll agency meticulously arranged the results in an animated presentation, all analyzing one thing: the rise and fall of his approval ratings.

On a good day, Prime Minister Rahav felt like he could sing. Today was not a good day. According to the pollster:

42% of the test group preferred his second-in-command, the wonderfully charming Minister of Finance.

58% felt that he was dragging his feet with internal policy

57% felt that his coalition stank

A very bad day.

And there was nothing he could do. With a government this shaky, he couldn't so much as choose his breakfast cereal without rushing to seek the coalition parties' blessings.

And then there was the Pack Mule Scandal.

The night before, on national TV, he had been asked an innocent question about Israel's debt to the Druze community. The Druze were fiercely loyal soldiers, an enormous asset to the IDF. But in an attempt to praise them, Rahav had unfortunately stated that "The Druze were as tough as pack mules. They bravely shoulder the army's difficult workload in these troubled times. A crucial resource that I am most thankful for."

His personal assistant received the first text message within a record-breaking twenty seconds of the gaffe. By the nine o'clock news, the networks were flooded by insulted Druze leaders, fuming over Rahav's comparison of their finest to beasts of burden. By ten o'clock, rioting began in the Druze township of

Halil, and for the rest of the night, Rahav and his massive team were stuck in the office making calls to placate and smooth ruffled feathers.

He managed to sleep for two hours before he was woken with more dreadful news. A suicide bomb attack at the Gaza border. Eleven dead.

It all felt personal; they were punishing him to make him fail. It just wasn't fair. No matter how he tried to steer the country's course, it all backfired on him.

Wearily, he listened as his house pollster gave him the numbers. Once the ordeal was over, he sat at his desk, staring unseeing at the fabulous Jerusalem vista that was framed by his window: ancient olive trees, a stone sundial, the walls of the Old City. A stunning backdrop he might appreciate in a better mood. He sighed as he nervously fidgeted with a gold lighter on his desk. He desperately craved a cigarette. The whole residence, gardens included, was a no-smoking zone. He had all the power of the country in his hands, but he couldn't light a damn cigarette in his own home.

His frustration reached boiling point. How had he sunk so low in the public eye? He had the best spokespeople in the country. He had the slickest spin doctors. He had won the election by a huge margin. The people used to love him! The cabinet members used to fear him. He used to be king.

All those paid advisors, those marketing phonies—
they were supposed to save him. Yet, despite all their
efforts, he was sinking fast. In less than a minute,
Rahav's mind had settled on the obvious conclusion:
this whole mess was their fault. He slammed the gold-
plated lighter onto the desk and barked into the
intercom.

"Get me Rosen and Yarkoni. And tell Yarkoni to
bring his whole damn team. Tell them I expect them to
be here in an hour!"

The crisis management session started off poorly.
Fourteen frazzled public relations pros sat in the room,
all of them having raced to Jerusalem at breakneck
speed from their breakfast tables in Tel Aviv, covering
the ninety-minute drive in less than sixty minutes.
None wore ties; some hadn't even had time to shave.

Rahav didn't bother with pleasantries. He ripped
into them immediately, tearing apart their shoddy
work and declaring a two-hour ultimatum: find a way
to fix it, or you're all out. Within seconds, a lively
debate was in session. Buzzwords and catchphrases
were thrown across the room—words like *stickiness,
storytelling,* and *traction,* spoken enthusiastically in a
tone that suggested that the group was just one slogan
away from saving the country.

Twenty minutes into the heated discussion, the last invitee appeared. He was about fifty, bald, overweight, and dressed as if he had just walked off a Milan runway. His cool, red designer glasses framed world-weary eyes. All conversation halted as he calmly crossed the room, sat down in the last vacant chair, and began checking his social feeds. If the marketing loudmouths in the room had been wearing dresses, they would have all curtsied to the man. He was a legend.

Finally, Prime Minister Rahav broke the silence. "You're late."

The man didn't even look up. "I was eating breakfast."

A visible tremor went through the other fourteen councilors. They all wished that they could talk back to the Prime Minister like that. But there was only one man in the country who could eat breakfast first and then answer the summons.

Robert Rosen.

Media and public-relations genius Robert Rosen had joined the Rahav election campaign when polls were predicting an embarrassing defeat. Rosen's conditions for joining were concise and simple: If I come on board, you will do as I say, and do the exact opposite of what you have done until now.

His demands were met with insulted outrage. Financial backers threatened to withdraw support, party members ranted about the irresponsibility and suicidal stupidity of changing your messaging mid-race. But Rahav was savvy enough to sense that Rosen's advice seemed logical. If you're sure to lose the race, you've been doing it all wrong.

Rosen went on to create a faultless campaign for Rahav, one that would be taught in business schools and marketing courses for decades to come. Instead of desperately trying to keep the peace, Robert Rosen instructed Rahav to aggravate and annoy the Palestinian leadership. Instead of promising social and educational reform, Rosen had Rahav push the message that hard times were ahead. Instead of currying favor with the Arab population, Rosen had Rahav blame everything on them, turning every Arab citizen into an enemy.

Two sleepless months later, the state of Israel witnessed one of the biggest comebacks in political history. Overturning what was expected to be a landslide defeat, Rahav was elected, thanks to a campaign that showed him to the public as a "brave, realistic, no-nonsense leader for the challenging times ahead." Once Rahav entered office, Robert Rosen remained on the party payroll as media consultant and personal guru to the Prime Minister.

Rosen sat down and, as if on cue, the lively discussion resumed. While the ideas flew around the table, Rosen sat calmly and used the time to answer text messages he had ignored during breakfast. Rahav kept shooting him dark looks until eventually he could hold it in no more.

"So, Robert, any good ideas?"

Rosen put his phone down.

"No," came the exasperating answer. Robert Rosen had a way of creating deathly silences.

Then his phone vibrated. With all eyes watching, he picked up his phone and read the new text message. He stood up.

"If you'll all excuse me, I need to go." He slipped his phone into his back pocket and left the room, stopping only to mutter into the Prime Minister's personal assistant's ear: "I think I have something. Call me when he's done with these schmucks."

Chapter 21

Hashim

He was sitting in a kitchen. A kitchen that was inside the Zionist settlement of Sedera. There was a father, a mother called Nava, and their son, who had somehow lost his vision. And he—Hashim Abu Tir— known as the dangerous, IDF most-wanted Mohandas, was now being treated as a Druze border patrolnik.

"Here, you must be still hungry. Have some more meatballs," Nava insisted, already dishing more food up for their guest.

Hashim smiled at Nava and accepted the extras, even though he felt like he would choke. Until this point, he had managed not to talk. He had picked up very little information about his situation. He had been misidentified as a Druze border patrolnik at the border. That was all he knew. So although he couldn't eat one more grain of rice, he smiled politely and accepted his third helping. Any excuse to keep him from having to talk.

"What's your name, son?" the father asked.

Hashim swallowed slowly before answering. "Asher."

Asher was a good, solid, Israeli name—one of Jacob's twelve sons. Hashim remembered meeting several Ashers during the days when his father did business with the Israelis. Some were Druze.

The son looked in his direction. "Asher? Do I know you from anywhere else?"

"No."

A few long seconds passed in uncomfortable silence. The father turned to him.

"So, where do you live? We need to call your folks and tell them you are okay. They must be sick with worry!"

Sitting at the table, his fork halfway to his mouth, Hashim stared at the father. He had no idea how to answer. They were probably already suspicious. Any minute now they would call the army to come and get him. It was over. He was about to be exposed.

The father repeated his question. "So, from which Druze village do you come?"

Then, a ray of hope shone as a faint memory flashed through his mind. The majority of guards at the Erez crossing were Druze Border Patrol soldiers—a mystic sect, followers of a secret religion known only to the elders and priests. Hated by the people of Gaza even more than the Jews, there was a chant that the children sang about how one day they would have their revenge on these Druze soldiers, and how they would burn their houses in the small village in the Galilee called...

"Hurfeish. I live in Hurfeish."

"What a beautiful place," said Nava. "We stayed there three years ago for a weekend.

"And you're a Border patrolnik, eh?" the father smiled encouragingly.

"Yes," Hashim nodded.

"We owe you guys a hell of a lot."

Hashim just nodded, his eyes on his plate.

"Why would I have been hanging on to you?" The son was looking in his direction. An uncomfortable silence filled the room.

There came a knock at the front door that made them all jump. The mother went to see who it was, and after a short, mumbled conversation, she returned to the table with two men in tow. One of them wore red-framed designer glasses perched atop his gleaming bald head.

"Asher, these people are from the Prime Minister's office," Nava explained. "They want to talk to you. You and Roni."

Chapter 22

Hannah

Something told Hannah that she did not want to wake up. She desperately tried to hold on to the blackness that enveloped her, but a far-off, monotonous beeping was getting louder, dragging her out of the darkness.

Hannah's eyes fluttered open, and a harsh white glare seared her vision. She squeezed her eyes shut, but the damage was done. Her head throbbed. The sterile smell of antiseptic and stale food filled her nose.

Why am I in a hospital?

The light in the ward was painfully bright as she opened her eyes again, but she forced herself to squint through the glare. The first thing she noticed as the world came into focus was that her clothes were covered in blood. A sudden feeling of elation filled her.

The protest. We did it!

She tried to sit up, but a searing pain tore through her torso, forcing her back down. She looked down at her clothes again and realized with horror that the blood was *not* cow blood—it was her own. She looked around and noticed that she was in an intake room. The pale-green bedspread covering her was branded with the Soroka Hospital logo. She was in Be'er Sheva.

Her chest tightened. Why was she here? What happened?

A nurse hurried to her.

"You're bruised and bleeding. Try not to move, honey. That's better. So, good afternoon, miss! How are we doing? Here's a little something that will make you feel better in a minute." As she spoke, she injected a clear liquid into the IV drip connected to Hannah's arm.

Hannah barely registered the cool sensation. "What happened?"

"I'm so sorry, sweetie," the nurse answered, "but I am afraid you were caught in a bad suicide attack at the Erez Border Crossing."

Hannah's stomach lurched. "Suicide attack? But we didn't…" Hannah stuttered. "What attack?"

"A female suicide bomber. She managed to get right up close to the soldiers at the crossing."

"What?"

"Yes, I know, it's awful. Apparently some crazy demonstrators were throwing bags of blood at the guards," the nurse continued, oblivious to Hannah's growing panic. "Because of the distraction, no one noticed the bomber approaching. But it's all over, and you'll be fine. The doctors have checked on you twice already, and there's no cause for concern. We'll just finish the paperwork, and then you'll be able to move into a smaller room." The nurse patted her arm reassuringly, as if that would help. "You take your time and have a nice rest. In the meantime, I couldn't find your phone or any ID. What's your name, lovey?"

"Hannah."

The nurse tapped her name into a tablet computer. "Surname?"

"Greenburg," Hannah lied. "Why am I here?"

"A few bolts and screws from the bomb blast hit you. But you were very lucky, honey." The nurse gave her a sympathetic smile. "Just a few flesh wounds, a nasty bruise. Your CT showed a slight concussion— you must have hit your head when you fell. Nothing that can't be fixed with a few nights of healthy sleep. Hannah Greenburg. Can you give me your ID number and home address?"

Hannah ignored the nurse's request. "What happened at the crossing?"

"Eleven dead, I'm afraid. It was terrible. Ten soldiers and a civilian. So sad."

"Eleven?"

"Terrible, isn't it? All of them so young. The nurse shook her head. "And all because of those crazy protesters. If it weren't for that ridiculous demonstration, those kids would all still be alive."

Hannah's pulse roared in her ears. "What about the protesters?"

"One is dead. He was with the soldiers when it happened."

Dead?

"They haven't found the others yet," the nurse continued, tapping at her tablet, but don't worry—there are cameras all over that place. They'll have his mates ID'd and in the bag faster than you can say *meshuga*…. "

"The protester is dead?" Hannah felt she might vomit.

"Yes. Killed by the very same *wonderful* Palestinians who he loves so much…. How's that for justice?"

A stout woman poked her head into the room. "Tzippi, they need you urgently at intake room B."

"We've got quite some work here this evening." The nurse, Tzippi, smiled at Hannah. "I'll be back in just a minute. Try to sleep."

Hannah didn't answer.

Fifteen minutes later, when Tzippi returned, Hannah was gone.

Chapter 23

Assad

It was all very confusing.

The Lion sat atop a secluded dune overlooking the sea. The bombing attack had been one of the most successful operations in many years. The Sheikh's niece had walked right up to the border crossing while the Zionists had been distracted by a demonstration. Eleven Israelis gone. Ten of them soldiers. It was a stupendous blow against the Zionist army. A wave of joy had erupted, sparking festivities within minutes throughout the whole Gaza Strip. From where he sat, the Lion could hear the city rejoicing—car horns blaring, gunshots fired in victory, the sound of women's ululations echoing through the streets. Families were gathering on rooftops, passing around plates of ka'ak and dates, smiling at strangers as if it were *Eid*. And yet, the Lion could not feel the elation so many of his people shared. He felt—nothing. Was it because it should have been him? Was it because, instead of fighting, he had just stood by and watched a pretty sixteen-year-old girl blow herself up? Was it exhaustion? Post-adrenaline hangover? He had suffered from that many times in the past.

No. This time it was different. He could feel it.

He exhaled, watching the setting sun glint off the waves. Two fishing boats dawdled past, their black silhouettes leaving a trail of diamonds in their wake. For a few minutes, the sun's golden rays blotted out the plastic bags and debris that peppered the Gaza beach, and in this moment of beauty, the Lion was filled with a powerful yearning. How he longed to rest, to finally escape this wretched life on Earth and enter the gates of Paradise.

A devout Muslim, the Lion knew he could not simply take his own life without being marred by sin. The only way he could reach *janna*, the permanent abode of the righteous, would be by doing his utmost in battle against the Zionists.

He could take an AK-47 rifle and storm the crossing single-handed. Or throw a grenade and wait as the border guards cut him down. He could steal a car, crash it into the crossing, running over as many Israelis as possible before anyone stopped him.

These were all simple solutions, direct paths to martyrdom. But he couldn't take the easy way out. He clenched his jaw as the words of the Sheikh echoed in his mind: the people needed him.

The sun began to dip into the Mediterranean, and a dark emptiness filled his soul. It took all that he had to find the strength to walk down to the waterline for the sunset prayer's ritual ablution. The sea was warm; the waves lapping at his ankles as he cupped his hands and let the water flow over his skin. Once he was cleansed, the Lion returned to the high dune where his prayer mat was waiting.

Not for the first time, he missed the simple joy of praying together with his family and friends. How he would love to be a part of society once more. No longer a warrior, ever on guard, ever on the run. Lonely.

He tried to empty his mind as he kneeled down, his body facing Mecca, and began reciting *salah* for *maghrib*. As he softly chanted the prayer, something shifted. It was as if only now he understood the true meaning of the prayer that had passed his lips a thousand times before. Ending the last *raka'ah*, the Lion sat with his back straight, his feet folded under his body. He turned to the south, one side of Gaza City spread before him, and recited: *"As-salamu alaykum wa rahmatullah."* He turned to the north and repeated the blessing upon the other side of the city. Peace be upon you, and God's blessing.

The words hung in the air. *Peace. Blessing.*

Was he bringing peace and God's blessing to his fellow Palestinians? His every waking hour was focused on *jihad*. When would it be enough to bring peace? In the past twelve hours, he had seen the young

Mohandas captured and a beautiful young girl dead. All by his direct actions.

Could it be that he had dedicated his life to do the exact opposite of everything he had just recited during evening prayers?

The Lion pensively rolled his prayer mat and slung it over his shoulder. Silently, he slid down the back of the dune. He realized he needed counseling. It was risky, but he had to speak to someone who understood. And there was only one man he could trust.

Chapter 24

Roni

Roni still could not understand why these two men were here. The one had introduced himself as a communications manager. Roni's father, Sami, seemed to know the man and was quite impressed by his presence. The other man was introduced as a psychologist. Both claimed to work personally for the Prime Minister. If that was true—what did they want with him?

At his father's insistence, the two men had joined his family for dinner. For almost half an hour they had made polite conversation, discussing real estate prices in Tel Aviv and whether Hapoel Be'er Sheva had a shot in the upcoming soccer season. Now the plates had been cleared, and his mother had set the wooden table with small bowls of cubed watermelon, salted peanuts, and sunflower seeds.

The man with the red glasses smiled warmly at Nava. "The meatballs were perfect, Nava. I must ask for the recipe before we go. I actually cook quite a bit at home."

His mother gave a nervous nod, tucking a strand of hair behind her ear. "Thank you, Robert. It is actually very easy to make."

Roni felt Robert lean toward him, all geniality and charm.

"Roni, we need to ask you a few questions." His tone was casual, his smile wide. "Important questions. Questions that could have serious implications in Parliament. Think we can have a little chat?"

Roni nodded, his voice polite but strained. "I hope I can give you the answers you need."

"Can you tell me how you got to shield Asher at the attack site?"

Roni blinked. "I don't know."

"Roni—were you trying to save his life? Were you trying to screen him with your body?"

"I don't know; I can't remember the attack," he answered, frustration creeping into his voice.

Next, Roni heard the psychologist's voice. "Let's take a step back. Try to trace your memory to the last thing you remember. Can you visualize the morning of the bombing?"

"No. It's... I think we were on our way out of the Strip."

"On your way out?" The psychologist's voice was steady. "What were you doing in Gaza?"

"I can't remember. I don't remember anything." Sami squeezed Roni's arm, his strong hand offering support.

The psychologist didn't let up. "You were in Gaza on a mission. Do you remember what it was?"

"No," answered Roni

"Do you remember your briefing before you left for the mission?"

"No."

"Do you remember arriving at your base camp?"

"No," Roni repeated.

"Do you remember leaving home?"

"No." Panic. His breath quickened. He felt like he was slipping into something dark and heavy—

Sami took up the questioning. "Son, do you remember the Crusaders?"

Roni suddenly raised his head. "Yes! They didn't come."

An energy spike swept through the room.

"And do you remember why they didn't come?" asked the psychologist.

"Yes! Because of the missile attack." Roni turned in his father's direction. "We were attacked, Dad. A missile landed in the kindergarten Friday morning. I remember that! We went there to see it! I remember!"

Chapter 25

Hashim

Hashim felt as if a sledgehammer had struck him in the chest. These people were talking about his missile. The missile he had fired with his own hand had landed right here. In a kindergarten?

It was too much. He wanted to run away, to escape, now. But there was no way out of this house. Even if he somehow slipped out unnoticed, even if he made it past the street, he would be alone in hostile Israel. He didn't stand a chance.

He needed time, and right now his best chance was to wait in this house until he found a solution. Somehow, within seventy-two hours of the launch, he had found himself on the other side of one of the most sealed borders in the world, sitting and eating watermelon at the impact site of the very missile he had launched.

He had always been told that Allah works in mysterious ways, but at that moment, he felt it would be nice if Allah, in His infinite wisdom, would throw him a clue as to what was going on.

Chapter 26

Assad

"Allah, in His infinite wisdom, will guide you." The old priest smiled kindly at his sparse flock of followers as they stood.

The Lion waited in the shadow of a giant pillar as the last few worshippers slowly fastened their sandals and shuffled toward the exit. Only when the heavy silence settled did he step forward.

His old imam. The only person in the entire Gaza Strip whom he could approach. The imam had held the largest influence on the Assad's upbringing. As a child he had been brought to this mosque morning and night. In those days, the place had overflowed with worshippers. The emerald-green tiles and turquoise geometric patterns of the carpets had been beautiful, almost magical, to his young eyes. The soaring arches seemed endlessly high. His father would bring him early, trying to catch a place as close to the imam as possible. The imam had been younger then, but his message was the same: He preached the love of Allah and mankind. The communal worship of hundreds had filled the Lion with a warm feeling of purity, of strength, of belonging.

But times had changed. The mosque now seemed much smaller, and the imam's message of brotherhood and unity widely seemed outdated and naïve. The fire-breathing, jihad-inciting imams had captured the minds and spirits of the younger Gazan generation. Month by month, attendance had dwindled until all that remained of the once-great congregation was a few dozen loyal old men who worshipped together in the half-empty mosque. Funds for upkeep were lessening, tiles were missing from the beautiful walls, and the once awe-inspiring building sorely needed renovation.

"*Assalamu Alaikum,*" he greeted his old imam.

The old man turned toward the Lion. He stared at him for a few seconds before his face lit up with a magnificent smile.

"Assad! *Wa'alaikum Salam!*" The imam's voice brimmed with warmth. "It has been a long time…"

Assad nodded. "I hope you are in good health and spirits?"

"Me? Oh, I'm fine. I feel like one of the lucky ones—Allah has been merciful to me," the old man responded, still smiling joyfully.

"I need your advice," Assad began. "I've been having thoughts… it's… I think…"

The imam raised a hand, stopping him mid-sentence. "Assad, let me stop you for a moment. I've just been preaching for an hour, and I would gladly give all I have for a cup of coffee. Would you mind if we go into my chambers and talk while the water in the *cezve* boils?"

"It would be my honor."

The imam smiled. "I fear I am terribly addicted to the brown bean."

Slowly they made their way to the modest chamber that was the imam's place of rest. It was a simple room, furnished only with a bed, a wooden cupboard, a large metal desk, and a small kitchen counter. Assad couldn't help comparing this small room to the Sheikh's mansion.

The old man refused Assad's offer of help as he scuttled about, heaping teaspoons of dark-brown Turkish coffee and sugar into an upright *cezve* kettle and adding water from the tap. There were once helpers who took care of the imam and his guests. Now he was alone.

Once the *cezve* was cooking over a gas flame, the old man sat down opposite the Lion, his fingers unconsciously clicking the colorful beads of a *misbaha* prayer chain hanging from the palm of his right hand.

"How are you, Assad? Why do you come to me today?"

Assad paused. How could he explain those dangerous thoughts that had entered his mind and wouldn't leave?

"I'm having trouble," he began.

The old man said nothing.

"Trouble. In my head."

Still, the old man said nothing. For a long moment, the only sounds were the hiss of the small gas fire and the almost inaudible, glassy click of the prayer beads as they ran through the old man's fingers. Assad took a long breath. The warmth emitted from the small gas stove and the potent smell of coffee and sandalwood enveloped him, calming his soul.

"I have been a fighter for four years, though it feels like a lifetime. I am ready to take my place in paradise, but…. I need to know." He looked up, meeting the imam's eyes. "Do you think I am on the right path? Am I indeed doing Allah's will?"

The old man leaned forward in his chair.

"These are dangerous questions to ask in the times we are living in," he whispered.

"I know," Assad admitted. "That is why I came to you."

"You have come to me so that I will strengthen you in your way, so that I will bless you in your current fight against the oppressors.

"Yes," Assad sighed.

The old man leaned back. "You have survived four years of daily battle, and your survival has created a power within you. You are one of the most celebrated fighters in Gaza. You see, Allah has a plan for you. The first step was to build an influential leader out of you."

"So, what is the second step?"

"Now, you use your power," the old man slapped the armrest of his chair as he spoke. "Now, you use the love your people have for you." He leaned in, his voice steady but urgent. "Now is the time for you to rise. Not as a fighter. But as a leader."

Assad stared at him. "What are you saying?"

The old man's dark brown eyes were dancing in the warm light. "Now is the time for you to leave the underground, to stop the violence, to rise *against* the terror." He was smiling, and Assad could not help but to smile back. The Imam's words had struck home.

"Show me how to do it. How can I know where to start?"

"My dear Assad, I think you know the answer to your question. It is your mission to spread the *true* ideals of Allah and his prophet Muhammad. Now the true battle begins. The battle for peace."

Chapter 27

Prime Minister Rahav

Prime Minister Rahav was propped up in his bed, multi-focal glasses perched on his nose as he read the short report. His wife lay beside him, snoring gently. A heavy sleeper, she had actually once slept through a missile attack during the first Lebanon War. The explosions had shaken the windows, but not disturbed his wife's sleep. Still, he turned the pages as silently as humanly possible, casting an apprehensive glance at her with each page turn.

Faint moonlight shone through the wooden slats of the windows. He could hear pine trees whispering gently in the night breeze. A short burst of radio transmission echoed but was quickly silenced, reminding Rahav that the peaceful residence garden was chock-full of patrolling Secret Service men.

The report held some good news. Robert Rosen, the Prime Minister's public relation advisor in chief, had made a wonderful discovery. Among the survivors of the terror attack that morning were two soldiers—one Jewish and one Druze. This was an incredible piece of luck. And the Jewish soldier had actually *saved* the Druze during the attack. This could easily be spun into PR gold. Rosen's plan for the Prime Minister was deviously simple:

"Get the Jewish soldier who saved the Druze soldier's life. Parade the two of them on as many national television and internet newscasts as possible. Get everyone talking about them. Create a frenzy in online media. Have everybody talking about the two. The Druze elders can no longer complain without seeming heartless.. For a moment, Israel will seem like a country living in beautiful harmony, a peaceful island in the bloody Middle East, and, by default, you can be the one to take credit."

Rahav smiled to himself. Simple. Beautiful. Effective.

He placed the report down and switched off his reading light. As he inched himself down from a sitting position, he couldn't help but smile.

Goddammit. Robert Rosen had done it again, the bastard!

Chapter 28

Hannah

A mere two kilometers away from the Prime Minister's residence in Jerusalem, Hannah stood motionless at the base of her building. She had hitchhiked back, still dressed in hospital clothes, the thin gown barely shielding her from the biting Jerusalem night air.

Looking up at the stairs leading to her apartment, she couldn't bring herself to move. For a full five minutes, she stood and breathed in the crisp night air, her forehead pressed against the smooth Jerusalem stone that covered the building. Eventually, she forced herself to climb, step by slow step. Halfway up, a wave of dizziness engulfed her, almost sending her tumbling backward. She barely made it by hanging on to the rail.

She woke a neighbor to ask for the spare key, entered the flat, and lowered herself painfully into bed. Her bruised arm sent wave upon wave of dull pain, and her head was now splitting. But the physical pain was minor compared to the torturous thoughts that pierced her soul.

Johnny. Dead! And ten soldiers. All of them dead.

How could it have gone so wrong? She tried to justify the terrible consequences of her actions to herself.

The Palestinians are under an oppressive occupation. They have no other way of communicating to the world than through violence. It is the only way they can resist the fascist Israeli regime. Johnny knew where we were headed. We both took risks.

The thoughts tangled together, looping in endless, fevered circles. Images of Johnny's face—alive, grinning, full of energy—flashed in her head. The thought of his body, lifeless and still, followed close behind. Somewhere in the chaos, the Tylenol PM kicked in, and exhaustion finally dragged her under.

It was early in the morning when the telephone yanked her from sleep. She turned on her pillow, and a mind-numbing flash of pain reminded her she was bruised, possibly bleeding. The ringing stopped for a few seconds, then began again. And then again. She wished the ringing would stop. After what felt like several hours, Hannah couldn't take it anymore. With a whimper of pain, she heaved herself off the bed and staggered across the room to where her phone lay. The screen displayed an unknown caller.

"Who is it?" she mumbled, voice thick with exhaustion.

"Hannah?" asked a deep voice. It was Yossi, leader of the Israelis for Palestine Brigade.

"Yes?" Hannah whispered.

"The police are on their way to pick you up. You must leave immediately."

"The police? But how do you know…" She was still groggy, trying to find clarity.

"Listen to me. You have got to leave now. This second."

"Leave? Where to? Where should I go?"

"Go to the market, meet me at the Fifth of May café," Yossi instructed.

"Yossi…"

His voice hardened. "There's no time. You've got exactly five minutes from now before they arrive. Just walk out the door now. You messed up, Hannah. You messed up big."

With a click, the line went dead.

Chapter 29

Hashim

Hashim was woken at 5:30 in the morning by a gentle knocking on his door. At 6:00 sharp, Robert Rosen arrived at the Uliel family's doorstep, escorted by two long-legged assistants, their heels clicking sharply against the pavement. Hashim had never seen a human being so beautiful. At least, not in real life.

Nava Uliel welcomed the team into the house, just as Dr. Yuri was preparing to leave after a quick morning checkup of the two boys, Roni and "Asher the Druze."

"Hey Doctor," Rosen called out heartily, "how are our two heroes?"

Dr. Yuri slung his bag over his shoulder. "Better. Just as I predicted, Roni's vision has improved immensely."

"Already?" Rosen spoke in feigned surprise as he turned to Roni, "Well done, young man. Can you see me clearly?"

Roni hesitated. "Sort of. It's all a little hazy at the edges. But I'm almost there."

"That's wonderful news!" Rosen continued jovially. "And you, Asher? Good as new?"

Hashim stared at his feet. "Yes. I think so."

"All we need is to dress you up. Here, go change."

One of Rosen's assistants handed Hashim a bag containing a pressed uniform, complete with the insignia of the Israeli Border Patrol.

"It's your size," said the ravishing assistant. She was as tall as Hashim, her hair tinted with blonde streaks, her red skirt ending mid-thigh, and on her feet she wore a pair of shoes with the highest, sharpest heels Hashim had ever seen. For a moment, he marveled at how she didn't topple over. The assistant felt Hashim's lingering stare. She smiled at him, her teeth a perfect white. Hashim was instantly bewitched.

"Why don't you go change?" she suggested.

Dreamily, Hashim took the uniform and went to the bathroom.

It took him a while to work out which button closed which pocket, and threading the extra-long military boot laces through the many eyelets was a bit of a riddle. In the end, he stuffed the surplus lace ends into his socks. He stood up to look at his reflection in the full-length mirror that was mounted on the door.

His heart went cold.

He was looking at one of the most feared and hated figures in Gaza—a patrolnik. If his family could see him now, he would be disowned on the spot just for dressing like this. Back home in Gaza, people wouldn't dare wear this uniform. Not even as a joke. The dark-green beret and matching dark-gray uniform, the shiny black shoes. A uniform that spelled vicious hatred.

He felt sick.

What have I become?

He was eating the enemy's food, drinking the enemy's Coke—he had drunk an entire bottle at supper, to the amusement of his hosts. He just couldn't help himself.

He had let himself be lulled into their world.

He was failing Gaza.

He was failing Na'ima.

A wave of self-contempt flowed through him. He had forgotten himself, who he was, where he came from. The past twenty-four hours in the Uliel household had been so comfortable, so warm and inviting, that he had surrendered to the easiness of it all. How swiftly he had turned from Hashim Abu-Tir, Mohandas and hero of Gaza, into Asher, the Zionist-loving pig.

Unless…

There was a long knife lying by the kitchen sink where Nava had been making sandwiches for them to take on their journey.

Could he do it?

Could he avenge Na'ima's death?

Could he kill them all?

Trying to imagine the murders, a thrill passed through his body. He imagined himself gripping the knife, stepping into the kitchen, taking the first silent strike. One by one. They would never see it coming. For the first time in his life, he felt the jihadi rhetoric filling his soul, and it felt good. The more he thought about it, the more it felt right. Righteous. His body tingled; he felt cleansed and pure. He was about to become a soldier in holy jihad, about to strike a mighty blow in the belly of the Zionist beast. *Allahu Akbar*! Allah is great!

Chapter 30

Hannah

Hannah hobbled down The Tree of Life road, which cut through the center of Mahne Yehuda, the largest and most chaotic market in Jerusalem. It was midday, and the *shuk* was crowded with hundreds of jostling customers all haggling with the loud store vendors. She passed storefronts boasting a myriad of mouthwatering goods: pickled sardines from Morocco; bitter olives from Nablus; mounds of baklava; dense cakes of halva; fruits and vegetables that gleamed in the sun. And in between the vegetable stalls, small, trendy cafés and bars had sprouted, attracting tourists and young Jerusalemites with promises of fresh salads, craft beers, and overpriced espresso.

Hannah wavered, unable to remember which hole-in-the-wall concealed the Fifth of May Café. The loud cries of the hawkers, mixed with music from the surrounding cafés, made her head pound.

"Hannah!" A hand grabbed her, causing her to jump.

It was Yossi.

"It's too loud to talk outside. Come, I've got a table for us in the back."

Still gripping her arm, Yossi led her into the narrow café, past the tiny, rickety tables crammed with students, Arab taxi drivers on break, and a group of European tourists hunched over their phones. At the very back, Yossi pulled out a chair and motioned for her to sit. As he leaned close toward Hannah, she could smell that he had been drinking.

"Tell me something, Hannah." His voice was low but taut. "Are you out of your bloody mind? What were you thinking? Do you understand how much trouble you have caused the Brigade?"

Hannah stiffened. "If you want to tell me what a bad girl I am, I'm leaving now."

"Get up and leave. I don't care. But before you go, have a quick look at these."

Yossi opened a large envelope and slid the contents onto the small table. Printed photos. Dozens of them. A crazed woman, face distorted in mid-scream, spittle flying out of her mouth, her whole body pointed at her enemies like a poisoned arrow in flight. When she realized what she was looking at, her heart skipped a beat. These were photos of *her* throwing bags of cow blood at the crossing.

"How did you get these?"

"We have sympathetic friends in important places."

Hannah looked up from the shocking photos.

"Friends?"

"Yes, Hannah. You're not the only one who believes in the cause. Now, I want to show you another set of pictures."

The second set of photos made her retch. She tried to turn away, but Yossi forced her to look at the photos.

"Look."

She saw two legs standing, frozen in place for a split second after the torso had been blown away. Pools of blood. Unrecognizable body parts, shredded by tiny, glinting ball bearings. Her stomach cramped, but as she hadn't eaten for hours, nothing came up but balls of foul air erupting from her hollow gut in silent burps.

"This is all your work." Yossi tapped the photos angrily. "All this death is your fault. If you had not caused a diversion at the crossing, the bomber would not have had the chance to get so close to Israeli citizens."

She shook her head, whispering, "No…"

"When the police get to you and link you to the Brigade, it will destroy us. It will ruin everything we've been working for. We'll be branded as terrorists. We will lose all our backers and all our funding. And Johnny—his family will demand justice; they will spend millions just to close us down. Do you understand what you did?"

"What can we do?" she whispered.

"We? *We* do nothing but deny having any connection to the protest. That's what *we* do. But you—you have to disappear. You have to go now."

"Go? Go where?"

"Out of the country. But the airports and train stations are all monitored. You'll be picked up seconds after you walk through an entrance."

"So what do I do?"

"The brigade council had an emergency meeting earlier, and we have come up with a solution. We pulled some favors, and we are going to smuggle you out of the country. Your escort is already waiting outside."

Hannah's head was spinning. "Escort? Where is he taking me?"

"At such short notice and with the limited options at our disposal, there's only one place where you can disappear completely." Yossi's face darkened. "Until things cool down, we're sending you to Gaza."

Chapter 31

Hashim

Would the knife still be there on the counter?

Hashim opened the door and walked down the short hallway to the living room.

"Ready to go?" one of the assistants asked as he entered.

"I just need a glass of water." His voice came out as a whisper. He moved woodenly toward the kitchen sink.

"We don't drink tap water." Nava put her hand gently on his shoulder. "I'll pour you a glass of filtered water."

"It's okay; I don't mind."

The knife was still there. Lying near the sink, just as he remembered. A long, triangular-blade with a lethal point. His heart sped up.

Nava brushed past him.

"You fix your shoelaces, and I'll get you cold water from the fridge."

Hashim stared at the knife. It was now or never. Push Nava aside, grab the knife, and then… He felt his pulse beating wildly as he prepared to move.

A firm hand gripped his shoulder. He froze.

"Ready to go, Chief?" It was Rosen.

To get out of Rosen's grasp, he quickly bent over and fiddled with his shoelaces, his eyes still glued to the knife. Then he watched in dismay as Nava turned, picked it up, and fed it into the dishwasher, together with a few plates that lay by the sink.

His gaze darted around the kitchen, searching for something—anything—he could use as a weapon. But the moment had passed, and with it, any chance he had to strike them down. Deflated, he lowered his gaze to the glass of water Nava had poured for him. His hand trembled slightly as he lifted it, forcing himself to take a sip, the cool liquid doing little to quench the feeling of frustration burning inside him.

"Okay, folks, let's move." Rosen called out. "We'll do this so fast, you guys will be home by dinner."

Hashim and Roni were guided out of the door toward a large, air-conditioned Econoline van that waited at the gate. Hashim looked at the large black car that was about to whisk him away, further into Israel. The fury that had consumed him earlier ebbed, giving way to a creeping, icy fear. Time was running out; it wouldn't take long before someone would recognize him as the Mohandas.

The doors slammed shut behind Hashim, the engine rumbled to life, and soon they were speeding away from Sedera. Looking out of the window he watched the yellow, square-block buildings shrinking into the distance, fading in the hazy morning light.

Rosen turned from the front seat to face them. "It's like this, boys: I admire the hell out of the two of you. I believe that you two are goddamn heroes! Modern heroes. True warriors. The two of you experienced an atrocious attack yesterday, and yet—no complaints. No self-pity. Heroes!"

Hashim sat stone-faced.

Rosen went smoothly on. "And I want the entire country to hear your story. I want the world to know it. I want to remind every citizen of Israel that we are still the most moral army in the world, and that we value human life. And, most importantly, that we are one. Jews, Druze, Christians, and Arabs. And that is why you, Roni—a Jew—put your life on the line to save Asher's life."

A wave of dread coursed through Hashim. If he were to go on air, he would be as good as dead. Word would get around Gaza faster than the speed of a rocket. The great Mohandas was actually a spy for the Jews! There was no way in the world he would be able to explain his appearance on Israeli television or any of the other consecutive appearances planned for the two "heroes." His family would disown him. The Lion would mark him for death.

The van rumbled down the highway, taking him further away from safety.

An hour later, they had reached the southern outskirts of Tel Aviv. The van veered off the main road, and suddenly the Mediterranean was at their window, stretching out westward.

"The sea!" Hashim blurted out.

The pale-blue water sparkled with a million suns reflected on the small waves. The beach restaurants were still empty, the chairs stacked in pyramids. A Nigerian municipal worker in a neon vest picked cigarette butts from the sand and gently slid them into a biodegradable waste bag. Two old men wearing bathing trunks threw a weighted ball at each other, their bare, wrinkled chests slick with sweat.

Hashim gazed at an almost naked woman jogging on the promenade, her body covered by a tiny bikini bathing suit. His teachers had warned him about the depravity of the Jews, but until now, it had all been theoretical. Now he saw it with his own eyes. If their women ran around like that, unashamedly displaying their personal, sacred beauty for everyone to see, the Jews as a people must be rotten to the core. A nation without honor. He glanced at the others in the van. No one was even looking. Rosen and the two assistants were all on their phones; the only one looking out was him.

Once again, he stared out of the window. The same Mediterranean, the same sand, the same waves crashing on the same beach. Yet things couldn't be more different. And then a single thought filled his mind, calming his soul like cool water:

I am in the hands of Allah, playing a part specially chosen for me. Whatever happens, it is Allah's way. It is Allah's will.

Chapter 32

Roni

On the hour-long ride to Tel Aviv, Roni was relieved to find that his vision had sharpened, and he could already discern the surrounding view with greater detail. The soft kaleidoscope of colors was coming into focus with every passing hour—the headrest in front of him, the colorful miniskirts of Rosen's assistants. He could see the dark green uniform of the patrolnik one row in front of him.

Asher—the patrolnik who had survived the bombing.

They had held on to each other. That's what Rosen had told them while preparing them for the upcoming interviews.

I held onto him; he held on to me; we saved each other. But that's total bullshit. If that were the case, one of us would have absorbed the full explosion wave, while the other would have been relatively safe, shielded from the bomb. That's how physics worked. It doesn't make sense. Why was I holding on to him?

Rosen continued to coach them for their upcoming appearances.

"Now—we've got a great day planned for you two." Rosen shuffled a stack of papers, which Roni assumed detailed their itinerary. "Three national radio stations, both national commercial television stations, cable news, and a photo shoot for the *Jerusalem Post*. By the eight pm news tonight, you guys are going to be celebrities! We'll be starting with Channel 12, morning news. You are going to be chatting with Didi Dimor in exactly one hour from now."

As puzzled as he felt, Roni felt a jolt of excitement. They were about to meet one of Israel's most famed celebrities. Didi Dimor hosted the morning talk show and also the highest-rated game show—"Box-It!™, every Tuesday at 21:00, only on Channel Twelve!"—and when Didi was off-screen, he spent his time at one of his three ultra-trendy restaurants in Tel Aviv. He was smooth, good-looking, and extremely popular.

"First stop will be makeup. Your uniforms are looking sharp, thanks to your mother, Roni. From makeup, we move to the green room, where there will be sandwiches and drinks if you're hungry. You'll wait there until they call you to tell your incredibly heroic story."

Roni bit his tongue, unsure how he was supposed to describe something he couldn't even remember.

"And let me give you a small tip. If you want Didi Dimor to like you, try not to show your surprise when

136

you see how scrawny he looks. He hates that!" added Rosen.

"Scrawny?" asked a surprised Roni.

Finally, the van slowed to a halt at the Herzliya Studios entrance. A young guard quickly lifted the electric barrier, admitting the van into Israel's premier filming studio. They disembarked and were immediately led by a production runner through a long corridor that ran straight from the entrance to "hair and makeup." An assistant producer helped guide Roni, even though by now he could walk unassisted.

Once the makeup team were done with him, Roni was led to the green room together with the patrolnik, Rosen, and his entourage.

Roni looked around the large room. He could fuzzily make out a few couches and a wide table in the middle set with what the PA told him were sliced vegetables, diet drinks, and whole-wheat bread sandwiches.

They weren't the first in the room.

A petite woman with platinum-blonde curls seemed to hurl herself into Rosen's chest as they entered.

"Robbie, *Hayim shelli*, love of my life! How are you?!" Roni's heart skipped a beat as he heard the inimitable nasal voice and fuzzily recognized Orit

Katz, Israeli Academy-Award winner and leading lady in almost every movie made in the country.

She petted Rosen's stomach. "You gorgeous hunk, have you lost weight?"

The green room door opened, and another familiar voice called out, "Rosen, you loser, what are *you* doing here?" A small entourage swept into the room, at the center of which walked the striking Minister of Finance. The minister reached Rosen and shook his hands.

"I'm sure you know this beautiful lady?" Rosen asked.

"Can't really miss her, can you?" answered the Minister of Finance in a mock-complaining whine. "She's in every movie, every billboard, everywhere!"

Roni was surprised to see the great man behaving like a fifteen-year-old teeny-bopper.

The door flew open once more, and all heads turned to watch as Chef David Ballilli moodily entered the green room. Roni's mother adored Chef Ballilli. One of the hardest-working TV chefs, Ballilli had been the first professional chef to fuse French and Arab cuisines, creating a style of cooking unknown to the world until then. But in Roni's view, that was not why he had become a TV star. The reason he had become a celebrity chef was his ability to appear on television and keep a straight face while coughing up bizarre lines such as "A tomato is a tragic love affair," and "When I see a green pepper, it makes me want to go into a dark room and feel myself."

"David, daaaaarling." Orit Katz disengaged from Rosen and flew toward Ballilli.

Roni listened to their mutual gushing, excited at the exalted company he was in, adjusting to the sheer absurdity of it all. Smiling, he turned to share a glance with the patch of olive green that was Asher, the patrolnik. But there was no olive-green patch where he should have been. There was no olive green anywhere in the room.

He looked around. The patrolnik was just slipping out of the green-room door. Without thinking, Roni shoved his chair back and went after him.

Chapter 33

Hashim

The room was full of distractions—people laughing and shouting, hurried instructions, producers barking out notes. No one was paying attention to Asher, the patrolnik.

No one was looking at him. It was now or never.

He inched toward the open green room door, craning his neck to see what lay behind it. The sun-dappled path outside stretched ahead. At the end of the tree-lined path, a lone security guard stood by the studio gate, idly killing time by whacking the ragged edges of a green shrub with a branch. Hashim tried to assess his chances. What would happen if he just coolly walked out of the gate? The uniform would do the work for him. He was just another soldier. A border patrolnik heading home.

One thing was certain—his window of opportunity was short. The segment recording would be starting any minute. He had to move now. Quietly he stood up, took a deep breath, and edged toward the door. No one noticed. Silently, he slipped out the door.

I'm out!

Swiftly, he made his way toward the exit gate. He had only taken a few steps when a hand caught the shoulder strap of his shirt.

"Where are you going?" It was Roni.

"Home. I want to go home." He tugged at Roni's arm.

"But we're going on air in a few minutes. Don't you want to appear on the show?"

"No, I think I'll just go now," said Hashim. But Roni held onto him with an iron grip, eyes searching his face. A flicker of something—recognition.

Roni's fingers curled tighter around his shirt. Hashim tried to pull Roni's hand off, gently at first, then more and more violently as Roni tightened his grasp, holding him with two hands.

"You... I remember you. We got you in Gaza. You're..."

Hashim switched tactics. Instead of trying to release Roni's hands, he went on the offensive, snapping his hands around Roni's throat, fingers digging into flesh. Their small battle was deadly earnest and deadly silent. Roni gasped, his hands flying up, grabbing at Hashim's wrists, prying and pulling.

"Hey! What the hell are you two doing?" Hashim saw Roni's eyes dart sideways. Approaching them was the nationally famous ratings king himself, Didi

Dimor. For a split second, Roni loosened his grip in surprise. Hashim wrenched himself out of Roni's grasp and, finally free, bolted toward the studio exit.

"What are you doing to the other soldier? You guys go on air in ten minutes," shouted Dimor, red blood vessels managing to make an appearance through his heavily spray-tanned face. Dimor's shouting drew Rosen and the rest of the green room occupants. Even the Minister of Finance dashed out to see the commotion, a paper tissue shielding his starched white collar from his heavy makeup.

Hashim ran. Just five more steps, and he was out.

"He's not a soldier," he heard Roni gasping behind him. "He didn't save my life. He is a wanted terrorist. He's the Mohandas."

Two more steps.

Shouts erupted behind him as Hashim reached the gate. But before he could clear the exit, a sticky, leaf-encrusted branch came flashing out of nowhere, tripping him up and sending him flying into the guard booth. The impact with the booth wall was so strong that stars shot in front of his eyes. He dimly saw a cluster of figures running toward him. His strength drained; he slid down the booth wall and sat on the ground, waiting for them to capture him.

Chapter 34

Roni

"Hello, is this Roni?"

"Speaking."

"Hello Roni, this is Ya'akov Rahav speaking, how are you?"

"Mr. Prime Minister?" Roni's mouth went dry. He was sitting in a small production room behind the studio. Rosen was sitting opposite him, watching him with what seemed like quiet amusement.

"Roni, first, I want you to know that I admire what you did on that terrible day. You showed guts. Guts and courage."

"Thank you, sir, I really didn't do anything—"

"I want to tell you a little story. Can I?" Roni knew this wasn't a request.

"Of course, sir."

"When I was in the Naval Commandos, it was a time when Israel had its back to the wall. We were standing alone against five Arab states who wanted us annihilated. There were three million people living in Israel, fighting against twenty million Arabs.

"In those days, we used to go out on secret missions three, sometimes four times a month. We had no red tape, no procurement units breathing down our necks. Ops would dream up the most outrageous missions, and we would suit up and go get the job done. You've heard about *Shayetet 13*, the naval commandos, yes?"

"Of course, sir," Roni answered.

"Good. Anyway, where was I? Ah, yes!" Rahav's voice was warm, nostalgic. "It was a golden age, Roni. Some of the operations we pulled off back then are taught to this day in military academies around the globe. Sandhurst, West Point, Langley. Hell, even the Pakistan Military Academy, and they really hate Israel. And do you know why we were so successful?"

"Why, sir?"

"Because we asked no questions. We got the orders from ops, we trained, and we won."

There were a few moments of silence. Roni, thinking that maybe the PM was waiting for an answer, quickly coughed up a "Yes, sir!"

Rahav's voice softened. "Roni, I have a favor to ask of you. It's not a simple one, but nevertheless—I have decided to ask you this favor. I want to give you a chance to serve your country in a way that few ever do. Are you willing?"

"Anything, sir!"

"The man you know as the Mohandas."

There was another long pause until Roni tentatively said, "Yes?"

"I need you to forget for the moment that he is the Mohandas. I need you to believe that he is Asher, the patrolnik whose life you saved. I need you to go through your television appearance in a few minutes and say exactly what Rosen told you to say. I can't go into the specifics, Roni, but I can share that—this is a matter of national security, highly classified."

"Of course, sir!"

"So, can you do it for Israel? Can you do it for your country?"

Roni hesitated. Just for a second. Rahav quickly carried on. "Whatever Rosen asks of you, no matter how strange it may seem, please understand that he speaks for the government of Israel, and you are to do as he says. Are we clear, Roni?"

"Yes, sir."

"Well done. Now you focus on your mission, and if it is successful, I'll pull some strings and see if I can get you sent to officers' training school. How does that sound? A lieutenant in the Paratroopers Brigade."

"That sounds excellent, sir."

"Good. Then do what needs to be done. Good luck, soldier." The line went dead. Rosen leaned forward and plucked the phone from Roni's hand.

"Come on soldier, let's go make television history."

If anything, Roni was surprised by how unremarkable his first-ever television appearance felt, given the super-remarkable circumstances that had brought him there. But once the little red 'ON AIR' light flickered on the camera, and the audience, incited by a manic floor manager, started cheering, Roni felt at ease. He had seen plenty of "behind-the-scenes" specials, and that—together with Didi Dimor's unique ability to make you feel like the only important person on Earth—made him quite comfortable. Pretty soon, he found himself chatting away as expertly as the oldest hack on Israeli TV.

He smiled politely at the Minister of Finance, believed actress Orit Katz's description of her new movie as a masterpiece, and salivated at the scent of sauteed onions, pine nuts, and minced meat floating from Chef Ballilli's little kitchen corner ("Touch it. Feel the onion still pining for its earthy womb.")

Roni's only moment of queasiness came when he was asked to describe his heroic deeds at the crossing, introduced by his gushing host as "Boldly shielding the Druze patrolnik." Four lies in a five-word sentence. He wasn't bold, he didn't shield anyone, and the Mohandas was no Druze, let alone a patrolnik. But

146

with the PM's words still ringing in his ears, Roni swallowed the sour little lump that had formed in his throat. And thus was history reconstructed.

"So, you shielded each other. Wow! That's amazing! A real story of modern-day heroes. It's so rare that we have a story this huge on our little show."

The crowd tittered at Didi Dimor's false modesty.

"It's a small story that reflects so much about our society!" The Minister of Finance remarked, flashing his famous smile. "To all those who believe this administration has been neglecting the Druze, or anyone who has anything but the highest regard for the IDF's strongest and most courageous Druze warriors, I say—we are all one! And I think that Roni here proved that with his own body, risking his life to save a fellow soldier with no regard for race or religion." The crowd erupted in wild cheering.

The minister's monologue surprised Roni. Could it be that the Minister of Finance had been brought all the way here just to add weight to Roni's story?

"I have so much to ask you, Roni, but it's time for this falling-to-pieces studio to make a few shekels, so let's take a break for a couple of...." The crowd joined Dimor: "Co-mmer-cials!"

Roni smiled at the camera, trying to look as if he deeply appreciated all that had been said about him, even though he knew that a crushed and bruised

Hashim was sitting only a few meters away in the green room, covered by the studio guard's taser.

Chapter 35

Rosen

"Do you want me to call the military police? Regular police? What do you want to do with him?" The studio guard stood by the Palestinian, taser pointed menacingly.

Rosen didn't answer right away. He stood, hands on his hips, staring at the crumpled figure on the sofa.

"Don't call anyone. Leave me alone with him."

"Are you sure?" his assistant asked, casting a wary glance at the boy. "Is it safe? Isn't he, like, a terrorist or something?"

"Go," Rosen growled. "Both of you."

The blonde assistant melted out the door together with the studio guard.

Rosen took a slow step forward, then another. Hashim sat frozen, hunched in the far corner of the sofa. He looked like what he was: a frightened child. Not some hardened militant. The kid was crying, for god's sake.

"What's your name?"

No answer.

"Come, I will not do you any harm," Rosen tried again. I'm not a soldier, nor a policeman. What's your name?"

A long silence stretched between them. Then, in a shaky voice: "Hashim."

"Where are you from? Gaza?" The boy nodded.

"How old are you?"

"Eighteen and a half."

"And a half?" Rosen asked in a bemused tone. "Why do they call you the Mohandas?"

"I swear on my mother's life! It's all a big mistake!" the boy mumbled through his tears.

Rosen tilted his head. "I'm sure it is. Just one big mistake."

"Yes!" Hashim's gaze snapped up, desperate. "I just said something about the fins. That's all. I'm not a Mohandas. I've only just graduated from high school."

"Fins?"

"They were doing them wrong, so I told them—"

"Hang on." Rosen held up a hand. "Slowly. Who was doing what wrong?"

"At the factory. They were doing the missile fins wrong—"

"Factory? You mean a Qassam missile factory?"

"Yes. Of course."

"Good lord. What the hell were you doing in a missile factory?"

"I was running deliveries for Hamas. They made jokes about me, and I got mad."

"Oh God. And you told them what?"

"That the fins were wrong. Not aerodynamic. And we tested one, and I was right. So everyone started to call me the Mohandas."

Rosen let out a soft whistle. "You poor idiot. You improved the Qassam. The army is going to really have fun with you in interrogation."

He turned to leave. Who should he call? Probably the Israeli National Security Service—Shin Bet. This was their turf. He walked to the door, opened it, and then looked back. The Palestinian hadn't moved. He just sat there, staring at him, tears still spilling silently down his face.

Rosen stepped back into the room. To his surprise, he was feeling something he hadn't felt in years. Somewhere under the thick, blubbery layers of dead feelings, at the very depth of the black void that filled his soul, a miracle had happened.

Looking at the frightened Palestinian boy in front of him, a tiny pinprick of a lightbulb had suddenly flickered on in a place that, for over a decade, had seen nothing but darkness.

Chapter 36

Hannah

Hannah stared out the dirty windscreen at the endless, gray-black plains. Just forty-eight hours ago, she had driven down this exact highway with Johnny Melamed, her heart pounding with exhilaration, the protest ahead feeling like the start of something momentous. Forty-eight hours ago, she was a free woman—proud and idealistic.

Forty-eight hours ago, Johnny was alive.

And now she was going back, this time as a fugitive, at the mercy of strangers, on her way to Gaza.

She had already been passed from vehicle to vehicle twice, and she was sure there would be more yet. With each careful step, she was getting closer to Gaza, each transfer digging her deeper into the underground. The first driver at the Jerusalem market entrance had been an Israeli. He was a silent, sour-faced Brigade activist. The second, an Israeli Arab, at least acknowledged her, murmured something about "good intentions gone wrong." This third driver was a proper Palestinian, that much she knew, but she could not imagine how he was connected to the Brigade. He was the nicest of them all. Friendly.

They flew past a signpost pointing toward Sedera. Lights winked from the blocks of flats closest to the main road. The driver gave her a beaming smile.

"Are you hungry? Want me to buy you some food?"

"No, thanks."

"At least have some water."

She hesitated. "Okay."

Keeping his eyes on the road, the driver stretched back and pulled out a plastic water bottle from under the back seat. He opened the bottle and gave it to Hannah. She took a polite sip. It was warm tap water. Re-bottled.

"You smoke?" the driver fished a Kent from his pocket.

"No, I don't."

"Mind if I do?" He popped the cigarette into his lips and waved a plastic lighter at her.

Normally, Hannah would have crucified the poor oaf there on the spot for smoking in a car. Normally. But she was outside the realm of normal.

"Sure, go ahead."

The driver lit his cigarette; its stink soon filling the car. Noticing Hannah's discomfort, he politely opened his window a couple of millimeters to allow some smoke to escape. Hannah could not summon the energy to open the window on her side.

"Bad times, eh?" he mused, shaking his head. "Bad times. You know, my father used to say to me, 'War is not fought by weapons. It is fought by hearts.' I can see you have a big heart, like mine. If more people were like us, there would have been peace ten years ago. At least. Maybe more, who knows?"

Hannah smiled obligingly.

"It is the politicians who have hearts of fire. Hearts full of hate. I see them, and I cry inside. Where is their love?"

Hannah slumped deeper into her seat and stared at the emptiness surrounding them. They drove for another hour through what looked like an empty wasteland. Every once in a while, they would pass small, sleeping kibbutz settlements surrounded by anonymous cowsheds and fruit orchards, all gray in the dark night. Finally, they slowed to a halt in what seemed like a random, empty patch of road. They weren't anywhere. No lights, no signs of civilization. Only the desert, vast and empty.

The driver turned off the engine. "We're here." He opened her door, and Hannah stepped out, breathing in the pure night air in thankful gulps. She looked around her. The night was dark, a toenail clipping of a moon giving out a faint light. Broken rocks, a few scrawny trees, and endless sands.

Her driver flashed a white-toothed smile, and then, suddenly, as if queued by an invisible signal, he stamped out his cigarette and, with a quick movement, his hand shot out, grabbing her arm.

"Come." He started to pull her away from the car, out into the empty dunes.

"Where are we going?"

Hannah had met many Palestinians before. Being a political activist, she had joined forces with Palestinian students and politicians, all of whom were overjoyed to have this blonde, Jewish Israeli on their side. She had slept in houses in Nablus, eaten hummus in Ramallah, and attended rallies in Jenin. On returning to Jerusalem, she had told anyone who would listen how she had felt a oneness among them, a true feeling of mutual trust and admiration. Her time in the West Bank had given her the sense of a genuine bond between two peoples, a hope that peace in our time was within reach.

But here in the dark, being dragged into the desert by the driver, she felt terrified of this man. She realized she had, on some level, been terrified every time she had visited her Palestinian friends. There was no mutual trust. No sugary feeling of unity and brotherhood. She had lied to herself.

"Where are we going?"

"I'm taking you to the meeting place. I stop here. You will continue with my cousin, Akram."

They reached a tall dune. Her chaperone started climbing, and she wearily followed. Once they had ascended, the driver pointed eastward.

"That is Egypt. You will be taken in and then smuggled from the Egyptian side into Gaza. Be careful; Egypt is crawling with Zionist agents. The only place you will ever be safe is in Gaza City."

"Safe in Gaza City?"

The driver smiled at her. "Everything is relative in life. At least you can be sure that there will be no Zionist police to look for you there…"

He took a few quick steps, and suddenly he was close to her. Much too close. He was still smiling. He reached out and took her hand. Surprised, she didn't resist, and before she could realize his intentions, he yanked it forward, pressing it against the stiff bulge in his pants. Hannah tried to pull away, but he was stronger. His grip tightened, his other hand locking around her wrist, forcing her fingers over him.

"I'm here to help you, don't you see?" he asked.

He began rubbing her hand up and down his trouser front. Hannah tried furiously to slip out of his grasp. He undid the top button of his black trousers and sucked his stomach in. Hannah knew what was coming. Using her last ounce of strength, she kicked him squarely in the shin. He howled in pain, staggering back.

"You bitch! You daughter of a whore! That hurt. We were only having a little fun."

In two bounds, he was beside her, but this time he slapped Hannah across the face, sending her reeling to the ground. He ended their friendship with a well-aimed gobbet of spit, after which he climbed down the dune back to his car.

A few seconds later, she heard the car engine growl to life. Headlights flared, illuminating the dunes for an instant. For the next ten minutes, Hannah could hear the car motor diminishing through the still desert night, until there was nothing left but silence—an eerie, absolute silence that pressed against her ears, amplifying the rapid thud of her heartbeat.

Chapter 37

Roni

Roni couldn't help but chuckle at the bewildered expressions on the faces of Rosen's entourage when they were told that they would be left behind.

"I'm taking these two, and I'll drive the van myself. You all can go back to the office now," Rosen had instructed. They just nodded and asked no questions. Not a word. Looking through the back window of the van, Roni could see the stranded group of marvelously dressed and spectacularly stylish PR pros staring rather pathetically at the disappearing vehicle. They looked like expensive furniture abandoned on the side of the road. He sat behind Rosen, while Hashim—silent, stiff—rode shotgun.

"Where are we going?" Roni asked.

Rosen kept his eyes on the road, one hand lazily gripping the wheel. "We're going for a ride until I can think of our next move."

"What move? You told me we're taking the Arab to your military contact. You said we were turning him in."

"Well, we can't turn him in." Was Rosen's answer.

Roni blinked. "We can't?"

"You remember that little chat with your prime minister before the program?"

"Yes…?"

"That call started a chain of actions and reactions, and you, Roni, are one of the biggest links in that chain. The Prime Minister asked for your help, and you agreed to do anything that was needed. Are you still willing to do your supreme commander's bidding?" Rosen glanced at him in the rearview mirror.

"Of course!"

"Good. So what I need, what *we* need you to do, is work with me."

Roni couldn't understand where all this was leading, but it all seemed contrary to the solid facts. Fact one: The Arab was the bomb-maker they had been sent to extract three days—or a million years—ago. Two: The Palestinian had escaped Israeli custody because of the suicide bomber attack at the border. Three: By now, Hashim should have been locked up in a detention center. Those were the facts.

But he also knew that Rosen was Prime Minister Rahav's right-hand man, and he remembered what the PM had said to him. Very confusing.

Rosen swerved the van onto the shoulder of the road and stopped the car. The powerful engine hummed quietly as Rosen turned to face Roni.

"Can I trust you to work with me?"

"Yes." Roni met his gaze.

"Excellent! What we need to do now is lie low for a couple of hours." Rosen shifted back into drive, and they were moving again. "Have you guys ever been to the Dixie bar in Tel Aviv? They make the best spareribs in the country."

Allenby Street cuts through Tel Aviv, beginning at the sparkling beachfront and stretching all the way down to the blue-collar workshop quarter of Levinski Street, dividing the city like a jagged scar. Exhaust fumes clung to the humid air, mixing with the scent of frying falafel and sea breeze. Sitting at one of the many restaurants and bars along its pavements promised an endless parade of colorful characters. Harried bankers playing it cool in their designer suits, cinema students whizzing past on their electric scooters, penniless beggars whining for cigarettes from passing cars, a group of ultra-religious Hassidim dancing to house music pumping through loudspeakers on a battered van, their four-cornered, cloth prayer shawls flying in the air.

A noisy, colorful, and crowded street, it appeared to cow both Hashim, who had probably never seen such a busy street scene, and Roni, for whom Tel Aviv was the "Big City," a mecca of fashion, celebrities, and nightlife.

Rosen had seated the two young men opposite each other at a Dixie Bar booth. Across from Roni, Hashim was stiff, his shoulders hunched like he was bracing for an explosion. The two of them avoided each other's gaze, staring at their untouched plates. They had both declined to taste the spareribs offered by the waitress. Roni, because they were not kosher; Hashim, because they were not Halal. The both chose burgers and fries, but neither of them did any justice to the steaming hot patties that were served. Rosen sat at a table opposite them, talking on his phone, glancing now and then at Hashim, who squirmed under his gaze. Finally, Rosen got up and moved to sit with them. He laid the phone on the silver tabletop, staring at it as if trying to bore holes through the plastic keypad.

"How're your burgers?"

"Fine," the two boys mumbled in unison.

Rosen picked up the phone and dialed. There was no answer on the other end.

"Goddamn druggie! Won't be up before dark." Rosen violently pushed the end button on his phone.

Hashim, surprisingly, was the one to break the silence. "Sir, what exactly are we doing?"

Rosen turned to him and looked straight into his eyes.

"I'll tell you what. I have decided to take you home."

Roni's head snapped up. The Arab seemed just as surprised as he was.

"Home? To Gaza? But how?" said Hashim.

Rosen smiled. "I have a few connections from my army days. They'll help us get you in. One of my best friends was the strip commander back in the day. He knows every smuggling route, every tunnel. We'll meet up with him and make plans."

"When?"

"When the stupid bastard picks up his phone, I'll be able to answer that question. Meanwhile, get used to the idea." His face softened. "You're going home."

Roni stared at the bright light coming through the restaurant windows. Something was very wrong. The Prime Minister had told him to trust Rosen, to follow his orders no matter how strange they seemed. But this wasn't strange.

This was insane.

PART THREE

Chapter 38

Assad

Assad, the Lion, was on a natural high. He was high on freedom. For the first time in years, he was free from orders and missions. He had vanished. No phone. No messages. No handlers breathing down his neck. Just him, the streets of Gaza, and the thick scent of briny sea air.

Wearing dark glasses and a *keffiyeh* that covered most of his face, he strolled through the old markets, past the pushcarts of tomatoes and onion, the butcher shops with their swinging lamb carcasses, the children kicking a half-deflated football against cracked concrete walls. The afternoon heat shimmered off the pavement, but he barely felt it. For now, he was free as never before.

He made his way to the Al Shira beach café, chose a small table in the back, and ordered a scented "mud" coffee. He watched as an ice-cream vendor weaved his way through the green flags planted by Hamas militants. Surf was up, and a few boys rode the waves on battered surfboards, watched by fascinated young children on the beach, who were in turn watched by their black-robed mothers.

He had come to this exact spot as a child. Things had changed so much in such a short time. He remembered his mother rolling up her denim jeans and dipping her toes in the water, a colorful scarf tied around her neck, a white, buttoned shirt gleaming in the bright sunlight, her toenails painted red. Today, she scurried across dead alleyways, wrapped in a full-length black *abaya*.

He sipped his coffee, staring out at the water.

The surfers, the children, the mothers–they were all on that beach doing exactly what he was: escaping the horrid reality of life in Gaza. They were all taking a few short moments to forget their day-to-day struggles, letting the waves and the watery blue horizon mute the never-ending roar of overpopulated, turbulent Gaza City.

The old man had been right. Assad was in a unique position to help these young children on the beach. The people trusted him. They listened to him.

Burrowing into his pocket, he threw a two-shekel coin onto the table, got up, and left. It was time to change the future.

* * *

"You're back!" The Hamas al-Qassam Brigade commander clapped Assad on the shoulder, beaming.

"Very few of our soldiers are fearless and—most importantly—intelligent like you, ya Assad! I was afraid we had lost our best warrior!"

"I needed a little time off." The Lion smiled.

"I can understand, my brother," the commander chuckled. "Three days ago, when I heard you had smashed your cell phone and blocked all contact with the organization, I was a little surprised. But I can understand. I feel the stress myself every minute of every day. We are soldiers in an army that is in a constant state of war. Always on the run, always trying to remain one step ahead of the Zionist intelligence—we can never rest. But now, are you ready to jump right back into the deep end?"

"Of course," Assad answered.

"That's great news! Come, have a seat. I just got my lunch delivered. It's your favorite: *sfiha*!"

"Thank you." The lion sat down as his commander began sliding steaming flat-bread covered with fried mutton out from oily paper bags.

"Here. Eat!" The commander held up a piece of *sfiha*. Assad smiled politely and popped the steaming morsel into his mouth.

The commander tore a piece off and chewed as he spoke. "How about a little light security work? Ease you back in? A simple assignment. Security work. A shipment of TNT is coming in through Abu Yusuf's tunnel in Rafah."

Assad let out a low laugh. "Abu Yusuf? You're working with that thieving bastard?"

"He's doing it for free." The commander smacked the table, delighted. "What does your lawyer brother call it? When he works with no pay?"

"*Pro bono*."

"That's it! *Pro bono*." The group commander exclaimed.

Assad raised one eyebrow. "I'll believe that you don't fart in your bed anymore before I believe that Abu Yusuf is helping us *pro bono*."

The group commander erupted in a fit of laughter.

"Ya Assad! It is so good to see you back. For a few days there, I truly thought you were gone. May Allah forbid we ever lose you!"

Assad just smiled.

The commander pushed a plate toward him. "Eat!"

"It's very good," Assad took another polite bite out of the mutton-topped flatbread. It really was his favorite. Dripping with olive oil and crushed hyssop, the warm bread base was soft and chewy, and the chopped mutton was superb. It was a truly good *sfiha*, but the joy of eating a good *sfiha* paled compared to the excitement that filled his belly. He couldn't have asked for better orders from his leader. Today, he would take the first step on his own personal mission.

He wiped his hands on a paper napkin and leaned back. "I would like nothing better than to pay a visit to Abu Yusuf. When is the shipment coming in?"

Chapter 39

Rosen

The Lunch Club was as Tel Aviv as it got—trendy, exclusive, and unapologetic. It opened long after lunch hours, and not only did it not serve lunch, it didn't serve food at all. The only items on the menu were drinks at the bar, dancing on the floor, and—if you were talented enough—fast sex in the pristine, unisex bathrooms.

It was still early. The dance floor was empty; the lights that would flash under the glass floor tiles had not yet been turned on. The video screens that covered the balcony wall were showing loops of soothing psychedelic patterns, occasionally interrupted by fluorescent dolphins leaping through waves of electric blue. But even in its pre-party silence, it was a most stunning place to experience.

Rosen smiled as he caught the Palestinian kid gaping at the LED light chains running along the ceiling: a flowing, pulsing river of pure light. The mayor's son was ogling the long and varied collection of bottles lining the bar shelves—vodka, rum, cognacs, and whiskies—the mirrors at both ends making them seem endless. The two young men wilted

under the cool, judgmental gaze of the bartenders—
striking in their black clothes, mascaraed eyelashes,
and haughty stares. Military men were not welcome in
this club. *Not in uniform, at least.* Rosen was certain
that if Roni and Hashim had chosen to arrive stark-
naked, they would have drawn less attention than they
did now in their neatly pressed IDF uniforms.

He lit a cigarette and blew smoke toward the
monumental DJ console, set on a giant, illuminated
podium. Immediately, a puffy black shirt materialized
at his side.

"I'm sorry, sir, but this is a no-smoking zone.
Please put out your cigarette."

Rosen didn't even register the request. He just
stared into the distance, a strange, faraway smile on his
face.

"*Adoni?* Sir?"

Roni and Hashim stared at the conflict between the
pouty bartender and Rosen. When he didn't answer,
they exchanged an amused smile, then quickly looked
away, remembering who they were smiling at.

The bartender flitted off, defeated.

Rosen was in a world of his own. It was as if an
iron clamp on his heart had suddenly loosened, and
blood—real, warm, human blood—rushed back into
places that had been dead for a long, long time. He
now understood how that dreadful day, over twenty

years ago, had consumed his innards, nibbling away at his soul until there was almost nothing left. The panic attacks, the months swallowed by depression, the sleepless nights. He had trained himself to keep drowning out the echoes of the past with work, power, and distraction. But nothing—not the finest whiskey, not the greatest political victory—could keep out the one thing that had always found a way back to him: the children.

They had never left. They haunted him every day and every night.

Could this mad idea help ease the pain? Taking this bewildered Palestinian boy back home—could it somehow change things? Maybe not—-Rosen was old enough to know that some things can't be undone. Yet he was already feeling something. A strange, reckless hope.

Loud music suddenly erupted from the overhead speakers, snapping him back to the present.

He glanced at his phone. They had been waiting for almost two hours. It was dark outside, and the club was set to open in twenty minutes. He was losing his patience and was about to unleash his temper on one of the bar staff members when the doors swung open, and in walked a crew-cut, tall, monster of a man wearing a shiny green silk suit.

"*Achi*." My brother. The giant stepped forward and grabbed Rosen in a warm hug. Rosen himself was quite tall, but clasped in the man's arms, he looked like a child. After a few long seconds, the two men let go of each other.

From the corner of his eye, Rosen saw the Palestinian kid staring at his friend in what seemed like… fear? He didn't blame him. His friend was physically impressive, the perfect manifestation of the Aryan male ideal: just under six-foot-eight-inches tall, a razor-sharp nose, blue eyes, and Marine-style, close-cropped blond hair. The only thing that stopped him from being a perfect specimen was his crooked buck teeth, which—although a perfect shade of white—gave him a slightly comical look.

"Love the suit." Rosen took a step back to inspect his friend's outfit. "What shade of green is that? No, let me guess—Fluorescent-vomit? Ultra-frog?"

The giant smiled, unaffected. He looked at Rosen with true friendship in his eyes.

"*Achi*, I called your office. Rumor has it you've flipped out? Left your employees to hike back to Tel Aviv and disappeared in a TV production van?"

"Come on, Gil, you know better than to believe rumors."

"And that is because you were in a hurry to get to…?" Gil raised a questioning eyebrow.

"Gaza," answered Rosen.

"Gaza?"

"Gaza."

For a moment, the giant just stared. Then he let out a short, incredulous laugh. "Gaza! It warms my heart to see that some things never change. You're still insane."

Rosen leaned in, lowering his voice over the growing pulse of the club's music. "I need your help. Can you get us into the strip? Are you free for a bit of action as of… well… as of now?"

"No, I need to look after my stamp collection."

Rosen smiled. "Good. So, why don't you change out of that slimy green thing you're wearing? We need to get going."

Chapter 40

Assad

Assad stared down the wide hole, waiting for the familiar scraping sounds and bobbing lights. Abbu Yusuf's tunnel ran under the Egyptian-Gaza border. It was a wide, comfortable tunnel for the smugglers, but at the Gaza end, it opened out into an empty field, leaving the receiver dangerously exposed.

Today's shipment was running late, and the Lion was getting worried. The moon was about to rise. No chance he'd wait once the field was illuminated with moonlight. Too exposed. The recent bombings had made the Israelis edgy and vindictive. There would be a retaliation strike; that much was sure. And the Israelis loved bombing the tunnels. *Allah Yustur.* Cover us with Your protection.

They had sent him with just one backup soldier, a young boy named Ahmed. The kid had lied that he was seventeen. He couldn't have been a day over fourteen. The Lion looked back and tried to make out the young boy's silhouette, but the kid had learned his lessons well. The only clue to the fact that he was even there was the smell of cigarette smoke coming from a burned-out house fifty yards away.

The black desert sky was a three-dimensional light show, the Milky Way smooth and ethereal above him. They were waiting in the usual burned-out remains of what had once been a Zionist settlement, a few hundred yards away from the Egyptian border. Not for the last time, the Lion sighed at the terrible waste. This used to be a beautiful, thriving Zionist settlement, built by Palestinian laborers and designed to meet Israeli standards. It had been a gem of a place, but before they retreated, the enraged Zionist settlers had razed the small desert oasis to the ground. They stripped any building materials they could load onto a truck and then bulldozed the remaining upright structures. Thirty houses and a tiny community center, just large enough to house a mini-market, post-office boxes, and a culture hall.

Behind the community center, rows of greenhouses once stretched toward the horizon—high-tech structures that grew high-tech tomatoes and flowers. They were all torn down by the retreating Zionists. All that remained were shredded nylon sheets clinging to rusted metal frames.

And what the settlers didn't demolish, the Hamas militants burned down the day after the retreat, doing their best to pretend that they had evicted the Zionist intruders with their mighty military prowess. They sought to project an aura of brave and fearless warriors fighting the Israeli tanks in the name of the Gazan people. That the Israeli retreat was unilateral and that the tanks were long gone did nothing to lighten the heavy fighting rhetoric, later transmitted worldwide by the Arab TV channels.

A greenhouse plastic sheet that had been spared from the fires was flapping mournfully in the light breeze. This place could have housed so many Gazan families. It could have lived on, a positive symbol of the Middle East finally leveling out of its permanent imbalance. But maybe that's exactly what it was—a symbol. Not of a healing Middle East, but of the hatred that marred this land.

His thoughts were cut off abruptly as he finally heard the scraping sound of a wheeled cart reaching the bottom of the tunnel entrance. He let out a short hiss in Ahmed's direction, warning him it was time to get cracking. There was TNT to carry.

Chapter 41

Hannah

The night air felt fresh on Hannah's skin as she poked her head out of the tunnel exit. Barely lit, the stuffy tunnel had amplified her claustrophobia, turning her into a shivering, almost catatonic creature. She didn't care that she was now on the wrong side of the border. She didn't care that she was a lone woman being led by three men she had never met. All she wanted was to breathe the open air, to see the horizon.

With one last painful pull, she hoisted herself out of the manhole and sat on the edge of the deep stairwell. She closed her eyes, enjoying the wind on her face.

"*Yalla*!" The Palestinian guide behind her pushed against the soles of her feet. "Come on, move."

She climbed up the last rungs of a ladder that had been haphazardly placed at the tunnel exit. Once out, the small group stumbled through the darkness over the rocky ground stepping through what seemed to be the ruined frames of demolished hothouses. Then, a short, stocky man appeared suddenly out of the shadows. Her three chaperones fell onto the short man with delighted, whispered blessings and joyous hugs. Finally, the short man turned to her.

"Come with me," he whispered in perfect Hebrew.

A young boy appeared out of the darkness. The short man and the teenager hoisted two heavy sacks onto their shoulders, straightened up, and started walking northward, away from the Egyptian border. Hannah's three guides quickly made their way back to the tunnel on their return trip to Egypt.

"Where are we going?" she asked, stumbling after her new guides.

"Gaza City," answered the short man, "I've been directed to take you up to—"

Then the man suddenly stopped short. He stared forward, his head cocked sideways. He blinked.

"Run!" he bellowed.

The two Palestinians suddenly scrambled forward. Hannah stood rooted to the spot.

"What?" she asked, dumbfounded.

"*Run!*"

A low growl filled the air, growing louder and louder. She ran, the escalating roar terrifying her. It was like nothing she had heard before—a sound that induced pure terror.

Seconds later, the deafening scream ended in a crash of lightning, striking the tunnel entrance. The desert exploded in a hellish fury of fire and molten rock. A wave of debris expanded from the center of the attack, engulfing Hannah as she ran, her ears ringing. It was raining boiling sand.

Twenty minutes later, they were resting with their backs against a concrete sewage pipe, the two Palestinians just managing to hold on to the heavy sacks. Hannah stared at the pillar of smoke that was still rising from the demolished tunnel, not three hundred yards behind them. The Lion followed her gaze.

"The three men who brought me over?" she asked.

"Dead, *Allah Yirahmo*. The bomb took out the whole northern side of the tunnel. Five-hundred-pounder. The Zionists call it Steel Rain."

"How do you know it was a five-hundred-pounder?"

The short one smiled at her sadly.

"Because we are still alive."

Chapter 42

Prime Minister Rahav

Prime Minister Rahav smiled at the Finnish ambassador's wife, nodding with the well-rehearsed look of a man pretending to listen. It was Finnish Independence Day, and normally Rahav wouldn't have given the event a second thought. A junior minister would have been sent for a brief visit, and that would be that. But a lucrative Finnish tender for a cellular research and development center was reaching the final lap, and Israel needed the extra jobs. So there he was, wife in tow, with a line of Finnish businessmen waiting to meet and greet him. He was bored, he hated vodka, and he hated herring even more, but unfortunately, that was the 'artistic concept' the caterer had come up with for dinner.

God almighty—even caterers were bloody concept artists these days.

He glanced at his watch. He'd hold out the obligatory twenty minutes before he could be whisked away back to his residence. That was the magic number—long enough to be seen, short enough to avoid pointless small talk.

Ten minutes into the cocktail party, one of his aides approached and, with a barely perceptible nod, signaled for Rahav to step aside. Once in relative privacy, the aide handed Rahav a secure phone with a text message.

> *Target 1115 hit. Strike successful. Three to six opposition casualties.*

He nodded and handed the phone back. He remembered that morning's intelligence briefing—Target 1115 was a Gazan tunnel running into Egypt.

Thinking of Gaza rekindled his fury. Rosen had messed up — a colossal mistake. How could he have misidentified a known terrorist? And even worse was having to butter up that soldier just to get him to play along for the cameras! Prime Minister Rahav was used to sucking up to political activists, but kissing that young soldier's ass because of Rosen's stupid mistake was too much. He'd had enough of Rosen's sneering attitude. But where in hell was he? Rosen had disappeared off the radar, vanished. Rumor had it that he left the TV studios in a production car, leaving the rest of his staff behind.

Rahav turned back to his aide, his voice low.

"I want you to find Rosen. Find him as fast as possible. I want to know where he is and what his plans are. If you have to, get the whole of the Shin Bet on it. Have their tech department monitor his private phone and anyone he came into contact with in the last twenty-four hours. This is now a matter of national security."

The assistant gave an almost imperceptible nod and melted away.

Rahav took a deep breath. He knew he was overdoing it. Using the Shin Bet for his personal vendetta was extreme. Not for the first time, Rahav mentally kicked himself for letting Rosen have such a hold over him. His wife had scolded him for the same at least five times that day.

"You're the bloody Prime Minister, and he's an advisor—a damn consultant!" she had snapped at him that morning. "One of many. How do you let him get away with all the shit he does?"

"Honey, he got us in here. You wouldn't be First Lady without him."

"And since then? What has he done for us? He's hypnotized you. He has you bewitched! I swear, you talk about him like you're in love with him."

"Don't talk nonsense, honey. I owe him a lot. He put us here, remember? We owe him a debt of loyalty…"

"We *owe* him? Bullshit! Thanks to *our* success, his clientele has quadrupled. He's making more money than you or I will ever see. You've made him a millionaire, and you think you owe him? You're so bloody useless!"

"I'm useless?! I'm the Prime Minister! You call me useless?!"

And then the shouting had started. Insults and blame were flung from one side of the room to the other like glass plates, shards of contempt stinging and cutting into the skin.

"Pickled herring, sir?"

Rahav snapped out of his reverie. A waiter was standing in front of him, silver tray balanced on one hand.

"No, can't stand the bloody stuff."

The surprised waiter nodded dumbly for a moment before making his escape.

Chapter 43

Rosen

It was peak hour at the Lunch Club. The small group sat in the Lunch Club VIP room overlooking the crammed dance floor. The Palestinian kid had his nose glued to the panoramic, two-way window, his breath fogging the glass as he stared at the dancers. Rosen looked out to see what the kid was staring at. The lights were hypnotic. The women were beautiful. The men were beautiful. Rosen wondered if the Palestinian had ever seen anything like it. The kid was spellbound. The music was Mediterranean house: a mixture of wild darbuka hand drums, Arab violins, over-dramatic vocals, set to a fast drum and bass. Every few minutes the Palestinian would turn around to steal a glance at Gil. Rosen had the feeling that the kid recognized Gil somehow. He shifted his gaze toward the mayor's son. The soldier was sitting a few feet away, watching the Palestinian, his brow furrowed.

Rosen crossed the small room and sat next to Gil at the private bar, built to accommodate the ultra-celebs for whom the VIP room was a sanctuary. It was time to make plans.

"Are you done? Can we go now?" Rosen asked.

"So—you want to smuggle, what's-his-name?" Gil asked.

"Hashim."

"Hashim—back into Gaza?"

Rosen nodded firmly.

Gil let out a short chuckle. "And you think I can help you do it?"

"Well, you were the Gaza Division boss," Rosen answered, smiling. "You knew every rock and tree and family in the strip. You had contacts everywhere. You were Gaza Gil."

"I haven't been Gaza Gil in quite a few years. I'll need to make some more calls."

"So, make some more calls."

Gil grinned at Rosen.

"What?" asked Rosen.

"It's just…" Gil shook his head slightly, still smiling. "I wouldn't have expected you to be doing this. Surprised, that's all."

"You know better than I do what will happen if we hand him over to military intelligence." Rosen replied and shook his head, trying to block the mental image.

Gil shrugged. "It's not that bad, Rosen. So, what? He'd be interrogated, shaken up a bit, smacked a bit. Do his time in prison, released next time there's a swap. And he'll be the hero returning home. I really can't see what all this is about."

"He's just a kid, Gil! He's too soft; he'll die in prison. He'll be some inmate's wife within two minutes of his arrival. He's not a warrior—he's a geek."

Gil looked at Rosen for a long moment, then he spoke in a soft undertone.

"It's the children, isn't it? They've come back."

Rosen looked up as if stung by Gil's words. A shiver went up his spine and into the base of his head. It had been so long since he, or anyone around him, dared to speak aloud about the children.

"Maybe I've found a way to make it right."

Gil shook his head distractedly. "It won't bring the children back. You know that."

"I know," Rosen admitted. "But maybe I have a chance to start paying my debt. A life for a life."

"A life for a life?" Gil contemplated Rosen's answer. "I'm not quite sure it works that way. But okay, I'll make a few calls. Jonah Levi is the Gaza boss now, you know him?"

"Jonah Levi? How the hell did he make Gaza chief?"

"Jonah? He's the master at sucking up to the right people." Gil looked down at his size 14 loafers as he continued. "I know it's a stupid question, but you wouldn't be in his good graces these days, would you? Could make the whole operation really simple."

"Jonah? Loves me!" Rosen smiled wryly. "*Meshuga* about me. And I'm sure he loves me even more since he discovered I advised *against* making him Gaza Division commander."

"Rosen," Gil sighed, shaking his head. "You have the finesse of a fucking rhino. How the hell did you ever make it in this business?"

"Must be my looks."

"Must be. Let me make a few calls." Gil patted his breast and trouser pockets. "Shit. Where's my phone? I could have sworn I left it on the bar."

Rosen picked up a phone that was lying on a nearby table and dangled it in the air. "Looking for this?"

"Yeah." Gil grabbed the phone from him. "I'll make some calls. Meanwhile, you turn off your mobile."

"Way ahead of you. I switched it off back at the studio."

"Good. They are looking for you. For all of us."

Chapter 44

Hannah

Hannah's entire body ached. An ancient Toyota truck had been waiting for them in the burned-out shell of a building—an Israeli gas station, maybe, though there was little left to confirm it. She shifted in her seat, trying to find a position that didn't send sharp currents of pain up her spine or into her bruised shoulder. But she soon realized that Toyota had not built this specific model with luxury in mind.

"Where are we going?" she asked, her voice hoarse from exhaustion.

"A safe house in Gaza City. We should be there in about forty minutes."

Hannah looked out of the window. Funny. It was the first time she had ever set foot in the Strip. She had argued, fought, shouted, heckled, and championed the Gaza Palestinian cause, but she had never actually *been* there. Until today.

She peered through the smeared window. Although they were riding along a main highway, there were no streetlights. The occasional car flashed past, headlights illuminating quick glimpses of a densely populated, sandy landscape. It looked totally uninteresting, uninviting, dry, and dirty.

Why, in God's name, would someone want to live here? To kill and die for this bland view? Where was the logic to it all?

And, lying on the back seat of the jolting Toyota—her arm and shoulder shooting sharp currents of pain up and down her back—she realized that there was no logic. She tried to imagine being forced to give up Jerusalem. She had no attachment to the so-called holy rocks and sacred stones that nations tore each other apart for. And yet, the idea of losing Jerusalem, of someone else laying claim to the city where she had grown up, where she had built her memories, made her sick to her stomach. The city was a part of her.

Maybe that was it. Maybe logic had nothing to do with it. Home wasn't something you could weigh or measure, or bargain away. It wasn't about politics, or policies, or ceasefires. It was simply about belonging. And if both sides felt that same unshakable pull toward the land, then what hope was there for peace?

She let out a groan of pain and frustration. She wasn't supposed to be here. She should be in Jerusalem, at home, reading a Nick Hornby novel at her kitchen table. She should be working; she should be out in the world, seeing people. She had been searching for purpose and belonging her whole life but had neglected to actually *live*. The search itself had become her life; her purpose.

Could she start again, or was it too late? All signs pointed to the fact that it was. Her path had led her to this broken-down Toyota, a wanted fugitive shielded by terrorists. Since her meeting in Jerusalem with Yossi, her Brigade's commander, she had been constantly active and on the move, without a moment to think and analyze her situation.

Watching the broken view from her window, depression took hold of Hannah like a black tide, swallowing her whole. She was so immersed in her grief that she didn't notice the car slow to a complete stop.

The driver turned to her.

"We need to make a quick delivery."

Then a warning:

"Stay here."

Chapter 45

Prime Minister Ya'akov "Yaki" Rahav

"Stay here, sir."

The Secret Service agent opened the front car door and stepped out, leaving Prime Minister Rahav alone with the secret service driver, who sat alert at the wheel, scanning the street with a soldier's trained vigilance. The Jerusalem night sky burned a muted orange as demonstrators lit up the street with diesel-fueled bonfires. Fireworks popped and sizzled overhead, sending blue streaks through the smoke-drenched air.

"What's going on?" Rosen called to the driver through the partition.

"Protesters have swarmed the intersection; they're blocking the route between the Knesset and your residence, sir."

Fifteen agents jumped out of the various cars in the motorcade, creating a cordon around the Prime Minister. They were not openly displaying their firearms. Not yet.

Rahav leaned forward. "Do we know who these people are and what they want?"

The driver didn't turn. His eyes remained locked on the growing crowd. "Yes, sir. It's nationalist demonstrators. They are demanding you bomb Gaza following the attack yesterday morning."

"Nationalists...?" Rahav gestured toward the mass of furious civilians. "These are *my* voters?"

"Yes, sir. Seems like it, sir."

Rahav rolled down the window. A chorus of megaphones boomed above the crackling fires, their chants rolling into the vehicle.

Yaki, Yaki, where's your spine?

Bomb Gaza now! It's way past time!

Rahav rolled the window back up. The rhythmic shouting continued, muffled but still grating against his nerves. He'd had enough. His ungrateful voters could all go and collectively jump in a lake. They did not deserve him. How he wished he could storm out of the car and face the demonstrators. He was not afraid of them. He would tell this ungrateful, moronic mass of sheep what he really felt about them. For almost two decades, he had spent every minute of every day keeping the coalition happy, the Americans happy, the European Union happy—admittedly, he knew the EU would never be happy with anyone—and above all: his voters. And this is how they repay him. This is what he got for the years of dedication, sleepless nights, and non-stop politicking. He longed, for once, to say what he truly felt. But he swallowed the urge and fumed in silence. He well knew every protester was holding a phone at the ready, waiting for something newsworthy to happen.

And the worst part? He had been looking forward to a quiet night in front of the sports channel. Beitar Jerusalem soccer club versus Maccabi Tel Aviv. Yaki was one of Beitar's most voluble fans. He had prayed that morning for his beloved Beitar to whip Tel Aviv's butt tonight, to shut up their smug, media-darling fanbase. But instead of watching the game, he was trapped, listening to illiterate demonstrators and their sing-song rhymes.

The door opened, and the agent reappeared.

"We've commandeered a florist's van. We'll use that to smuggle you in through the suppliers' entrance.

Rahav exhaled sharply through his nose, his patience already worn thin. A florist's van. *Kol HaKavod*, congratulations to the number one citizen of the country, the most powerful man in the region, reduced to sneaking through a back door in a vehicle filled with goddamn tulips.

His jaw clenched. *This could never happen in Russia.*

Exchanging the six-car motorcade for a single florist's van had made Rahav's security detail jumpy and over-protective. Crushed in the small Peugeot van with no less than six security agents, Rahav was ignobly transferred to the residence, the van inching through the crowd unnoticed. By the time Rahav made it to the residence TV room, the first half of the game was over. Beitar had scored twice, and Rahav had missed both goals.

A beautiful cut-glass tumbler awaited Rahav on a small table by his recliner, together with an ice bucket and a bottle of Macallan 31-Year-Old Single Malt, a gift from a campaign backer with excellent taste.

It had been a bad day. He would allow himself a double.

Just as he settled into the chair, the secure line flashed on the room's phone. Wearily, he leaned over and picked up the handset. As he leaned back, he noticed a smudge of yellow pollen that had stuck to his suit trousers. He brushed it off angrily.

"What?" he snapped.

"Sir," the receptionist didn't flinch, "it's Shin Bet. They have something for you."

"Regarding what?" The second half of the game had just started, and the ice was melting in his tumbler, diluting the expensive whisky.

"Not sure, sir, but it's the head of the service."

The head? Something must have happened.

"Patch him through."

Seconds later, the gruff voice of the head of Shin Bet came through the headset. "Rahav, I hear you put in a request to locate Robert Rosen?"

Rahav's heart gave a heavy thump. *Rosen!*

"I did," he answered carefully. "Any news?"

"Following your orders, we set up electronic surveillance on a few promising sources. One of them was Mayor Sami Uliel, father of the soldier that Rosen disappeared with."

Rahav swallowed hard. If anyone ever discovered he was ordering surveillance on Israeli civilians out of sheer political vengeance, he was finished. The Shin Bet commander continued.

"We intercepted a very strange call from the soldier, Roni Uliel. It seems that Roni has been with Rosen all day. Probably still with him."

"Rosen was in charge of handling Roni and the Druze patrolnik's media appearances."

"Exactly. Except…" the chief's voice faltered.

"Except what?"

The chief's voice dropped to an undertone. "Roni said something about the patrolnik not being an actual patrolnik."

"What?!" Rahav's stomach clenched. This could not be happening. Until now, only he and Rosen knew the real identity of the patrolnik. Once the Shin Bet worked it out, it could lead to a political catastrophe.

"It was hard for me to understand exactly what Roni was saying." The chief continued. "There was loud music in the background. Like a club or something. And the kid spoke fast, like he was afraid of being caught."

"Who was he hiding from?"

"I think, Rosen." The Chief's voice dropped even lower. "It was hard to hear, but we think he said something about it all being a lie. We cleaned the audio up enough to hear him say that: 'The *patrolnik is the Mohandas and that I should tell someone at the IDF.*' Does this mean anything to you?"

Oh yes, it meant a great deal to Rahav. *The Shin Bet chief had just offered him deniability on a silver platter.* Rahav leaned back, exhaling slowly, letting the weight of the moment settle over him.

"So, the Druze patrolnik is actually a Palestinian terrorist?" His voice was perfectly measured. Just the right amount of outrage and surprise.

"Correct," the Chief's voice was firm. "We believe his name is Hashim Abu Tir, aka the Mohandas. The Cherry Commando unit picked him up 48 hours ago in Gaza."

"What is Rosen up to?" Rahav continued to act dismayed. "If he is aiding a known terrorist, we must locate him as soon as possible. Did the soldier tell his father where he was?"

"No."

"Can you locate the phone he called from?"

"We were monitoring the father's phone, not the phone Roni called from. But we have the number, and it is being added to the system as we speak."

"Good. So, how long before you locate Rosen? Give me a rough estimate." Rahav demanded.

"Just before Roni rang off, he told me he's going to do his best to stick close to Rosen. I have a team on the way to Sedera, just in case he calls his parents again. I think by morning we'll have them all in custody."

"Keep me updated."

"Sure, Yaki." The Shin Bet chief ended the call.

Rahav stretched out on the recliner and sipped from the whisky. He had just managed to wash his hands of the whole Mohandas disaster. It was all on Rosen now.

Beitar had scored a third goal during the call.

His day had been a mess, but it was ending beautifully.

Chapter 46

Hannah

The pain had become unbearable.

Hannah tried to shift her weight, pressing her spine against the rough seat of the ancient Toyota, but every movement sent sharp, electric jolts through her battered muscles. Before they had exited the vehicle the two Hamas militants had ordered her to stay put, but she couldn't. If she sat still for one more second, she would scream.

She waited for the two men's footsteps to fade into the distance and, hardly daring to breathe, she slowly reached for the door handle. The latch clicked softly, a sound far too loud in the silence. Holding her breath, she eased herself out of the truck, biting her lip as her body protested. Her boots sank slightly into the cool sand, the tiny grains rolling beneath her weight. The air smelled of salt and distant fires, the kind that burned low and reeked of plastic.

They were parked on a broken, unlit road lined with non-functioning streetlamps—relics of another era. She had once heard a speaker at a Brigade meeting claim that, since the Israelis had left, no one had the funds to replace the mercury vapor lamps. One by one, they had flickered out, leaving Gaza's roads darker, the shadows deeper. But there was a beneficial angle to this neglect. The moonlight shone incredibly brightly, making the pale yellow sands surrounding her glisten and shine. The night was hauntingly beautiful.

She rolled her shoulder, stretched out the stiffness, and took a few careful steps away from the truck. It did her good to move her legs after the painfully cramped ride. She could smell the salt in the air. She began moving toward what she hoped was the sea. She fought her way up a small sand dune. As she reached the top the view opened around her. In the moonlight, she could just make out the small waves lapping at the long, sandy beach.

Then... voices. She crouched low against the dune's ridge. Her two chaperones were walking down a dusty, rock-strewn path toward the car. The sacks they had brought from the tunnel were gone.

She was about to slide down the dune and limp back to the dreadful Toyota when she saw the shorter of the two men stop. He turned to his younger companion, muttered something, and then—without explanation—walked back the way they had come. From her vantage on top of the small dune, Hannah could watch both men. The short one turned behind a small ridge, and once out of sight of his younger partner, began to run. She watched as he paused, then crouched toward small, dark lumps on the sand—the smuggled bags. A tiny, orange pinprick of light flickered to life, dancing like a crazed firefly. The short man stood up and ran back toward the car, slowing down to a walk as he came into view of his partner. Further behind the two, the small, orange firefly was still dancing in the darkness.

Having done her two years' compulsory military service, like all young Israeli women, Hannah knew what that firefly meant. The short man had lit an explosive fuse. He was going to blow up the bundle of bags. Something very strange had just happened, but she didn't have the time to figure it out. Gritting her teeth, she turned and half-stumbled, half-slid down the dune, making it to the car just as the two men came into view. She made no sound as the two climbed into the truck. The short one fired up the engine and pulled back onto the road. The younger one was laughing at something—some crude joke in Arabic. He seemed completely unaware of what had just happened behind them. She raised her head and stared back at the receding dune. She was still staring sixty seconds later when a brief orange flash lit up the night sky behind them. The bags—and whatever was in them—were gone.

She turned to see whether her guides had seen the explosion. The younger militant was looking forward, oblivious to what she had seen.

The short driver was staring in the rearview mirror, his eyes locked onto hers, glinting with an unspoken warning.

Chapter 47

Prime Minister Rahav

The game had ended, and the Macallan was nothing more than a lingering warmth in Rahav's chest. He stood up and stretched. The plan was for an early night. In bed by eleven, up at 5:00 a.m. A solid and extremely rare six hours of sleep—if nothing urgent happens. He bent over to slide his feet into his house slippers when the phone by the recliner lit up. Rahav could easily guess who it was.

Well done, boys. That was fast.

He picked up the receiver. "Yes?"

"Sir, we have the Head of the Shin Bet on the secure line."

"Good. Patch him through."

A beat of silence.

Then the familiar, gravelly voice, laced with unmistakable smugness. "*Layla Tov*, Yaki."

If he were calling now, it could only mean one thing. "You find him?" At this late hour, there was no time for pleasantries.

"We found him," the chief confirmed. In the background, Rahav could hear the quiet hum of a busy operations room—ringing phones, clipped radio transmissions, the murmured coordination of men at work. "We traced the number the soldier called from," the chief continued. "It belongs to Gil Hamami, one of Rosen's best friends."

Rahav inched up both eyebrows. "Gaza Gil?"

"Correct. The former commander of Gaza Division. The soldier used his personal phone."

A triumphant grin appeared on Rahav's face. "And where are they now?"

"Looks like a building on Allenby Street. We cross-referenced the satellite overlay, and we are pretty certain they are hiding in a building that houses a club—a place called the Lunch Club. That would account for the loud music in the background of the soldier's call. I'd say there's a 99% certainty the call was made from there."

"Excellent work! Who is on standby at General HQ?"

"We have the Cherry Commandos ready for action."

Rahav loved the Cherry Commandos. Known for their ruthlessness and toughness, they specialized in hostage recovery and surgical strikes inside the Palestinian territories. They were perfect for this mission. He remembered they were the unit sent to pick up the Mohandas, the very same terrorist who was being shielded by Rosen. Now they would pick him up again. Rahav relished how the story was about to come full circle. And now that he had made sure that he was in the clear, Rahav was more than happy to send them in.

"Call the Cherry Commando commander. Tell him to mobilize immediately. Lunch Club. Now. Bring me Rosen and the Mohandas!"

Chapter 48

Roni

Roni forced himself to look down at the partying mass as he tried to calm his breathing. They hadn't noticed. He'd made the call without Rosen or Gil realizing. It had been close, but he had managed to drop Gil's phone onto a table seconds before Gil missed it.

Once he steadied himself he turned around.

Gil and Rosen ended their hushed conversation, and Gil left them. Then, Rosen called Roni to the VIP bar, the neon glow from the liquor shelves bathing them both in an electric green haze.

"How are you feeling? How's your eyesight?" Rosen asked as Roni slid onto one of the shining black barstools.

"I'm okay."

"You're extremely lucky, soldier."

"I know." Roni answered, though he still wasn't sure why he should be feeling lucky.

Rosen smiled at him, leaning in slightly. "So, did the Prime Minister promise you anything?"

"Yes. He told me that if I did everything you asked of me, he'd help me transfer to the officer's academy."

"The *Academy*? Now, that is one worthwhile promise. You will have an incredible service as an officer. Paratrooper officers are the cream of the crop. Well done."

"Were you also in the Paratrooper Brigade?"

"No. I was Air Force."

"Air Force? You were a pilot?"

"Combat pilot. F16. First the A-model, then C-model when it arrived."

Roni stared in awe. Like many of his countrymen, he admired air force pilots, a fascination bordering on blind adoration. The cloth pilot's wings sewn onto air force khaki shirts were enough to make any Israeli male drool with envy, and any Israeli woman drool at the thought of matrimony. Air force pilots were modern-day Israeli heroes, a dream accessible for a very talented few.

"Do you still fly?"

Rosen's expression shifted—just slightly. "No. Haven't been up in twenty years."

"Oh."

A few silent seconds passed before Rosen continued.

"So, Roni, I think it's time for our paths to part. What do you say we get you a taxi to your home?"

Roni shook his head. "I'd like to stay with you. I'd like to help you, if that's possible." He was not the greatest of liars, and by putting on what he thought was an earnest, helpful expression, he hoped he could get away with it.

"You want to help?" Rosen asked, tilting his head slightly.

"Prime Minister Rahav ordered me to assist you in any way I can."

Rosen smiled. "Things have changed. Your part in this story is done; we will continue from this point without you. You'll have to wait here, I'm afraid. I've arranged for a taxi to take you all the way home to Sedera. It should arrive after we've left. I paid online, so you're good to go."

"Please, I want to come with you." Roni couldn't let them out of his sight. He knew that Rosen and his friend Gil were acting illegally. It was up to him to stop them.

"Trust me, Roni, this is for your own good. It's better if you don't know our plans. And anyway, we don't really need your help, so you might as well take the opportunity to go home. Stay out of trouble, have your eyesight return to normal, rest a little and start preparing for officer's school."

"My eyesight is much better, really! Almost normal," Roni lied. His eyesight had indeed returned at a fast pace, though the world was still slightly blurry around the edges.

"Thanks, kid." Rosen's face softened. "You've got real *neshama*, a good soul."

At that moment, Gil re-appeared in the VIP lounge. He waved a folded map at Rosen.

"I think I may have a way in."

Rosen glanced at Roni. "Good luck, soldier. Now, if you don't mind sitting at the other end of the bar, we need some privacy."

"Of course." Roni stood and crossed to a sofa at the other side of the VIP lounge. His mind raced as he desperately tried to think of something to say to Rosen. Was there a way to persuade Rosen to let him stay? He needed to stick as close as he could to Rosen and to the...

"Thank you." A shadow fell across the sofa.

Roni lifted his head. The Mohandas was standing in front of him.

"What?"

"I heard what you said to Rosen. Thank you. It's hard for me to understand why this is happening." The Mohandas's voice sank, almost inaudible under the pumping music. "I just want to go back home."

"Oh. Sure."

"I'm not really a Mohandas. You know that now, I hope."

"So you did not re-design the rocket that hit Sedera? You aren't working for Hamas?" Roni was

208

doing his best to contain the anger that was bubbling inside of him.

A few silent moments passed before the Mohandas replied.

"I did. I was. But I will never work for them again."

Of course you won't.

Roni kept his voice calm. "So, they're taking you back to Gaza?" he asked, his tone shifting just enough to sound curious, not too probing.

"Yes."

"Do you know how? Through which crossing?"

"No. But somehow, we've got Gaza Gil on our side."

"Gaza Gil? You know the big guy?"

"Of course. He was Gaza Division commander until a few years ago. Very tough on everybody—Gazans, his own soldiers. Everyone was scared of him. Me, I hated him more than any man on earth."

"Why?"

"He killed my sister." Hashim answered in a soft voice.

"What?" Shalev asked, surprised.

"Na'ima. My sister. She was caught in a gunfight between our people and the Zionists. The Zionists sent a drone to blow up the building our fighters were shooting from. Na'ima was hiding on the ground floor, waiting for a chance to escape. She had nothing to do with the war, *nothing*. Just a young woman on her way home from work. Gaza Gil and his soldiers killed her. Buried her in rubble. He is a Zionist terrorist who tried to exterminate every last one of us." Hashim took a deep breath and looked toward Gil, who was showing Rosen something on his phone. "But now he's helping me. It doesn't make any sense. Why?"

"Why blame him?" Roni asked, "He didn't personally bomb that building."

"He is a violent man. He had no limits, no borders. It was he who personally ordered our school to be bombed."

"Your school?" Roni asked, with a surprised glance at Hashim.

"The Azzadin El Qassam used to shoot rockets from our schoolyard. They thought the Zionists wouldn't bomb a school." A dry laugh. "But Gaza Gil didn't care. School, hospital, any target was a good target for him."

"What happened to your school?"

"Our school? The yard was obliterated. As were the Azzadin fighters. For two weeks, we were washing their blood off our school wall. Part of the teachers' lounge was hit, too. The bomb's impact waves crushed the windows on our physics--"

"You studied physics?"

"Yes. We didn't complete the full course. It took us months to rebuild the lab and set up all the equipment like it was before the attack. We missed too many lessons."

A minute of silence passed. Roni felt he needed to keep the conversation going if he was to stay close to the Palestinian.

"I studied physics, too," he finally said.

The Mohandas blinked. "Really? Did you just graduate high school, too?"

"Yes."

"How well did you do in the finals?"

"Pretty good. Only made one mistake in the optics chapter. Stupid mistake, too."

"I hated optics. I loved almost all the rest. Especially mechanics. I hope to one day study robotics. I think I've seen almost every robotics tutorial on YouTube."

"We did a short robotics course at Jerusalem University. Thanks to you, actually."

"Me?" Hashim looked bewildered.

"Well, not you specifically. We were evacuated to Jerusalem when your people bombed Sedera nonstop for a full month. The university volunteered to teach robotics to whoever was interested. We were there for almost a month. By the time we were sent back home we had managed to build a robot with volume sensors that could guide itself around the whole campus without bumping into anything."

"You built a robot?" Hashim's eyes gleamed with enthusiasm, mingled with a touch of envy. "We didn't have any equipment like that. Just theory and paper notebooks, and YouTube videos when the internet worked. And you built an actual robot..." Hashim shook his head in wonder, "How did you build it? From scratch? Did you solder sensors, Did it have tracks or wheels?"

Roni pasted a pleasant smile on his face as he began to describe to the Palestinian the technical details of his robot build. He knew he had to get closer to the Mohandas.

My whole team was murdered because of this terrorist. I have to make sure he pays.

Chapter 49

Cherry Commando Team Three

Team three of the Cherry Commando unit had been on call at their Tel Aviv headquarters. With blue lights flashing the nine man team had raced from the Kirya command center on Kaplan Street and made it to Allenby in less than five minutes. They deployed at staggered points around the target building, slipping into the city's nightlife like ghosts. Yet, despite their training and vast combat experience, the soldiers couldn't shake the sheer strangeness of it all.

A mission in Tel Aviv. Unbelievable.

They were used to operating behind Palestinian lines, moving through the dust-choked alleys of Nablus or the labyrinthine refugee camps of Khan Younis. Deploying inside Israel's borders was unusual enough—but a mission in the heart of Tel Aviv? That was unheard of.

And to make things even stranger, their mission, orders that came *directly* from the head of the Shin Bet, was to apprehend Robert Rosen, chief media advisor to the Prime Minister, along with the legendary Gaza Gil! Gaza Gil was a hero, well known to anyone who had ever been stationed at the southern borders. He had been one of the bravest, shrewdest commanders the area had ever seen.

So why was he being taken down like a common criminal?

On the ride over they had tried to guess what the two men had done to warrant an arrest by a special ops unit, but no one could come up with a sensible answer. Rosen? That one might make a little sense—he was a political operator, a shadow puppet-master, maybe he had stepped on the wrong toes. But Gaza Gil? It didn't add up.

Within seconds, all team members had blended into the Tel Aviv nightlife. One of the Cherry team's main strengths was an ever-growing collection of costumes, streetwear, wigs, and props designed to allow the team members to approach their targets without attracting attention or being recognized, even during the day. They would slip through markets in *keffiyehs* and knockoff Adidas, easily blending into the crowd. The only difference? Micro-Uzis and mini-Tavor machine guns nestled unobtrusively under their street dress. Their earbuds were all linked to a central comm system but could easily pass as regular headphones. Everyone was wearing them these days. Even in Gaza.

But this mission had stretched the capabilities of the costume collection. Finding fifteen sets of Israeli clubbing gear was a tall ask for their ever-patient quartermaster. He had ransacked 'the boutique'—their vast costume storage—grumbling about the injustice of being asked to perform miracles at the last minute. Somehow, he had delivered and now, fifteen of Israel's deadliest soldiers were scattered along Allenby Street, their weapons concealed under loose shirts and designer jackets.

Working efficiently and carefully, the team did a slow recon sweep that brought them in an ever-closing circle toward the Lunch Club, until all fifteen soldiers were just meters away from the building entrance. They could hear the bass pumping inside the club, the massive sound system making the air pulsate to the beat. A rich aroma of roasted nuts wafted from the all-night munchies shop across the road, its front stalls filled with cashews, salted sunflower seeds, hot peanuts, and dried watermelon seeds. Next door, a lifeless Subway franchise sat empty. In the land of shawarma and falafel, Subways were seen as a poor second choice.

The Cherry Commando team leader checked his watch. They were sixty seconds away from *Gamma*, the designated hour at which they were to enter the club. He spoke quietly into his radio.

"Command, this is One. We're on-site. Kill the lights."

The street lights along Allenby flickered, then died, plunging the street into darkness.

The team leader scanned the dark street one last time before quietly announcing: "All Smiley units, Gamma. Repeat, Gamma."

Silent as the shadows they had trained to be, the Cherry Commando team advanced on the club, weapons cocked and ready.

Chapter 50

Rosen

"You're kidding. That was you? You made up the disengagement?"

Rosen shrugged. "Yep."

Gil burst out laughing, shaking his head in disbelief.

For months, terror attacks had bled the country dry. Pressure from the left was mounting, the Americans were breathing down their necks, and then—just like that—the Prime Minister had stunned the world. Israel would withdraw from Gaza, leaving the strip to the local Palestinian population. Overnight, the country had erupted with protest. Streets clogged with settlers in orange shirts. Rabbis declaring divine punishment. The government had scrambled, desperate to keep the operation from spiraling into civil war. In an effort to smooth the public outrage, the Prime Minister's office had issued a tender for a PR package that included a branding campaign for the withdrawal and a reframing of the whole painful operation.

Rosen's company had won, and one of the first steps taken was a minor—yet significant—terminology spin.

At the cabinet meeting, he had delivered his pitch with the confidence of a man who knew exactly what people needed to hear. "Israel does not withdraw, so do not use the word withdrawal. We don't do that. What Israel is doing is *disengaging* from Gaza. Ladies and gentlemen, Israel is going to disengage."

The sheer gall of it had stunned the public. The Israelis were so stupefied to discover that its leaders thought them dumb, that the phrase 'disengagement' became the sole focus of the endless political arguments. Everyone was suddenly arguing about the word instead of the actual withdrawal, and within a few months the disengagement—née *unilateral withdrawal*—was over. And just like that, Gaza belonged to the Palestinians.

Rosen smiled at Gil. "Laugh all you want, but it worked."

Gil shook his head, still chuckling. "I've said it once, I'll say it again—you, my twisted friend, are a bloody genius!"

Gil's cellphone rang. He spoke for forty seconds before ending the call, then looked at Rosen and Hashim.

"We're ready. Rosen, where did you park your van?"

"In the back. We came in through the bar."

"The bar's insane right now. We'll go out the front door and around the back. Let's move."

Rosen turned to call the two young men. To his surprise, the two enemies who had tried to kill each other only hours earlier were now sitting together, talking animatedly.

Rosen took a moment to watch the mayor's kid. He hadn't expected him to offer his help. Maybe Prime Minister Rahav's promise of officer training had softened him up. Maybe. Yet Rosen couldn't get rid of the nagging feeling of mistrust that he felt toward Roni. He couldn't put his finger on the exact reason, but even though it seemed like the two boys were bonding, the sooner Roni was out of this, the better.

Chapter 51

Roni

This can't be it.

The Palestinian was speaking to him.

"Again, thank you," he said, speaking over the thudding bass rising from the club below. He held out his hand. Roni shook it, his grip weak. And then, just like that, the Palestinian turned and walked toward Rosen, who was already waiting at the stairwell leading to the exit.

This can't be the end.

He could not come up with a reasonable excuse to stay with Rosen. He had been told to wait a few minutes in the club, then take a cab home, while Rosen and Gil took the Mohandas toward Gaza. There was only one thing he could still do—he would escort Rosen out, memorize his car plate number, and quickly call his father. Not a heroic plan, but it was the best he could come up with. The Prime Minister himself had asked him for his help; the words were still ringing in his ears: *"Can you do it for Israel? Can you do it for your country?"*

And the Mohandas—well, he wasn't what Roni had expected him to be. He seemed so normal. A physics geek like himself. Someone who could have been sitting in his class, scribbling equations in the margins of a notebook. Not a jihadi executioner.

What would his father have done?

Rosen, Gil, and Hashim had already started to climb down the stairs when Roni shot to his feet, crossed the room, and joined them. His eyes still a little fuzzy, Roni didn't notice a low table that caught his shin on the way out. Trying hard not to curse, he hobbled out after the three, silently praying that he'd be able to make out the car's license number.

Rosen glanced back. "Roni? Your cab hasn't arrived yet."

"I know, I'll just see you guys out." Roni answered as he began descending after them.

He was just stepping off the last stair when the lights in the Lunch Club went out. A brief, stunned silence followed. Then, a cacophony of beeps as backup power units started kicking in.

"What happened?" Rosen asked, his voice tense.

Gil opened the entry door and glanced out. "Looks like a blackout. The whole road. The electric company must be doing maintenance or fixing something at the mains. Don't worry, just wait thirty seconds—the generator should kick in."

The crowd in the club began to noisily whistle and shout. A few drunks began shouting unintelligibly.

Only the DJ's laptops glowed weakly in the dark, the one visible light.

Gil flicked on his phone light and pointed it at Hashim. "Let's go. Now is as good a time as ever."

Chapter 52

Rosen

The dark Tel Aviv night was thick with the lingering scent of fried shawarma and cigarette smoke as Rosen stepped out of the building. He looked around him. The lights along the entire block were out. He began scratching in his pockets for the van keys.

"Stop!" He heard Gil hiss. The two young men, who were about to exit, froze in the doorway.

Rosen snapped his head up. "What's wrong?"

Gil tapped his phone light off. "They've found us."

It took a few seconds for Rosen to make out a group of men closing in on them in the dark—shadows shifting, moving casually, like ordinary pedestrians, except for the way they walked... too measured, too controlled.

"Run?" he asked in a low voice.

"No, we don't have a chance."

"Back inside?"

"No." Gil continued to scan the street. "You and me, we wait. We'll hold them up, buy time while those two get away."

Then, with a blinding flash of light, the entire club lit up as the generators kicked in, and the music thundered back to life. The group of men closing in on the club entrance stopped for a short moment, squinting in the bright light.

Gil spoke sideways toward Hashim and Roni. "Go out back, take the van."

Rosen stuffed the keys into Hashim's hand, pushed the two young men backward, and then closed the door, shutting them back inside the club.

"Robert Rosen? Gil Hamami? I'd like you to come with me, please." The voice was smooth and practiced. Authority in every syllable.

The man stood ten feet away, blocking their way forward, his posture easy, almost relaxed. Eight more men flanked him, their bodies rigid with quiet readiness. They wore civilian clothes—Tel Aviv evening casual—but nothing about them read as civilians.

Pros. Probably military intelligence. Maybe even Shin Bet.

"Who the hell are you?" Gil drew himself up menacingly.

The man slid his hand into his jacket and drew out a Glock 19 handgun. On-cue, the rest of his team did likewise.

"Who I am doesn't matter. You're coming with me. And tell the soldier and the Arab to come out."

Rosen raised his hands. "Okay, chief, we're coming. No need to…"

The shrill voice of a young lady cut through the tension. "Excuse me? We went outside for a smoke, look—we have the stamps." Two young girls wobbled up to Gil, dressed in short skirts and matching striped cat ears. It seemed they had mistaken him for a bouncer holding up a bunch of uninvited partygoers. The men quickly hid their guns.

"Show me your stamps, please." Gil smiled at the welcome distraction.

The two girls rolled up their sleeves and displayed ink stamps that had been printed on their arms earlier in the evening. Rosen almost laughed at the absurdity of it.

"Are you sure these are from today?" Gil frowned.

"Are you serious?" one girl huffed. "You're actually checking?"

"Standard procedure," Gil explained, taking his time.

The leader of the Cherry Team narrowed his eyes. "Let them in."

Gil exchanged a dark look with the man before turning back to the two girls. "Sure. You can enter."

As they stumbled inside, Gil looked straight at the man in charge, then a shadow of a smile crossed his face.

"There will be no need for the guns anymore, Lankri."

The man was visibly surprised. "You know me?"

"Of course I know you. Cherry Commando, right? We crossed paths when I was running Gaza Division." His gaze flicked across the assembled men. "Looks like you've moved up the ranks. *Kol ha'kavod*. Well done."

The leader stared at Gil with disbelief. "I don't believe you actually remember me from back then."

"Oh, I remember you, Lankri," Gil's voice dropped to a growl. "And I will definitely remember tonight."

"Look, Gil, I'm just the messenger." The atmosphere had changed in an instant. Lankri was almost apologetic as he continued. "I didn't want to be here. We all have nothing but respect for you."

Rosen stepped in. "Who sent you?"

"Shin Bet Commander himself. He ordered us to pick you two up, along with the soldier and the Arab. Prime Minister's orders." Lankri almost pleaded. "Do us a favor, tell them to come out. We don't want to have to find them ourselves."

From the corner of his eye, Rosen caught a flash of movement. The production van was swerving away from them, down Allenby Street.

Good boys.

He turned to the commando. "Okay. You win. They're inside."

Gil turned to Rosen with a questioning look. Rosen held his gaze.

Trust me.

Without a word, the eight commando soldiers entered the club, leaving their commander to cover Rosen and Gil. Minutes passed, and Rosen could see Lankri becoming increasingly impatient. It seemed that the reports he was receiving in his earpiece were not satisfactory. One by one, the soldiers trickled back out.

"They're not in there," Lankri stood opposite Rosen. "I saw you shove them back into the club when the lights went on. Where are they?"

Rosen chuckled loudly. "Look at that, Gil—a top commando unit can't catch two teens. And they say that the Israeli Defense Force is the smartest military force in the world."

"They are wrong." Gil smiled sweetly back.

Lankri's face turned a gentle shade of red. There was only so much mockery a fighter could take. Through gritted teeth, the team leader commanded his men, "Keep these two here. The rest of you—grab the cars and fan out. They couldn't have gone far. Move!"

Instantly, the soldiers dissolved into the night, and the manhunt began.

Chapter 53

Hannah

The ancient Toyota engine roared unnaturally loudly as it cut through the hush of the sleeping city, rattling over endless potholes, Israeli souvenirs from previous conflicts. Crumbling apartment blocks loomed on either side, their balconies sagging, rusted satellite dishes hanging at odd angles. Finally, they came to a halt in front of one of the anonymous gray apartment buildings.

"Here," said the short man. He climbed out and opened Hannah's door. "This is where you will stay for now."

Hannah sat frozen, staring at the building. It looked abandoned. Half the windows were boarded up; the rest were patched with tattered plastic sheets, fluttering weakly in the breeze. The walls were raw concrete, stained by decades of weather and war, the metal reinforcements exposed in places like broken bones. As if in a bad dream, she got out of the car and walked toward the entrance.

"Wait!" She hardly registered the sound of the driver's footsteps behind her. "Your bag!" He approached her. "Come, I'll show you your room."

Still holding her small bag, he drew a bundle of keys out of his pocket, separated one, and handed it to Hannah.

"This is yours now."

The main door creaked as she unlocked it. Her guide brushed past her into the entrance hall. He turned on a flashlight, the tight beam illuminating peeling paint on the walls and exposed wiring snaking along the ceiling.

"This way."

Hannah followed in a daze, trailing the wavering circle of light as they climbed. On the second floor, he stopped in front of a door. Another key. Another click. The door swung open.

The room beyond was unexpectedly intact. The suite was small, just two rooms—a living area with a few couches and a little kitchenette on one side, and a doorway leading to the bedroom. Yet somehow, there was a whisper in the air of happier times. A king-size bed lay in the corner of the bedroom, its plush mattress bare. The surviving cupboards in the kitchen had hand-crafted handles, adorned with colored glass beads. A broken dishwasher stood lopsided under one of the broken cabinets.

Someone had lived here. Someone who had cared about beauty, about comfort—about the small things.

Under the bright fluorescent light, she could see her guide clearly for the first time. His black hair was almost white with dust; his face streaked with sweat and sand. Two scars ran across his face, one on his forehead and one on his cheek. But it was his eyes—sharp, piercing blue—that caught her off guard, a stark contrast against his sun-darkened skin. They were sharp and clear, and there was something about them that drew Hannah in. The short man was standing back at the door's threshold, watching her.

"Whose house is this?" she finally asked.

"Was. The building belongs to a very old family. This suite belonged to their youngest son and his wife. There were four generations living in this home."

"Where are they now?"

"They deserted. Ran away to Europe, like most of the rich people of Gaza. They are in Belgium now." His voice became edged with bitterness. "The rich leave. They swear they'll return when we win—when the Zionists are defeated. They left us behind to fight their war for them." He shook his head, as if shaking the thought away. Then, he pointed to the kitchen cabinet.

"There is a little food in the pantry. Tea, some rice, a few cans of vegetables. I opened the mains so you have water in the kitchen. I couldn't find a can opener, but there is a big knife in the drawer you can use. There is a brand-new sleeping bag in the bedroom, and in the bathroom you will find mosquito repellent."

"You arranged all this for me?"

"I cleaned it, too. It was thick with dust and dead cockroaches." For a brief moment, his blue eyes twinkled. "I can't remember when was the last time I housecleaned."

Still standing outside the apartment door, he set Hannah's bag down and turned to leave.

"Wait!" Hannah's voice cracked. He stopped.

"What will I do? What will you do with me?"

"I was instructed to prepare the safe house and bring you here. That's done. May Allah protect you." He turned to leave.

"Wait!" Hannah pleaded. The man stopped and turned back to her.

"Please—where are we?"

"Gaza City, in the Rimal district. You are safe now."

"But who's going to help me? I need things. Can you help me?" she pleaded. His gaze softened as he noticed tears beginning to run down her face. A few long seconds passed before he spoke. His next sentence came out mumbled.

"Tomorrow. I can come in the morning if you wish. We will go to the market to buy whatever you need. I have to go now."

"Please. What is your name? How do I call you?"

The man stared at her. Finally, after a long pause, he answered, his voice soft. "Assad."

"Assad. Stay here. Just a few more minutes," Hannah pleaded. "I'm scared."

Assad took a long breath. "I will wait with you. A little."

But still he would not cross the door threshold.

Chapter 54

Roni

Roni was terrified. Kneeling on the leather seat, he pressed his face against the rear window, scanning the street behind them. His breath fogged the glass as his pulse pounded in his ears, muffling even the van's soft, steady purr.

They had barely made it out.

The moment he'd seen those men emerging from the darkness, he had frozen, his body rooted to the floor of the club. He wouldn't have been able to move if Rosen had not physically shoved him backward through the door. The impact jarred his ribs, knocking the breath from his lungs. Then, a rough hand clamped around his wrist. It was the Palestinian, who yanked him toward the dance floor, past the crush of sweaty bodies and the pulsating neon strobes that painted streaks of electric blue across his vision. He had stumbled after him through packed crowd of dancers, running through the back exit, half-expecting to hear the burst of gunfire at any second. Still dazed, he followed the Mohandas around the building to Rosen's van and climbed into the back seat, hardly daring to breathe. With the Mohandas at the wheel, they quietly rolled out of the parking spot and onto Allenby Street, in the direction that took them away from the club.

He scanned the road behind. As far as he could make out, there was no one after them. Yet. But every car that pulled in behind them made his stomach churn.

He forced himself to take a few deep breaths.

By the time they had reached the eastern outskirts of Tel Aviv, his pulse had slowed a little. Then he heard a loud sigh coming from the driver's seat. He pulled forward, gripping the dashboard as he slid into the passenger side.

"You okay?" Roni asked, "What's wrong?"

Roni regretted the last question. Moments ago, Hashim had been promised he would be returned to his home, his family. Now they were in a van, fleeing from a large group of armed men.

"I'll be fine. I just want to go home already." The Palestinian glanced at Roni, offering a tired smile. "How do they say it? So near, and yet so far."

They turned onto a wide freeway. Headlights swept around them.

Roni knew what his duty was. He could hear his father's voice as if he were sitting there in the van with them. *Your duty is to your country. Ten men and an Israeli civilian have died to bring this man to justice. You must turn him in at the first opportunity!*

And now, here he was—alone in a van with him. How proud his father would be if he, Roni Uliel, single-handedly brought the dangerous Engineer into military custody.

I should do it.

But the Prime Minister himself had asked him to keep quiet. His commander-in-chief had given him a direct order. He was a soldier, and his duty was to obey—even if it felt wrong.

It didn't help that, twenty-four hours after meeting the Palestinian, he just couldn't picture him as dangerous. The Palestinian had repeatedly and passionately explained that he wasn't a real engineer, and the whole affair had just been a fluke, blown all out of proportion. And looking at him, grimly holding the wheel, his slightly oversized patrolnik uniform making him look like a kid playing soldier, Roni felt something soften. The Arab couldn't be that good of an actor.

With a thrill of authority, Roni realized that the Arab's life and future lay completely within his power. If he stayed silent, the Palestinian would disappear back into Gaza. If he managed to alert the military, it would be prison. Roni had done time guarding prison camps during basic training. He knew how vicious and bleak life was behind the barbed wire. Could he condemn this boy, with the robotic aspirations and geeky dreams, to a cruel, perhaps unending, prison sentence?

Roni had never felt this much power over another human being—and yet felt so lost.

They drove on in silence, the hum of the tires the only sound between them, each young man deep in his own thoughts. Traffic on the Tel Aviv-Jerusalem Road was sparse at this hour of the night. The powerful van engine hummed as they crossed the Ben Shemen junction, where pine trees loomed on either side of the road, their dark silhouettes standing like silent sentinels.

"We should keep moving," the Palestinian said eventually.

"Yes."

"We can't stop. We must drive."

"I think you're right."

"Do you know where we are?" asked Hashim.

"On the Tel Aviv-Jerusalem Road."

"Jerusalem?" The Palestinian's dull eyes sparkled at the news. "How far away are we?"

"If we keep driving, we should be there in half an hour."

"Half an hour from Jerusalem?" His voice was hushed, as if he had just heard a miracle spoken into existence. He looked forward through the windshield, as if expecting the golden dome to rise on the horizon at any second. "*Subhan Allah*," he murmured, his fingers tightening on the wheel. "Allah be praised. I never thought I'd get to see the holy city in my lifetime."

Chapter 55

Assad

As he walked back to the car, Assad kept his eyes fixed on the ground, his brow furrowed. He was trying to understand—trying to name the unfamiliar sensation twisting inside him.

Ahmed, the young militant who had assisted him on the mission, was fast asleep, sprawled on the back seat with his thin legs dangling out of the open car window. His sandals hung loose on his feet, one of them tapping against the car door with every lazy rise and fall of his breath.

"Wake up." Assad grunted as he slammed the door shut. "We're done."

The boy stirred, groggy. His eyes blinked open, struggling to make sense of where he was. He stretched, yawning widely before glancing at his wristwatch.

"Took you a long time. Where were you?"

Assad ignored his young partner and turned the ignition key. The engine rumbled to life beneath his hands, vibrating through the metal frame.

He felt lightheaded. Off balance.

As a veteran fighter in a guerrilla war, the Lion had learned to always expect the unexpected. It was what had kept him alive for so long. But he had not expected this. The Israeli girl was the first adult woman he had ever had the opportunity to speak with. She was beautiful. Not in the way of the airbrushed women in Cairo fashion ads. Not in the way of the foreign reporters he had seen on Al Jazeera. She was beautiful because she was real.

He wanted to see her again. And what caused his pulse to rush was the fact that he knew she wanted to see him again, too.

Of course, in her case, it was because she was scared. She was alone, far from home, dependent on strangers. He knew under other circumstances there was no chance she would want anything to do with him. He had no illusions about his personal charms and physical appeal, but still, she wanted to see him. She had made him swear he would return, and she wouldn't let him leave until he had made a promise to pick her up the next morning to go purchase a few necessities.

He started calculating time, counting the hours. He had gone too long without sleep, running on strong coffee and cheap energy drinks. Thirty-six hours, maybe more. His body ached for rest, and he knew it would be best if he managed to grab a few hours of sleep. He had to stay focused and alert.

"Were you with the girl all this time?" asked the boy.

It was almost sunrise. He could sleep until seven, make the quick run to the Sheikh as he had been commanded. That meeting would take twenty minutes...

"What did you do with her for so long?" the boy pressed.

Then he had to deliver the package to headquarters—half an hour, maximum—then shower, change, another fifteen minutes...

"Did you kill her?"

That would keep him busy until five minutes past nine, and then—

"Wait, what did you say?" He broke off his chain of thought.

"Did you kill her?" the boy repeated, his tone casual.

Assad turned to look at him. "Why would I kill her?" he asked angrily.

"I don't know what your instructions were. You were gone for hours. Up there, with the girl. What did you do to her?"

"Nothing."

"Did you take her?" His voice dropped. "You could have called me."

"You think I raped her?" the Lion asked, his voice dangerous.

"You took your time." The young militant stared at him with defiance, his dark eyes flat and unreadable. There was no flicker of shock, no hesitation, just a quiet, unnerving expectation.

The cold, emotionless way in which the boy had asked such questions dismayed Assad. The Zionists had created generations of blacked-out youths for whom violent death was a close and ever-present reality. For a brief moment, Assad saw himself at that age. Young. Angry. Looking for revenge.

"Just shut up before I break all your teeth."

Ahmed stiffened. He sat up straighter, his pride prickling. But he wouldn't dare talk back.

Around them, the city was waking up. Fishermen carrying tackle sleepily shuffled toward their boats that were pulled up on the sandy beach. Dilapidated taxis cruised the main boulevards; fires were lit in bakers' ovens, filling the street with the scent of wood smoke; piles of newspapers were thumped down heavily by café doors and corner shops.

They cut through the city, each deep in their own thoughts. Assad knew the teen was fantasizing about how he could take Assad's place as the most

242

celebrated warrior in the Gaza Strip. But soon the Lion was back to counting hours and minutes. He would drive back and pick her up to go to the market. The drive to her flat from his current hideout would take about fifteen minutes.

So, if his calculation was correct, and nothing unexpected happened, it would be no later than nine-twenty when he would see the Jewish girl again.

Chapter 56

Roni

Jerusalem was waking up. The rising sun threw soft rays of light across the white stone buildings, making them glow a soft beige against the clear morning sky.

Once they had entered the city, Roni and Hashim drove around aimlessly, constantly on the move, keeping ahead of whatever might be behind them. Hashim was still jittery, gripping the wheel like he expected someone to ambush them at any second.

The city unfolded in twists and turns, its ancient roads winding through the modern sprawl. Without meaning to, they suddenly found themselves in the ultra-religious neighborhood of Mea She'arim, One Hundred Gates. Hashim was staring wide-eyed at the Hasidic Jews in their long black coats, their trousers tucked into their socks, wide fedora hats worn tightly on their. They moved with the same single-minded focus Roni had seen in soldiers during training—except here, the war was against time itself, the enemy a ticking clock counting down to *Shacharit*, the morning prayer.

Hashim's eyes darted between them, wide with fascination. "Look—there!" He suddenly pointed. "That Jew is married to a Muslim!"

Roni looked at a couple who were walking well apart from each other on the opposite side of the road. The man wore a black hat and a flowing black coat. The woman beside him had her head wrapped tightly in a beige scarf.

"She's not a Muslim; she's Jewish," Roni corrected.

"But she's wearing a *hijab*…"

"Roni chuckled. "Yeah, married, religious Jewish women wear that, too."

"They do? It's just like in Gaza. All women have to wear them outside the home."

"Here, some wear scarves; some wear wigs."

Hashim was momentarily thrown. "Wigs?"

Roni gestured toward a woman with smooth chestnut hair, curled at the ends, framing her face in a perfect bob. "See her? That's not her real hair; it's a wig. It's the religious women's way of keeping her hair private, but still looking the way she wants—wearing a wig."

Hashim squinted at the woman again, his eyebrows pulling together. He let out a short laugh—half amused, half baffled. "Hair over hair. That's the strangest thing I've heard in my life."

They drove about aimlessly, trying to make sense of the twisted, hilly layout of the holy city. The roads here were a maze—one moment a slick boulevard lined with glass skyscrapers, the next, a cobbled alley just wide enough for a car. Beautiful monuments and landmarks jumped out at them; the gleaming white chamber housing the Qumran scrolls, the Knesset parliament building, the Church of the Holy Sepulchre. Hashim randomly turned the large van onto a narrow road that climbed steeply up Mount Olives. The van crested the hill, and suddenly, the city unfolded beneath them.

The air was crisp, carrying the scent of damp earth and olive trees. Somewhere below, a siren wailed, followed by the sharp cry of a rooster. Jerusalem was waking up, layer by layer. Hashim pulled the van into an empty lot, the gravel crunching beneath the tires as he killed the engine.

Without a word, the two got out of the van.

"*El Aqsa! Qubbat As-Sakhrah!*" whispered Hashim as he spotted the two holy houses of worship. The black dome of Al-Aqsa Mosque stood tall and solemn, its ancient presence commanding the sacred mount. Standing adjacent was the golden Dome of the Rock, gleaming in the morning light. The contrast was mesmerizing: one dark and steady, the other glowing like a celestial beacon.

They left the car at an empty parking lot and walked in the soft sunrise to the panoramic viewpoint. At this early hour, they had the whole mountaintop to themselves.

Roni saw history rising with the morning mists, the energy in the air raising the hairs on the nape of his neck. Here was where Abraham had come to sacrifice his son, Isaac; here King David built his palace; Solomon raised his temple.

In kindergarten, Roni had sung about the city. In bible class, he had learned about the many historic events that had taken place on that one holy mountain since the binding of Isaac. In history class, he had learned about the city's five thousand years of stagnation and rebirth. He remembered the numbers by heart. Destroyed twice, besieged twenty-three times, attacked fifty-two times, captured and recaptured forty-four times. Sacked, burned, rebuilt, and then sacked all over again—the current cycle had finally ended with the third kingdom of the Israelites. There before him stood a view that encompassed everything he had ever learned about being a free Jew in a free Jewish state.

It was Hashim who brought him back to earth.

"Al Quds. Our capital."

Roni turned to him as if stung.

"Your capital?"

Hashim was still staring at the city below. "Our capital, your capital. Christian capital. So much war. Look—it's all just a pile of rocks and trees. It's beautiful, but why die for rocks and trees? Don't you think it's crazy?"

Roni opened his mouth to protest. But the simple logic rang true. For an instant, Roni could see Jerusalem for what it was. A land like any other. Rocks and trees, and buildings.

The feeling unsettled him. He shook his head. "I don't know if it's crazy. Hundreds of millions of people around the world believe in this city, in its holiness."

Hashim shrugged. "I don't."

Roni turned to the Palestinian.

"You don't?"

Hashim smiled back apologetically.

"No. I believe Allah doesn't only live here. He lives in my Gaza, too. And in Nabulus, Hebron, Mecca. There is nothing special about Jerusalem. Allah lives wherever his believers live."

Roni turned back to look at the old city which was bathed in the soft morning light. Jerusalem. *Yeru Shalem.* A name that literally meant City of Peace. Was there a reason he had been led to this mountaintop?

Chapter 57

Rosen

The Prime Minister's residence in the heart of Jerusalem was quiet at this early hour, mostly for fear of disturbing the first lady. The staff moved in practiced near-silence, having learned the hard way—disturbing First Lady Rahav before she was ready to face the day was a career-ending mistake.

Rosen wasn't officially under arrest yet, but he was not exactly free, either. They were sitting on low couches in a small, dimly lit waiting room that Rosen had crossed many times. In previous visits, his staff and entourage had escorted him. This time, six grim-faced Cherry Commando operatives, the same men who had picked them up at the club, flanked him.

A bit of a difference…

They stood on watch, their arms crossed, their eyes blank. When Rosen had asked to use the bathroom, two of them had escorted him, watching his every move like he was about to pull a Michael Corleone and take a gun out from the toilet tank, or at the very least escape through the barred window.

Gil, with his usual icy calm, had dozed off—his head propped against a corner wall, his mouth drooling slightly. The man could sleep anywhere.

They hadn't been told anything yet, but Rosen knew why they were there. They were about to get reprimanded by Prime Minister Rahav himself. And the reason they were still waiting was because it was seven in the morning—pollster time. Behind the large oak door in front of them, Prime Minister Rahav was having the daily sit-down with his pollsters, and Rosen knew that the severity of what awaited the latest results would largely influence him. If the numbers were high, it could end with a slap on the wrist. If numbers were down? A prison sentence could be on the table.

As the hours passed, and with no phone to keep him busy, Rosen's mind began to wander.

The Palestinian.

He was just a kid. A kid who had been swept up in something bigger than himself. And maybe—just maybe—Rosen had found a way to pay for the unforgivable. But the debt of the past wasn't so easily settled. As he sat waiting outside the Prime Minister's office, the memories crept back, like shadows slithering under a locked door.

"Arrow One to Sparrow, approaching final leg of patrol, please advise on vector back to base."

"Arrow One, hold position."

"Roger that, beginning left turn 360."

Formation leader Major Robert Rosen lightly touched the F-16 Fighting Falcon's stick. The airplane banked to the left, initiating a holding pattern. His wingman for this training mission was one of the squadron's latest newcomers, a rookie fresh out of the Hatzerim flight academy. Not everyone made it this far. In a country where thirty-thousand hopefuls fought for a slot in the Air Force every year, only a handful became combat pilots. Even fewer had *the gift*, the natural instinct that separated the good from the elite.

This rookie was damn good. Rosen had broken in many new pilots in the past: some good, some okay, some there because their dad was somebody important. But every now and then he would discover what he called a 'natural pilot.' This rookie had it. He was good, and he knew he was good.

"Arrow Two, this is One, we'll hold for a few minutes."

"Roger, Arrow Two initiating holding pattern, on your four o'clock."

It was late evening, sunset patrol. To their right, the Mediterranean gleamed brightly, blinding if you looked westward. Rosen slid down his black sun visor, shielding his eyes from the blinding reflection off the water. He checked the time flashing in the heads-up display. He had been in the air for more than two hours, sixty minutes of which had been spent in bombing practice. He was tired, needed to piss, and circling endlessly above the sea was making him cranky and aggravated.

After completing two wide, three-sixty-degree turns, Rosen called combat control.

"Sparrow from Arrow One, request vector back to base."

"Arrow One, stand by, please."

"Come on, it's simple, give me my course and we'll part as friends."

"Arrow One, stand by."

Rosen was about to rudely—and illegally—leave combat control's frequency when his radio crackled again.

"Arrow One, please confirm you have one live air-ground onboard?"

A wave of excitement surged through Rosen's body. "One live air-ground" meant the live multi-purpose air-to-ground bomb that hung from his left wing. Combat control wouldn't ask unless they were serious. This wasn't a drill. Someone, somewhere, was about to feel the full weight of Israeli air power.

"Arrow One confirming, I have one live onboard."

"Okay Arrow One, we have a job for you… head one niner five, stand by for target coordinates."

Rosen clicked the strike coordinates into the onboard computer. He was focused and calm as he prepared for an attack. He didn't need the computer to tell him that the coordinates were for a target just north of Gaza City.

"Arrow Two. This is One. Follow me closely. We're going to see a little action."

"Right behind you, Number One." Rosen was pleased to catch a slight tremor of excitement in the rookie's voice. So he was human after all.

The F-16s cut along the coast as attack details poured in from the combat controller. The target was a confirmed sniper nest.

As they approached the target, they swung westward toward the setting sun. A minute later they turned once again, aligning themselves with their target, the sun at their back. Rosen flipped up his sun visor and gently pulled the stick. His F-16 started climbing toward the darkening sky, his stomach and leg muscles flexing against the inflating pads of his G-suit.

Suddenly, Rosen felt as if someone had injected his spine with a warm liquid. Moments later, a shock of pain sliced his lower back, like a hot wire stabbing into his spine. His back locked up instantly. The extreme pressure had done something to his spine, but he was right at the zenith of the loop that comes just before the dive. At his side, the rookie was still following smartly, just out of his slipstream. He was damned if he would let a little back pain get in the way of his dive. He would push through the pain.

"Arrow One's going in." Rosen grunted, as he flipped the F-16 over and started the bomb run.

He was having a hard time concentrating. I was taking all he had to keep the airplane on its proper course. The pain increased as the dive continued and the g-forces dropped, and he knew that in seconds he was about to pass out. There was only one thing to do: abort and climb to an even flight angle. But then, to his joy, the bomb buzzer went off, signaling that it was the moment to release the payload. In a haze, Rosen released the rocket, feeling the familiar bump from the side of the wing as it flew off on its lethal trajectory. He pulled the stick upwards, but instead of climbing steeply, he leveled the aircraft parallel to the ground.

"We're too low! We're too low!" He heard the rookie shout over his radio.

"Two, pull up. I have a problem here."

"Pull up! Pull up!" The rookie was yelling.

Rosen couldn't. Another G of pressure and he would pass out. The bomb detonated underneath him, and a split second later, a wave of hot air shook the F-16, tossing it about like a marble in a washing machine. Rosen could hear bits of debris zinging and pinging as they hit the aircraft, and still he couldn't bring himself to pull up. He could hardly think with the pain, and he knew that one more point of pressure would make him pass out. He plodded on at a low altitude, hoping that he'd make it back. He didn't realize that he had neglected to double-check the flight computer before releasing the bomb.

Twenty minutes later, he landed safely at his home base, yellow emergency vehicles lining the runway, their lights flashing in the dark. Slowly and painfully, they lifted Rosen out of the scarred and scratched cockpit, placed him on a hard stretcher, and whisked him away in an ambulance.

As he was being wheeled into the base infirmary, his squadron leader joined him. He could see by the look on his leader's face that something was wrong. And then he remembered.

"Oh, God! The rookie. Did he get out? Is he…?"

"The rookie's fine. He pulled out on time and came back without a scratch."

Rosen frowned, despite the good news. "What's wrong, then?"

"Nothing for you to worry about…"

"Come on, I can see it in your face. What happened?"

"Rosen, I'll talk to you when the doc has finished his examination…"

Rosen lashed out and managed to grab the sleeve lapel of his commander's flight overalls.

"Don't bullshit me. What happened?"

His squadron leader looked coolly at him. "You missed the target. By two hundred meters. The bomb hit a kindergarten instead."

Rosen let the news sink in before answering in a quiet, level voice:

"But it's evening. The place must have been empty?"

"They were having an end-of-year pajama party. Twenty-two Palestinian civilians dead."

"Children?" Cold spread through his body.

"Eighteen five-year-olds, two teachers, and two other adults—probably volunteer parents, from what we've gathered."

Rosen tried to nod, to say something, but his mouth felt disconnected from his brain. If only he'd been on course. If only he had double-checked the flight computer. He should have aborted when his back began aching. The children would have been alive.

"Rosen?"

The voice yanked him back. One of the operatives stood over him.

"Prime Minister Rahav will see you now."

Rosen stood up wearily. The familiar numbness returned, his heart retreating to the black cell in which it had been trapped since that terrible evening, memories efficiently pushed back into darkness.

"This way."

Chapter 58

Hannah

"This way."

Assad pulled back a curtain of thick plastic strips, nodding toward the dimly lit passage beyond. Hannah hesitated for a fraction of a second before stepping through. The air inside was dense with the mingling aromas of sizzling lamb, garlic, and the sharp tang of pickled turnips. It was a kitchen—stainless steel counters lined with trays of half-prepared dishes, massive pots bubbling over open flames. The clatter of knives against cutting boards stopped the moment she entered. Six sets of eyes stared coldly at the strange, black-robed woman who had entered. Eyes that became all smiles as Assad followed her in.

The market trip had been intended as a quick errand, but Assad had turned it into a tour. The best stalls. The best coffee. The best baklava, dipped in honey so rich it stuck to Hannah's fingers. He avoided the crowds, slipping instead through back entrances, navigating alleys like a man who knew every stone, every shadow.

Hannah was amazed to see how every single person on their trip smiled happily when seeing her escort—shopkeepers, bakers, even a gang of bored teenagers kicking around an old soccer ball—at the sight of Assad, their expressions brightened, their postures straightened, like he carried some unspoken authority. She began to realize that the strange little man whom she was spending the morning with was a Gazan celebrity. There was something about Assad that the people adored. He radiated a mixture of devilish carelessness, raw intelligence, and—as she could see in his eyes—deep pain.

They had spent the whole of last night talking. He had gone out of his way to help her calm down by telling humorous stories, personal anecdotes, and asking her many questions about her previous life, all the while standing just beyond her doorstep. Even after two hours of earnest conversation, Assad would not come inside her flat. Not even for coffee.

That morning, he had picked her up as arranged. After the long hours in the dingy flat, the relief at seeing his face was enormous, as if a dear friend had arrived. She had to remind herself that he was a stranger, a terrorist whose job had been to smuggle her into Gaza. He had brought an oversized black dress with a matching black *hijab* to cover her blonde hair.

Now, in the gray light of the Gaza morning, she found herself almost—almost—trusting him.

They had stopped at a vegetable stall where tomatoes were stacked in pyramids, their skins taut and glistening.

"This is where you can buy the juiciest vegetables in the world. Planted and grown right here in Gaza," he proudly smiled. Baskets with onions and potatoes spilled onto the stall front, while chains of garlic and red peppers hung like shining jewels from the stall roof.

"Look." He picked up a ripe tomato, rolled it in his hand, and squeezed it. A spurt of watery seeds flew out of his fist straight onto her shirt.

"Oh! I'm so sorry!" He reached over to brush the juicy seeds off her shirt front, realized what he was doing, and reddened very much like the squished tomato in his hand.

"It's okay, Assad. That *is* a really juicy tomato." Hannah laughed.

"Hey! What do you think you're doing?! You pay for that!" A giant man barred their way, eyes shooting lightning bolts at them from under a thick unibrow.

"Of course, I'll pay; don't worry." Assad turned to the man and started fishing for change in his pocket. Then the outraged stall seller recognized the Lion, and his unibrow shot up in surprise.

"*Ya Allah*! It's you! Come, you must take some of these beautiful cucumbers. They're the best crop we've had this year, sweet as honey!"

Waving away Assad's attempt at paying, the man squeezed a variety of vegetables into a large plastic bag. Hannah noticed with amusement that the wrinkled bag was printed with the logo and design of a prominent Israeli fashion chain.

"Allah bless you." Assad smiled at the shopkeeper.

Now, they passed through the busy kitchen and into a small restaurant. Assad guided her to a corner table with a view of both entrances.

A waiter shimmered into view within seconds. Without a word to Hannah, Assad ordered a full meal for the two of them. Under different circumstances, Hannah would have felt slighted to not even be consulted on what she would be eating. But today she just smiled. She couldn't be angry with this man. And besides, the menus were in Arabic, and the dishes were mostly unknown to her.

Once he had ordered, Assad stood up.

"I need to run a small errand," he said after the waiter had disappeared. "I'll be back in a few moments. If you don't like the food, ask for something you like. They'll make you anything".

"Even if it isn't on the menu"?

Assad grinned. "Especially if it isn't on the menu".

And then he was gone.

For the first time in two days, she exhaled. Really exhaled. The tension in her shoulders loosened as she tore off a piece of warm pita, the dough soft, still steaming. The tangy tomato salad soaked into the bread, its heat mingling with the sharp bite of olive oil. The flavors were simple, perfect. It was surreal—less than forty-eight hours ago she had been dodging death, yet now, in a tiny corner of Gaza, eating bread and tomatoes, she felt calm. Almost safe. Stockholm syndrome? Exhaustion? Or maybe… maybe this was exactly where she was supposed to be.

A few minutes later, Assad reappeared at the restaurant doorway, a heavy-duty plastic sack slung over his shoulder.

She smiled at him.

Assad didn't smile back.

Something was wrong.

His entire body tensed, his gaze fixed on something just past her shoulder. The sack slid from his shoulder, hitting the tile with a dull thud. Then he was gone. No words. No explanation. Just a streak of black disappearing through the door. Hannah twisted in her seat to see two men racing out of the kitchen toward the door, one of them shoving aside the waiter, who had been carrying a tray of small mezze plates. Plates shattered on the tile floor. The waiter hit the ground hard, knocking over a chair as he fell. The two men stormed through the restaurant toward the front door, one of them speaking into his collar.

And then they were gone. For a few long minutes, no one dared speak. The waiter lay where he had fallen; the customers sat rooted at their tables, eyes wide with surprise and terror.

Hannah didn't wait to think. She stood up, grabbed the sack that only seconds ago had been propped on Assad's shoulder, ran through the restaurant, into the kitchen, and out the back door, disappearing into the noisy, chaotic market.

Chapter 59

Roni

He was beginning to work it out. It wasn't about what the Prime Minister had asked of him, or Rosen. It wasn't even about duty. It was about what was right.

And the right thing, he now knew, was to help Hashim make it back to Gaza. Back home.

The realization sat heavy on his chest. But how? He had no connections, no back-channels to smuggle someone across the border. He wasn't Rosen, and he sure as hell wasn't Gil. He could barely find his way out of Jerusalem without Waze. He needed help, and there was only one person who could give him a clear; who could help him decide what to do. His father. He would know what was best.

Mayor Sami Uliel was not a friend to Palestinians. The man had spent his career railing against Hamas, pushing for harsher security measures, and ensuring Sedera remained a fortress. He would never agree to help a wanted terrorist. Not unless Roni could make him see Hashim for what he really was—a kid, not a killer. It would take careful words, the right approach. But before he could plan, they had to keep moving.

The two walked back to the van.

"What should we do now? Where should we go?" Hashim wondered aloud.

"We need to think of an idea. And we need to keep moving," Roni replied. "I'll drive; why don't you sleep a little while I think about our next move."

"You sure? Is your eyesight..?"

"It's fine."

Hashim was out before they hit the next traffic light, his breathing deep and steady.

For the millionth time, Roni missed his phone, crushed at the border bombing. Mobile phones had almost completely wiped out the public phone booths. The sooner he could call his father, the better. He cruised aimlessly through the streets of Jerusalem, hoping to spot a public phone. And then, just ahead, he spotted it—not a phone, but something better. A red beret. Roni pulled over, causing Hashim to wake up with a frightened jump.

"What's happening?" Hashim whispered.

"I have an idea," said Roni. He rolled down the window. Hashim watched him carefully.

"Hey, *Achi*!" Roni called out to his paratrooper brother. The soldier, noticing Roni's identical red beret, smiled widely.

"What's up? Can you give me a ride? Where're you headed?"

"Sorry, bro, not going anywhere."

"Oh." The soldier sounded disappointed.

"Listen, I need a favor—my phone is dead. Can I make a quick call from yours?"

Hashim stiffened beside him. "Who are you calling?"

"It's okay. I want to call my father. He'll help us out. He'll know what to do."

Hashim didn't look convinced. "Are you sure?"

Before Roni could answer, the paratrooper was at their door. "You don't have a charger in the car?"

"No." Roni answered.

"This your car?" the paratrooper continued, with an impressed glance.

"No."

"His?" The paratrooper pointed at Hashim, who tried to act relaxed, but failed miserably.

"No."

"Then whose is it?"

"A friend. Lent it to me. Listen, I really need to make a phone call. Can I use your phone?"

With another look at Roni's red beret, the paratrooper dug down into his shirt pocket and pulled out his cellphone, which was encased in a red, heavy-duty protective cover with paratrooper wings embossed on the back. He quickly unlocked the phone, then handed it to Roni.

"My phone is yours, bro."

Roni leaned back into the driver's seat and quickly dialed his father's number, flashing Hashim a quick, reassured smile as the call connected.

The line rang twice. Then came the click.

"Hi, Abba," Roni said, exhaling. "It's me. I'm okay, listen, I need your help."

But the voice that answered Roni was not his father's.

Chapter 60

Hannah

It took Hannah over four long hours to make her way back to the safe house, a mere three hundred yards from the market. The streets of Gaza City blurred into one—the houses featureless copies of each another. Having arrived the previous night, before dawn, Hannah had barely registered what the safe house looked like from the outside, let alone how to get there. Wandering in ever-growing circles, slowly dehydrating in the harsh sun, her confidence ebbed away until she was sure she'd never make it. The street shimmered in the heat. Sweat slicked her back, soaking into the loose black robe Assad had given her. The *hijab* clung to her scalp like a wet bandage.

A large woman was staring at her from the doorway of one of the buildings, her black dress stretched across a massive stomach, a scraggly hen cackling between her arms. Hannah walked up to her. She didn't dare speak Hebrew, so she tried in English.

"Please, can I have some water?" The woman and her hen glared at Hannah with disgust. She muttered something in Arabic.

"Water? I need to drink water?" Hannah mimed a cup of water, her cupped hand pouring imaginary water down her throat. The woman's muttering turned into a shout, causing the hen to join in a terrified screech. Hannah quickly moved on.

Earlier, at the restaurant, she had instinctively grabbed Assad's white bag, but it was gradually becoming unbearably heavy. She thought of discarding the bag, but felt it was her duty to return it to him.

Dazed, she walked the streets, passing tall, minareted mosques, crossing wide avenues, and squeezing through narrow alleys. A car backfired, and she nearly jumped out of her skin. Hamas' morality police stopped her twice, their voices harsh, their fingers jabbing in accusation. She had no idea what they were saying. She only knew the way their eyes moved over her made her want to disappear.

Now and then, a building would look familiar. Confused, she had entered three different houses, only to discover that she was in the wrong place.

And then, finally, she saw it. The faded blue shutters on the first floor and the broken cement doorway painted a flaking red. Home. A sob escaped her throat, unbidden. She staggered forward, her knees buckling just as she reached the door. Pressing her forehead against the cool wood, she forced herself to breathe.

She trudged into the dark stairwell, her eyes blinded by the outside sunlight. Slowly she made her way up the rickety stairs to the apartment door and tried to insert her key into the lock. Suddenly, a voice whispered behind her.

"Hannah!"

Hannah spun around in fright, her elbow catching on the doorknob, pain radiating up her arm like fire.

"Sorry, sorry. It is me." The whisper was urgent but gentle; his eyes roamed over her, checking for wounds. "It's Assad. Sorry. Are you okay? I was worried something happened to you."

"Assad! You scared me so much." Hannah felt her heart racing.

Gently, he reached for the key still trembling in her hand, took it carefully, and slid it into the lock.

"Sorry. Didn't mean to frighten you. Here, it's open."

With her last ounce of energy, Hannah walked into the house, settled Assad's white bag on the floor, and fell into a chair. Assad stood outside the door.

"You're bleeding."

Hannah followed his gaze to the small pool of blood that was forming under her chair.

"It's your elbow."

"I'm okay." She stared absentmindedly at her elbow, then lifted her gaze toward him. "Are you okay?"

He was not okay. He felt terrible, stupid, and clumsy. He had been worried sick when he arrived at the safe house, only to discover that Hannah was not there.

He had staked out the apartment, anxiety growing by the minute. Did the men who had chased him out of the restaurant take Hannah into their custody? He knew very well who they were. Cherry commandos. Their Arabic had been perfect. He had been lucky to get away this time. If they had come while he was sitting with Hannah, her clean hair peeping tantalizingly close from under the *hijab*, they would have been able to nab him easily.

But she was here now. Waiting for her in the dark stairway, he had sworn to himself that he would stay away.

Do not go inside. Do not touch her.

He had tried to focus on working out how the Israelis had found him. But his thoughts kept wandering back to the girl. Hannah. He promised himself in Allah's name that when she returned, he would not cross the threshold of the apartment. But now she was standing there, weak and bleeding. He could not walk away.

"I'm so sorry." He said. "I'm just so relieved you made it back."

She swayed slightly.

He took a deep breath and stepped in. He would pour her a glass of water, bandage her elbow, pick up the bag, and leave. That was all.

Water, bandage, bag.

He walked to the dusty kitchen, opened a cupboard, drew out a glass, and filled it with water from a plastic bottle he had packed for Hannah.

"Drink this." Hannah took the glass of water he offered and drained it.

"Good. Now I'm going to bandage your elbow, and then you are to drink another glass. Okay?" Hannah nodded at him, and then—smiled. Assad smiled bashfully back, his face reddening. He turned quickly, rummaging through the box of supplies he had arranged for the flat. Finally, he pulled out a small Red Cross first-aid kit, crossed over to Hannah, and kneeled beside her chair. She flinched slightly when he touched her arm. He worked fast, cleaning the wound with practiced hands. He had done this before, in worse conditions. But never like this. Never kneeling before a woman who was looking at him like that.

"Please… stay with me," Hannah whispered. Assad felt his resolve melt away as the desperate look in Hannah's eyes pierced him.

"I can't."

"Please stay." Her uninjured hand reached for his, her fingers laced through his fingers. He should pull away. But he didn't. Still holding onto his hand, Hannah kneeled, her head resting on his chest. The touch of her body burned through his thin shirt. He could feel her firm breasts pressed against his stomach. She was breathing heavily. He had to go. He guided her back as he sank down to the floor, opposite Hannah. She moved toward him again and began to kiss his neck, his cheeks, his eyes, and he could not stop his hands from exploring her body. He began to shiver with tension and excitement. It was the first time in his life that he had ever touched a woman. He broke off and stood back, his breathing heavy.

Hannah smiled softly and stood up. Without a word, she turned and walked toward the bedroom. Assad watched her go, knowing it was over. The Lion, mighty warrior of Gaza, had no fight left in him, no willpower to resist.

Chapter 61

Roni

Roni gripped the steering wheel so tightly his knuckles turned white, sweat slicking his palms. The road blurred before him, his breath coming fast and shallow.

The call to his father had been one of the most jarring moments of his life.

It hadn't been his father who answered. It was a Shin Bet operative. The clipped, professional voice on the other end of the line turned his insides to ice.

"Roni, I'm from the Shin Bet. Stay calm, and if you are with the Mohandas, say: *Hi Dad. How are you?*"

His throat had gone dry, but he'd managed to force the words out.

"Hi Dad. How are you?"

"Good. He's there with you; that's excellent. Whatever you do, you must not raise suspicion. If you understand, say: *Dad, I need to talk to you.*"

"Dad, I need to talk to you."

"Excellent. Now—where are you? You can answer fully."

"I'm in Jerusalem. Don't know what street."

Roni could hear a rush of activity on the other end of the call. Radio static, urgent voices, digital bleeps of various unseen systems locking in to his location."

"Whose phone are you using?" the Shin Bet operative continued.

"I just borrowed a phone from a fellow paratrooper I just met."

"Excellent."

A few seconds passed. Then Roni heard a different voice on the phone.

"Roni, this is Gaza Division Commander Jonah Levi. I want you to listen carefully to what I am about to tell you. Do you know how to reach Bet Shemesh?"

"Sure."

"I need you to make your way there and stop at the Eshtaol junction. There's a petrol station at the entrance. Stop there for fuel. We'll do the rest. If you understand, say *Dad, I need to go; we'll talk later.*"

"You'll do the rest? What does that mean?"

"We are ending this conversation now. You just get there on time. That's an order. Now, say *Dad, I need to go. We'll talk later.*"

"What will you do?"

The Gaza division commander's voice grew angry. "That is no longer your concern, corporal. You just bring him in. Say: *Dad, I need to go.*"

Roni stole a glance at Hashim. Once again, he felt the heavy weight of responsibility for Hashim's life on his shoulders. Roni had no illusions about what Hashim would have to go through once picked up by the Israeli military. He would be living in hell, probably dead within a few months.

As he spoke the next words, Roni felt like he was outside his own body. Like he was watching himself from far away, hearing his own voice from a distance.

"I can't do that, sir."

A heavy pause. "What did you say?"

"I can't do what you ask me. This was all a big mistake. A big mistake."

With a dreadful feeling of impending disaster, Roni tapped the phone's end button and handed it back to his paratrooper brother. Slowly, he shifted the gear into drive and pulled away from the curb, trying to calm his breathing. His body felt heavy in the car seat.

"What can't you do? What did your father want? Will he help us?" asked Hashim.

Roni hesitated for a few seconds before answering.

"My father will not help us."

"Why not? You said he would help."

Roni stole a look at the Palestinian. Should he tell Hashim what had transpired during the call, or should he keep it to himself for now?

"It wasn't my father I just spoke with. It was Gaza Division. They have my dad's phone."

With a chill, Roni realized that he had just officially become a criminal. He had defied a direct order from the Gaza Division Command. He was now actively aiding an enemy of the state. There was no undoing this.

He wasn't a soldier anymore.

He was a traitor.

Chapter 62

Hashim

Hashim stared out the windshield, his mind whirling. The awe he had felt at being in Jerusalem—at seeing Al-Quds with his own eyes—had vanished the moment Roni had hung up the phone.

The Shin Bet was hunting them.

To Hashim, like all Palestinians, the Shin Bet was feared and hated. They had a god-like control of the Strip. They seemed to know everything, always watching. They could make people disappear, blow up houses in the middle of the night, turn neighbors into informants. Awesome and hated. Hashim felt a chill crawl up his spine as the full understanding of their escape hit him. He had escaped the Lunch Club, which had been crawling with Shin Bet operatives, and gotten out alive. That shouldn't have been possible.

Unanswerable questions flooded his head. How could they escape the web that was being spun around them while they just drove around aimlessly? Could they make it to the Gaza border? How would he cross the border once there? He felt he was drifting without a rudder, helpless and increasingly hopeless. He looked at Roni, and for a moment, felt flooded by a massive feeling of thankfulness. It was hard to believe. The Israelis had taken his sister, Na'ima, from him. They were evil, vicious people, hated by every single person in Gaza. And yet… here was an Israeli soldier who was risking everything to help him.

"Thank you for everything, Roni."

Roni smiled ruefully. "Thank me when you're back home in Gaza."

"Do you think we should maybe drive to the border and try to find a way to cross?"

"Won't work." Roni's tone was flat, absolute. "Every inch is covered by more than one security camera. Each camera is connected to a computer that alerts the patrol guards if anyone comes within twenty meters of the walls. The only way in is through the crossing, and they won't let you in without orders."

Hashim frowned. "But I'm dressed in a Zionist uniform. A border patrolnik."

"You don't have an ID. the military police'll pick you up at the first gate. Palestinian militants have tried that in the past."

Hashim cursed under his breath and turned back to the window. The old stone houses, which had looked beautiful and sacred just hours ago, now appeared gray and lifeless under the harsh sunlight.

"Where are we going?"

"I don't know. We need a plan. And until we figure one out, we have to keep moving."

Hashim glanced at the digital clock embedded in the dashboard. The red digits showed that they had been driving for twenty minutes since the phone call.

"You can't call your father again. Shin Bet is probably following every call made to him."

"I think so, yes."

He rubbed his temples. "Is there anyone else you know who has power? Like your father?"

Roni's head snapped up. "I wonder where Rosen is now."

"Rosen?" Hashim asked, surprised. "Those gunmen picked him up. He's probably dead."

"Dead? Why do you think he's dead? "

"Rosen is with the Shin Bet. He is dead for sure."

"Nonsense." Roni sent a quick glance at him. "They don't have a reason to kill him; they were looking for you."

Hashim let out a dry, humorless laugh. "How can you be sure?" It seemed unreasonable to Hashim that Rosen had survived. Back home, if the Hamas came knocking on your door, you would never be seen again. And as far as Hashim knew, Shin Bet was so much more ruthless.

"I'm not sure if he was released," Roni explained. "Just guessing. Rosen is a big man here, very important, very connected. I'm willing to bet you he was released five minutes after we escaped. We should try to reach him."

Hashim hesitated. It wasn't much of a plan, but it was better than driving aimlessly into a trap. "I suppose we can try. We can go back to Tel Aviv, wait outside his office until one of his employees comes out, and then we can ask."

"Good thinking."

"And we need to hide this van as soon as possible. It feels to me that every minute we wait here, they're coming closer to us."

"I wouldn't worry too much; they're not that efficient."

"They aren't?" Hashim raised his eyebrows.

"You watch too many movies." Roni chuckled. "There are no satellites closing in on us with death rays."

Hashim turned in his chair to Roni. His voice was low and tense. "My brother, last week I was sitting at home with my family. No one knew who I was. If there is one thing I've learned in the last week, it is that your army can find anything."

Roni didn't answer right away. When he finally spoke, his voice was quieter. "Good point. We'll get close to Rosen's office and ditch the van. Make the rest of the way on foot."

Hashim nodded. "Let's go."

Roni swung the wheel, and the van made a sharp right onto Golda Meir Avenue, wheels screeching. Hashim scanned the road signs, which were printed in Hebrew, English, and Arabic.

"I can't believe we're heading back to Tel Aviv."

The car picked up speed as they rolled down the Jerusalem hills. To their right, the ruins of the deserted Lifta village loomed over the valley like a ghost town, the abandoned stone houses crumbling into the hillside.

On the opposite side of the highway, the Jerusalem morning traffic honked and crawled forward; lines of cars stretched down to the horizon.

The road ran smooth and wide as it snaked through the Jerusalem forest, the tall pines casting shifting shadows over hidden traffic cameras, all focused on once mission: find Robert Rosen's production van.

Chapter 63

Hannah

Hannah sat at the small kitchen table, her body draped in a white sheet. Across the room, Assad dressed in silence, his movements quick and methodical, his back turned to her as he buttoned his shirt. The air between them had shifted—heavy now, filled with something unspoken. He hadn't looked at her since they had pulled apart, hadn't said a word. Tears were forming in her eyes.

"Assad, are you okay?"

"Yes," he said, his tone flat, automatic.

"Why are you going?"

"I have to move." He reached for his belt, tightening the buckle with a sharp tug. "I can't stay here."

"Will you come back?"

He turned to her. She was confused to see pain in his eyes.

"I don't know."

A shiver of fear ran through Hannah as she felt she was about to lose the only anchor to her sanity and wellbeing.

A lump formed in her throat, panic rising. "Please come back."

"I can't!" The sharpness in his voice startled her.

"Why not?"

"I shouldn't be here." He rubbed his eyes, exhaling hard. "I should not have come inside."

"But why not?"

"You must have realized by now that I am a wanted man. I am a Hamas military fighter, and that means that the Israelis have my picture and are looking for me. I have already outlived my life expectancy by over a year. A full year. And you know how I survive?"

She shook her head.

"By moving all the time. By being light on my feet. By not attaching myself to anyone or anybody. I have seen my family only once in the past twelve months, and they live not four blocks away from here, from this very house. Do you understand?"

She stared at him, searching his face. He was trying to convince himself as much as he was trying to convince her.

"Then let me come with you." She pushed back her chair and stood barefoot on the cold tile floor. "I have no ties here—I can move with you." Hannah implored, "I'll go wherever you tell me. Just don't leave me alone in this place."

"You'll be taken care of. There will be others who will take care of you, who will look after you."

"I don't want them." She took a step forward. "I want you."

His gaze softened. The shield cracked, just a little.

"Inshallah, the battle between our peoples will be over one day. And if I'm still alive, we will meet again."

"What if it never ends?"

"I'm sure it will. It has to. It is Allah's will that we live in peace on his earth."

"Is that why you blew up the package the other night?" She was trying to keep him from leaving, to keep talking. There were just two people in the world now, Assad and herself.

"I saw everything. The bag those poor men brought through the tunnel that night—you blew it up. You weren't delivering weapons, Assad. You were destroying them. You don't want to fight anymore; you want it all to end. "

A few long moments of deathly silence passed before Assad spoke. His eyes burned into hers.

"You followed me?"

"Not intentionally. I stepped out to stretch my legs, and I saw it all. I know what you're doing, Assad. While I was coming back here today, I looked into the bag you had dropped. I saw the wires that are inside;

285

they're all shredded. I know what you're doing. You're stopping the violence. I can help you. We can make Allah's wish come true together."

Assad turned and walked to the door. He picked up the white bag, staring inside like it held an answer he couldn't find. Hannah stood up and faced him, the white sheet slipping from her naked body.

"Please don't go. I can help you. Maybe that's why I'm here. Maybe this is what Allah intended. Please…"

Assad opened the door and stepped out. He stood outside the door for a full minute with his back to Hannah before closing it with a determined slam.

The tears she had been holding back ran freely down Hannah's cheeks as the pain of her loss rendered her powerless. She was alone in the world. Completely.

She crumpled back into the chair, her heart aching like never before.

And then the door creaked opened.

He stood in the doorway, an intense look on his face. Hannah didn't dare speak. She quickly covered herself with the sheet. After a pause that felt like a lifetime, Assad broke the silence.

"Get dressed. We have one hour to reach Rafah."

Chapter 64

Roni

"Wait, you guys have an actual football league in Gaza?"

Hashim laughed. "Of course! I love soccer! I love Shabab Rafah. I think they are the best team to ever come out of Gaza. Do you know them?"

Roni chuckled. "I never knew there was any soccer at all in Gaza. I am a fan of Be'er Sheva. And, of course, Real Madrid."

Hashim clicked his tongue in mock disappointment. "Then we cannot be friends. The only true football club in the world is Barcelona."

"Oh well, I'll just drop you off here, then."

The two young men burst into carefree laughter—the first time in hours that the tension had lifted, however briefly. Then the dashboard chimed, and the moment evaporated. Roni pointed at a flashing orange light on the dashboard. "We're running low on gas."

"We've been driving for hours." Hashim's voice was tense. "Do we have enough gas to get to Rosen?"

"I hope so."

"Do you have any money?"

Roni's father had stuffed a few bills into his pocket the previous morning. "About enough for half a tank, but I'd rather not stop."

"I'll check if there's anything in here." Hashim began rummaging through the glove-box, flipping open compartments, searching for anything that might help.

Roni suddenly braked the car. "Shit!"

Hashim looked up. The traffic ahead of them had slowed to a complete stop.

"Why are they all slowing down? Accident?"

Roni squinted at the flashing blue lights. "I count three police cars ahead. Could be an accident, or it could be a roadblock. We need to get out of here."

A tourist board sign announced the Latrun Trappist Monastery at the next exit. Roni squeezed his way across two lanes and drove onto the embankment. After a short, bumpy ride, they turned onto a gravel path that led them away from the traffic.

Minutes later, the Latrun Monastery appeared on their right, looking the part: a serene Holy Land vision of clean, white stone, neat olive groves, and healthy grapevines stretched out in orderly rows. On the left side of the road, a 1950s Sherman tank was standing atop a ten-meter-high pedestal, a memorial to lives lost in previous wars.

Hashim, still nervous, took in the surreal scene. Tank one side, peaceful vineyards on the other.

"What is this place?"

"Latrun." Roni checked his mirrors. No sign of pursuit—yet. "We can drive to Tel Aviv from here, but it's the long way."

"Roni, we don't have enough gas for the long way. There's a station up ahead. We'd better fill up now."

Roni rolled the van into the station, a tiny four-pumps-and-shack setup surrounded by grapevines on one side and olive trees on the other. Apart from an attendant, the station seemed empty. Eerily so. He stopped the van by the self-service pumps, got out, and walked toward the low shack. The young attendant was sitting behind a filthy table, reading a free daily newspaper and delicately sipping a boiling-hot cup of muddy Turkish coffee.

"Is there anyone here?" Roni asked the attendant.

The man lowered his paper, blinking.

"Huh?"

"Is anyone here? Did anyone arrive in the last twenty minutes?"

The attendant scratched his stubbled jaw. "There were a few people. They got gas. You need gas?" The attendant stood up heavily.

"No. I…"

The sound of a heavy motor cut through the silence.

Then Roni heard Hashim's voice as he shouted from the car.

"We need to go, Roni!"

Roni began edging back toward the van, then stopped and stared as a giant tractor rolled into the station. A Trappist monk, fully clad in a white tunic and black scapular, sat at the wheel, and a group of his brothers, similarly dressed, sat in the wagon behind him.

Hashim leaned out of the van. His eyes were wide with disbelief. "What are these people? Are they real?"

"Something feels off." Roni murmured, his eyes never leaving the Trappist monks. "Let's go. We'll find another station."

Roni began walking away from the monks, who had now parked by one of the pumps. They were staring at him in the sudden silence while their leader stepped down and began refueling the tractor.

Then a rumble came from the main road, and seconds later, three unmarked vans screeched around the corner into the petrol station. Roni ran to the car, but before he could reach it, Hashim had opened the car door and bolted into the olive grove that bordered the station.

The vans stopped, doors opened, and a team of fifteen soldiers spilled out. One of them, obviously the commander, ran to Roni.

"Where is he?" he barked at Roni, "Where's the target?"

"What target? I don't know."

"Is he armed? Is he carrying a weapon?"

"What? No. He's not armed. Please, I'm telling you, he is not armed. How did you find us?"

The soldier ignored Roni's question. He turned to his men and bellowed, "He's in the trees. Spread out and start searching."

The well-trained squad spread out and, within seconds, disappeared from view into the grove. One soldier remained by the cars, watching over a stunned Roni.

For a full minute, nothing and no one moved or spoke. The monks stared motionless at Roni as if they were made of unblinking balsa wood. The attendant stood at the shack door, his face a picture of excitement and surprise. The only sound heard was the gas pump filling diesel into the squeaky-clean John Deere.

Then—crack. A gunshot split the silence. Followed by another. And another.

Chapter 65

Hashim

Hashim ran, not daring to slow down, as he ducked under low branches and leaped over exposed roots. He was terrified, and the adrenaline pumping through him gave him almost superhuman strength and speed. He could hear the soldiers hunting him, a thunder of military boots and cracking branches closing in.

"*Wakef walla ana battuhak*!" a soldier shouted in Arabic. It was the one Arabic sentence that every Israeli soldier knew by heart. *Stop, or I'll shoot.* And Hashim, like every citizen of Gaza above the age of six, knew the script. It was the first line of the rules of engagement, binding all Israeli Defense Force soldiers. Three times a "Stop, or I'll shoot" warning, then a shot above the head, then a shot at your legs, then… Hashim tried not to think. He knew he had another two shouts before the shooting started.

But he was wrong.

A shot rang out, clipping a branch a mere foot from his head.

In an instant, Hashim understood—they were not trying to capture him. A second shot rang out, missing him again. The third shot found its mark, ripping into his shoulder. The pain he felt was beyond belief, as if his shoulder had been sliced open with a blunt knife, the raw nerves smashed with a five-kilo hammer. The pain sent circles of red lights across his eyesight, causing him to lose his footing and go crashing into the last olive tree in the grove. He closed his eyes, trying to battle the exquisite pain he felt. He gasped, blinking past the stars dancing in his vision. Footsteps surrounded him. He forced himself to open his eyes. He was staring straight into the black barrel of a Tavor rifle.

The soldier at the other end of the rifle spoke in Hebrew this time, his Arabic vocabulary spent:

"It's over, Mohandas. You're finished."

"Na'ima," Hashim whispered, "I'm coming, sister."

Chapter 66

Rosen

Prime Minister Rahav's knuckles turned white as he slammed his palm against the heavy wooden desk. "Where the hell is the Engineer?!"

Rosen sat across from him, unblinking, staring at a random spot on the bookshelf behind the Prime Minister's head. "I don't know."

They were alone in the Prime Minister's study. The room was an awkward mix of styles—antique chairs, modern Swedish mass-produced cupboards, North African artwork, and a giant, suspended fireplace. Designed and arranged by the first lady, it lacked both personality and warmth. Rahav banged his desk again, this time causing a brass vase to fall onto a shaggy IKEA carpet.

"You don't know? You don't know?!" Rahav bellowed. "You messed up, and you messed up fucking big."

Rosen had never heard the Prime Minister curse this roughly. The morning polls must have been bad.

Gil, leaning casually against a bookshelf, shrugged, unfazed by the Prime Minister's rage. "It was just a misunderstanding, Yaki. Rosen went down to Sedera himself, even took a shrink with him. It was Mayor Uliel. He told Rosen the kid was Druze. Just calm down a minute and let's—" Gil was quickly cut off.

"You?! What in God's name are you doing here? How did you even manage to stick your nose into this?" The question was clearly rhetorical—Prime Minister Rahav was in no mood to listen to Gil's reasoning.

"Listen, Rahav," Rosen cut in. "Nobody knows that the Druze is actually a Palestinian. Nobody. If we just keep it quiet, it will go away. It worked. The Druze are happy. You came out on top."

"Nobody knows? Nobody knows?!" Rahav's voice rose with each word. "Let's just make a quick list of these 'nobodies' who know."

He ticked them off on his fingers:

"First off, we have Mayor Sami Uliel, an unstoppable gossip and a political opponent. Then we have the Cherry commandos; we have the entire Shin Bet, down to the girl who runs the phones. Then we've got every soldier who has ever been stationed at the Erez border busy adding two and two, trying to work out who the mysterious patrolnik is. That long list is the 'nobody' who knows that your Druze hero is the Mohandas. I give it forty-eight hours before the news goes viral."

Rosen had nothing to say. He knew Prime Minister Rahav was right.

"Now I have to decide. What do I do with you?"

Rosen sighed. "Why don't you let Gil go? He has nothing to do with this."

Prime Minister Rahav looked at Gil. "I'm sure you're both in on it. I know you're in on it."

"In on what?" asked Gil pleasantly.

"You crossed the line. You've been hired by the opposition. You're ruining me from the inside. You're a pair of double agents! Do you think I'm stupid?"

"Damn right, you're stupid," bellowed Rosen, causing a throbbing vein to pop out of Rahav's forehead. Rosen quickly continued before the storm erupted. "Think of it—I worked my ass off to get you elected. I am on your damn payroll."

Apart from his wife, no one had ever shouted at Rahav like this, at least not since he was elected Prime Minister. For a moment, Rahav's fury froze—a flicker of doubt in his eyes. Rosen continued.

"So what reason could I have for crossing the lines?"

"I don't know, Rosen." Rahav snarled, "You tell me."

Rosen held his gaze. Neither of them blinked.

Then, Rahav let out a long breath. He rubbed his temples. His anger wasn't gone, but it was cooling.

"Listen, I've had enough of this bullshit. You're going to wait here until—"

The door opened, and Rahav's assistant walked in briskly.

"Who let you in here? I'm —"

The assistant wordlessly handed Rahav a small, folded note. Rahav scanned it, his face swiftly transforming from sheer rage to a sneaky smile.

"Your fairy godmother is smiling upon you once again, Rosen, you lucky bastard."

Surprised, Rosen looked at Rahav's beaming face, his expression questioning. "We've found your two precious heroes. We'll have them here within the hour."

Chapter 67

Assad

Assad stood at the entrance to one of the largest and oldest smuggling tunnels in Rafah. The tunnel mouth—a gaping cement hole four meters wide—had been dug into the middle of the basement floor of an apartment building. A single, flickering lightbulb cast harsh shadows across the rough concrete walls, the air thick with the scent of damp earth and gasoline. Behind him, Hannah shifted slightly. She was quiet, waiting. He didn't know if that made him respect her or fear her more.

This tunnel was one of the most valuable in Rafah; goods flowed in and out like blood through an artery. Sacks of grain, counterfeit Barbie dolls, cola bottles, chocolate bars, livestock—sometimes even entire cows—were ferried through, slipping beneath the Egyptian border less than a kilometer away. The building's inhabitants acted as a human shield. There were ten families, two per floor, each with at least four children. They were paid a sizable salary to live here, a necessary expense to ensure the Zionists hesitated before reducing the structure to rubble. Assad knew the price of protection. This tunnel was one of the

Strip's most valuable, its use restricted to those who could pay the steep toll set by the entrepreneur who had built it.

Today's shipment was a large one. Four impatient businessmen were waiting outside for the Lion and his partner, pacing and murmuring, their hands restlessly fiddling with prayer beads and cigarettes. Each had tens of thousands of shekels' worth of goods coming in, but everyone bowed before the militants. Hamas was served first. Only after the Lion had received his package could the other men be permitted to enter the basement and receive their packages.

"Isn't this dangerous? In broad daylight?" Hannah whispered.

"It's always dangerous. The Jews' spies follow us day or night. No difference."

She was about to press him further when Ahmed, Assad's young partner, appeared at the door carrying a plastic bottle and a tin box.

"Walaa made me bring you this," he muttered. "She said to tell you that they only have water in the house, but it's cold water."

"What's in the box?"

"Biscuits."

Assad turned to Hannah. "*Jamillah*, do you want to drink? It's from one of the families living here."

Hannah shook her head. Assad noticed she smiled every time he called her *Jamillah*. When he had asked her name, she had answered Hannah, but Assad had never called her that. To him, she was Jamillah—beautiful—and he used the name whenever he wanted to see her smile.

"Why is she here?" Ahmed asked in Arabic. "What did you bring her for?"

Assad appeared to ignore the question, though deep down, he was asking himself the exact same question. Why had he brought her? He glanced at the girl, dressed in a long black robe, her head covered with a black *hijab*. He had tried to rationalize his decision. Having a woman with him would make him less conspicuous as a target. Israeli planes filming them would see a couple with their young son, not a combat cell. And she was strong; she could help him...

But could he trust her?

Everything had happened too fast. She had clung to him, begged for his protection, for his time. He had never spent time with a woman before; the rules were strict. But with the Jewish girl it was different, and making love to her had opened a stream—no, a fierce *river*—of needs that had been dammed up inside him. She was an oasis of calm in his hellish, violent reality. But, maybe it was too good to be true. Was it rational that, within forty-eight hours, she had managed to connect so strongly with him?

What if she was a spy?

It seemed that everything he knew and believed had changed. He was sabotaging his own organization, he was spending his days with a Jewish woman, and he was lying to his superiors while telling the most damning truths to a woman he barely knew. He was caught in a whirlwind, but—in the eye of the storm it was so calm.

"They're coming."

Ahmed slid into the tunnel entrance, grabbed onto a thick rope connected to a pulley above the entrance, and lowered himself down. Seconds later, the rope jerked twice. Assad gripped it and pulled until the package emerged—a large, white, zip-up plastic bag. Hannah stared at the bag. "What is it? What's inside?"

"We don't ask. Our job is to move it to its destination."

"But before we deliver it, we'll…" Her words were cut short by Assad tugging urgently on her sleeve, signaling for her to stop talking. She heard a scraping sound, and she turned to see the young boy climbing out of the tunnel exit. He swiveled his thin long legs out of the tunnel shaft, stood up, and dusted off his clothes.

Assad's eyes flicked over him, sharp and searching. In one step, he closed on the boy and patted the his shirt. He slid his fingers into the boy's shirt pocket and withdrew a Galaxy chocolate bar.

The boy looked defiantly at Assad. "They have enough down there. I deserve this."

Assad studied the chocolate bar, then threw it back to the boy. "You stole it; it's yours."

Assad and young Ahmed lifted the bag by its handles, and together, they started up the stairs. The four businessmen who were waiting outside stamped out their cigarettes. They had been waiting for quite some time, and with each passing moment, the risk of being located grew. But this man was the Lion himself. For him, they would wait as long as it took.

"Ya Assad," one of them called. "Can we go in?"

"Yes. Your packages are waiting for you," Assad nodded.

The four men scurried quickly down the stairs to the cellar, stealing glances at the strange woman who had gone in with the Lion. One of them turned back suddenly and shouted, "Inshallah, you stay safe, blessed hero."

"*Shukran* my friend, thank you for your kind blessing."

The car they were using this time was an inconspicuous gray Mazda. Hannah sat in the back, her fingers resting against the white plastic bag, but not opening it. She sat unmoving, her gaze pointed the other way, at the dunes outside her window.

At the city's outskirts, Assad stopped the car at the side of the road. He turned to his young partner.

"You can go. I'll take the package to the Sheikh myself."

The young man stared, surprised at Assad.

"But we do this together."

"I don't need you. The Sheikh prefers it if I come alone. You go rest."

"But how will I get home from here?"

"*Yalla*, get out!" Assad barked at the boy.

Ahmed hesitated, then shot a final glare at Hannah before slamming the door shut. Assad drove away without a second glance. They drove alone for another ten minutes, Hannah still sitting in the back. Then Assad suddenly pulled over.

"What's wrong?" Hannah asked.

He opened the glove compartment and pulled out a dirty, rolled-up T-shirt. He shook it out, and a gleaming wire cutter fell out.

"We've don't have much time. Open the bag."

Chapter 68

Hannah

Hannah's fingers trembled slightly as she unzipped the white plastic bag, the thick material stiff and rough against her skin.

Inside, nestled among layers of plastic wrapping, was a large silver canister. The metal was cool to the touch, heavier than she expected. She passed it to Assad, who took it without a word, his movements efficient and practiced. In return, he handed her a thick black garbage bag.

"Hold this open," he said.

Assad twisted the lid of the canister and, with slow precision, began pouring out heavy, yellow flakes, each piece cascading into the garbage bag with a soft, rustling sound, like dry leaves.

"What's that?" She asked.

"TNT."

"That's TNT?" she asked, the disbelief evident in her voice. "It looks like cornflakes. I thought TNT was... you know, red sticks, fuses sparking?"

"You've watched too much *Tom and Jerry*," Assad smiled, "but the tubes you're talking about are just containers. This yellow material is what's inside those containers."

She swallowed. So, this was real. This harmless-looking pile of flakes had the power to kill dozens—hundreds—if placed in the wrong hands.

Once the canister had been emptied, Assad pulled out a second nylon bag from under the driver's seat. From that bag, he then began to pour similar yellow flakes back into the silver canister, talking to Hannah as he worked.

"This is imitation TNT, made of yellow stone. We use this in training for explosives specialists. Same color, same weight. No one will notice the difference."

Understanding dawned on her. "You're switching it."

He nodded.

Her eyes narrowed. "But when it doesn't explode, won't they be able to trace the switch back to you?"

"This will most probably be used in an explosive vest on a suicide bomber. They'll strap it to some kid and send him into a checkpoint. He'll press the button, and nothing will happen. The Israelis will grab him, confiscate the belt, and wonder what went wrong. Allah willing, no one will trace it back to us. Just one failed 'martyr' and a whole lot of confusion at Israeli Intelligence."

"But what if they *do* find out what you did?"

Assad stopped working for a moment. His blue eyes looked softly at her. "*Jamillah*, my life is in Allah's hands. He has kept me alive for a reason, and finally I have found my path. If it is Allah's will, then I will die trying to fulfill my mission."

Hannah's face clouded with concern. Assad quickly continued. "But let's not get carried away with too much of this joy and laughter, okay?" He chuckled. "I'm here, you're here. We have this moment. Together." Gently, he leaned over and kissed her. She couldn't help but smile.

She watched as he delicately resealed the canister and placed it back in the white plastic carry bag.

Twenty minutes later, they pulled into a shadowed alley near the Sheik's residence. Assad cut the engine, the car settling into silence.

"Here." he whispered. "I'll have to cover you up. I will be back in five minutes." He reached for a gray military blanket from the back seat and draped it over her.

Time passed slowly. Hannah rolled onto her side, holding the rough, gray military blanket in place. She peeked at the dashboard clock. He had said five minutes. It had already been ten.

Where is he?

Her bruised body had begun to ache. She fully realized how lucky she had been. So many people were killed at the crossing, and she got away with a few bruises…

The terrorist attack.

God almighty.

Since the suicide attack at the crossing, Hannah had hardly had time to think, to process all that had happened. Johnny was dead, killed alongside ten more young soldiers. And it was her fault. Those poor boys would have been alive today if she hadn't gone through with the cow-blood stunt. The suicide bomber wouldn't have had a chance to get close enough to detonate and take out an entire squad.

The protest had been her idea, and she had known that Johnny would only be too happy to become her accomplice. And now he was dead. And for what?

The car door flew open, causing Hannah to jump under the blanket.

"Stay down, *Jamillah*, they're watching us. Stay down."

Chapter 69

Rosen

Into the cold, dark recesses of his mind, a faint flicker of light appeared, glowing with sudden and unexpected warmth. It was the beginning of a wild idea.

A way out.

Rosen opened his eyes and lifted his head. Gil was slumped in a cheap plastic chair, watching him with concerned eyes. The two were being held in a small courtyard, situated behind the kitchen at the Prime Minister's residence. Dripping kitchen appliances surrounded them, the stainless-steel surfaces dulled with age and use. One wall was stacked with cleaning detergents labeled in bold Hebrew letters, meticulously arranged by size and type. Against another stood a humming walk-in refrigerator, its heavy metal door slightly ajar, a sliver of cold air curling out like mist dampening the tile floor.

The security officer assigned to watch over them stood by the only exit. Rosen stood up, crossed over silently, and whispered in Gil's ear.

"Whatever happens, go to the Erez Crossing and wait for the Palestinian kid there."

Gil nodded.

Rosen took a steadying breath, squared his shoulders, and strode toward the security guard, forcing confidence into his step.

"I need to talk to the PM now."

The man barely reacted.

Rosen tilted his head. "Why don't you talk into your jacket and tell them that I want to see Caesar One."

Rosen purposely used the Secret Service code for Prime Minister Rahav. Rahav was "Caesar One," Mrs. Rahav was "Caesar Two," and their two boys were Caesars Three and Four. The Minister of Defense's Secret Service codename was "Swallow," and Rosen knew for a fact that the minister's most urgent desire— more urgent than Middle East peace, more pressing than the budget crisis—was to have his Secret Service call sign changed. "Eagle One" had a nice ring. "Iron One" sounded strong. Hell, he'd even settle for "Rock One."

The Secret Service man turned away out of earshot, and Rosen saw him muttering something into the mouthpiece hooked into his jacket lapel. He turned back to Rosen.

"PM can't see you now."

"Tell him he has to. Tell him he's about to make a giant error and that I can help fix it."

Once again, the Secret Service man turned away. After a longer low-voiced exchange over the radio, the man turned to Rosen.

"What mistake?"

Rosen shook his head. "I'm not going to tell you."

"Then they won't let you in." The security agent shrugged.

"Tell your boss that he's about to make the biggest mistake of his career. Tell him to say the following sentence in Rahav's ear: *Three points for free*."

The officer muttered something into his lapel mic and walked off, leaving Rosen to sweat in the silence. Five minutes stretched painfully long before the man returned.

"The PM will see you. Wait here."

Rosen smiled. You could always trust Prime Minister Rahav's greed for public approval.

Fifteen minutes later, a second security guard appeared in the kitchen courtyard to escort him. As they passed through the service corridor, the scent of sizzling meat filled Rosen's nostrils. The kitchen was already prepping lunch—vegetables being chopped, cumin-scented rice steaming in massive pots, chicken skewers lined up on metal trays. Prime Minister Rahav's wife had installed a new regime in the mansion's kitchen—a low-carb, low-fat menu designed to restore her husband's pre-election waistline. It baffled her that not only had the Prime Minister's waistline not receded, but it was steadily growing by the week. Rosen looked at the low-fat salad dressing and chuckled. If only the first lady knew about the cheese bourekas and soft chocolate rugelach that were the staple catering of all sealed government meetings. Dr. Saadi, the government medical officer, had nearly keeled over when he saw the numbers—since the last election, the government had collectively packed on two hundred extra kilos. That was a fact that Prime Minister Rahav kept very close to his ever-expanding chest.

Rosen was pushed through the service door and down a short passageway, through which he caught a short glimpse of the next shift of Secret Service men checking and rechecking their various guns and rifles. The number of staff and security personnel had outgrown the beautiful old house, and there was a feeling of stuffiness and claustrophobia in the back passageways and corridors. Up a carpeted stairway, down another stuffy passage—more Secret Service members, more pushing—until, finally, they were at the entrance to Rahav's office.

"Wait here." Rosen's chaperone shoved him roughly onto the same couch he had sat on just a few hours earlier that morning.

Rosen sighed. He knew what would happen next. It was a gambit he himself had taught Prime Minister Rahav: the Wait Gambit. Never *ever* see someone right away. Let them wait, let them stew a few minutes. Make them think you don't care about meeting them. And although it was the oldest, most worn-out trick in the book, it was still efficient. Except now, the gambit was in play against him. Infuriating. Time was short, and Rosen needed every second.

Finally, the door opened, and the Prime Minister's personal secretary walked out toward him.

Rosen stood up. He was as cool as ice and as focused as ever, even though he well knew that the next twenty-four hours would seal his career. He was about to gamble everything. His career. His reputation. Maybe even his freedom. There was a good chance that, by his actions, he would also be ruining Prime Minister Rahav's career. But if that happened, so be it. There was certainly no shortage of pompous, lying snakes just waiting to grab Rahav's place.

"The Prime Minister will see you now."

Chapter 70

The Sheikh

The Sheikh sank into his La-Z-Boy with a satisfied sigh, easing the lever back into his favorite viewing position. He extended his arm toward the little table by his side, reaching for his glasses and then the remote control, all the while balancing a plate of pistachio nuts on his stomach.

He flicked the widescreen TV on, and after a few exasperating false starts and long, puzzled stares at the remote control, he managed to navigate to the files area of the TV's hard drive. He found yesterday's recording and pressed play.

The screen lit up with the image of more than one thousand men bowing their heads in prayer. One thousand believers. The video's sound quality wasn't great, but in the stillness of the moment, he could hear the imam mumbling in the background. He fast-forwarded, skipping past the prostrations until the moment when the congregation sat upright again, ready to listen. It was showtime.

He noted with satisfaction that this was the edited version. Five cameras had been networked throughout the central nave of the mosque, and his assistant had already stitched together a multi-cam version.

The Sheikh could hear his own voice filtered through the PA system, but the edit did not show him standing at the pulpit. He didn't need to see himself on tape. He wanted to see the effect of his words on the crowd listening. It was a technique he had heard American presidents used when campaigning, watching a mixed audience's response to different ideas and keywords. But the Sheikh wasn't campaigning. He didn't need to. He watched the recordings because they stimulated him. Seeing hundreds of men staring at him with adoration, hundreds of minds being led by him—it was exciting and arousing.

The various cameras zoomed in and out as they panned over the crowd of barefooted men. All eyes were gazing at him with admiration. He remembered his own sermon verbatim, absentmindedly lip-synching it as he watched. Today had been a great sermon; everything had worked as planned—the rousing sentences were rousing, the dramatic pauses dramatic, the inciting paragraphs inciting.

The knock on his study door couldn't have come at a worse time.

"What is it?" he snapped angrily.

The door cracked opened just enough for his servant's head to appear.

"Apologies, Your Excellency, but there's a boy…" the servant meekly informed him.

"A boy?"

"Yes, sir. He says he is from your family. Ahmed."

The Sheikh's brow furrowed as he ran the name through his mind. Ahmed. Could be any of twelve Ahmeds, ranging from distant cousins-in-law to his sister's grandchild.

"He says he's the Lion's combat partner," added the servant.

Ah. That Ahmed. He sighed heavily. His sister's grandchild.

"Show him in."

Grandnephew Ahmed. His eldest sister had dogged the Sheikh to fix her beloved first born grandchild with an honorable position among the fighters, and Allah protect us—she could nag, the cow. She called him day and night until, finally, just to get her off his back, he had paired the boy up with the Lion, figuring that was the safest place to put a well-connected but inexperienced boy. He hadn't heard from his sister since, which had been a small blessing.

But now the boy was here. Wearily, the Sheikh stood up, slipped into his sandals, and walked down to the bare, humble reception room. Only a few hours previously, he had met the Lion in this very room. He hoped all was well with the boy. He couldn't stomach facing his sister again.

"As-Salamu alaykum, uncle." The boy was already inside, standing stiff-backed, his hands at his sides, trying to appear disciplined.

"What do you want?" the Sheikh asked irritably.

Young Ahmed appeared a little cowed by the cold reception, but nonetheless proceeded. His words were halting as he stumbled through what seemed to be a practiced statement.

"I have reason to believe that the Lion is not true to the Islamic spirit and the Palestinian cause."

This, the Sheikh was not expecting. He folded his arms.

"You do? How so?"

Ahmed continued with his rehearsed speech. "He has a woman, a Jewish woman, that he takes on military missions. And he does not let me fulfill our missions. He would not let me come here today. He prefers her. She is not his wife. It is against Islam."

The Sheikh said nothing at first, studying the boy.

"He takes the Jewish woman on missions?" he asked at last.

"Yes." Ahmed nodded vigorously.

The Sheikh pondered this piece of news for a few seconds. "You did well to come to me. You can go now."

The young man stood for a few moments, apparently not having expected to be dismissed so quickly. Finally, he turned and left. The Sheikh climbed back to his viewing room, deep in thought. He had known about the Jewish terrorist girl, of course. He had arranged the deal himself with Yossi from the Brigades, charging a hefty sum to smuggle her into Gaza. You could always squeeze good money out of the Brigades; those naïve do-gooders, they were always so eager. He didn't know exactly how long Yossi was going to be paying him for watching over this girl or what they would do with her once the Brigade terminated payments, but payment for the first week had been generous. To protect his investment, the Sheikh had requested that the Lion, his best man, be the one to escort her and set her up in the safe house. And that was supposed to be the end of it. But clearly, it wasn't.

This must not continue.

The Lion was one of Gaza's most revered warriors, a role model to thousands of Palestinian youths. He couldn't be seen in public with a Jewish woman, of all people! He would lose all honor.

Absentmindedly, the Sheikh picked a pistachio and cracked it with his teeth. The girl was bad luck. The Sheikh considered how badly things had been going since they took her in: two deliveries blown up by Israelis, sacks of materials spoiled by acid, hundreds of meters of faulty wiring discovered...

A chilling thought struck the Sheikh.

Was it just bad luck?

The materials they used were often of very poor quality, and four out of five deliveries were usually defective in the best of times. But the Lion's shifts.... Was there a pattern he had been missing?

No. Impossible. The Lion? A saboteur? Unthinkable. And yet...

"Bassam!"

His servant appeared at the door.

"The TNT that came across today. Get it."

"It's out, sir. It's already been sent to the factory."

"Then get it back." The veins in his neck bulged. "Get it back now!"

The door closed as a frightened Bassam raced away at his master's bidding. The Sheikh lowered himself back heavily into the La-Z-Boy. He punched play, and the on-screen sermon continued. Once again, he watched as hundreds of sparkling eyes adored him.

But he could not enjoy it now.

The magic was gone.

Chapter 71

Assad

She was asleep. It was now or never.

Assad slid out of bed, the warmth of her body still lingering on his skin. He reached for his clothes, careful not to let the fabric rustle against the sheets. He donned his underwear, and with the rest of his clothes bundled under his arm, he inched toward the door. It was time to end this. What had he been thinking?

"Assad?"

Hannah looked up sleepily and smiled.

"Are you going? When will you come back?"

Assad didn't answer. Hannah stretched a little, her voice still sleepy as she spoke.

"Assad, let's disappear. Let's just leave. Chile. How's Chile sound? We can blend in there. No one will know. They'll never find us."

"Chile?" He let out a short laugh. "Why Chile?"

"I don't know." A sleepy smile crossed her face. "It's beautiful there. Green. I've had enough of this desert and dust. In Chile, you can drink water straight from the streams."

Assad smiled. She was wonderful. "Sounds like a good enough reason. Water straight from a stream. Let's do it. Let's go now."

"Stop laughing. I'm serious." Hannah pouted.

Assad knew he was in trouble. He had sworn that he would cut himself off. That he would leave while she was sleeping and never come back. He knew he had to go. This was getting too dangerous for both of them. His survival instinct was screaming at him to leave and never come back. But he hesitated.

Maybe just one last coffee before he left. Just a few more minutes with his Jamillah.

Hannah sat up in bed, pulling up the sheet to cover her exposed breasts. She looked at him with a worried smile and voiced his concern as if she could read his mind. "I'm serious, Assad. What we're doing is dangerous. It can't last long before they'll find out, and then they'll kill us both."

He looked into her eyes. How could he explain? He knew she was right. He was wanted by the Israelis, and soon he would be hunted by his own people, too. There would be a price on his head from all sides. It was tempting to just run away. Leave the horror behind; start again.

But she hadn't sent that pure girl in white to go up in a flash of fire and ball bearings at the Erez crossing. She had not seen Mohandas' face as he was torn from his family. It all had to end. But first, he had to leave this flat.

He stood up.

"You're right. You have to leave as soon as possible."

She stiffened. "And you?"

Assad sighed. "I'm sorry. I have to continue what I have started."

Tears welled in her eyes. Collecting the white sheet around her, Hannah stood up and walked to him. She touched his hand gently. He felt his resolve begin to melt away. Using every ounce of strength he had, Assad took two steps to the door.

"I can't stay. There is nothing I want more; please believe me. But I have to go. I'll arrange for you to be taken out of Gaza. You'll be safe."

"But I don't want to leave you."

"I'm sorry my Jamillah."

She reached for his hand, her fingers grazing his. His whole body ached to stay. To throw everything away and run. Instead, he forced himself to pull away, turned the knob, and stepped through the door. He looked back just once.

Then he closed it behind him.

Chapter 72

Hannah

Hannah stared with unseeing eyes at the door, her body stiff with fear. He was gone. She had lost him. Panic surged through her as her mind replayed their last conversation, finding a million things she shouldn't have said. Chile? Running away? Why had she said those stupid things? She should have told him she wanted to be by his side more than anything in this world. That she was willing to help him fulfill his mission. And, if necessary, she would die with him...

No. Assad was too talented to let anything happen to them. Determination flared in her chest. She wouldn't let him walk away. Swiftly, she stood up, threw the black dress over her body, and picked up the *hijab*. She slipped on her shoes and ran to the door.

And then—she froze. Assad had not gone! She could hear him standing there. He couldn't leave her.

Tears of joy silently ran down her cheeks. She opened the door.

Her smile faltered on her lips. It wasn't Assad who was standing behind her door. It was Yossi. Her former commander, the man who had recruited her into the Israelis for Palestine Brigades. For a few moments, she stared at him, unable to understand how it was he who was standing at the door.

"Yossi? What are you doing here?"

Then, a thousand red lights lit up in her mind. He was smiling at her, but it was not his usual smile. He seemed elated, even gleeful. It was all wrong. How could Yossi be here? How could he have entered Gaza? He was an Israeli civilian, a protester like she had been. How would he know to find her?

Suddenly, Yossi's hand clamped onto her arm and viciously shoved her backward into the flat, closing the door behind them.

Chapter 73

Prime Minister Rahav

Prime Minister Rahav stared into space, trying to 'visualize it.'

It made sense. Rosen always made sense. He was still furious with the man, but he had to hand it to him—the plan was a good one. It was worth three points in tomorrow's poll, easy. Three, maybe four. Even five.

"Run it again," Rahav ordered, for the third time.

Rosen started again, showing no sign of impatience.

"We will arrange a special press conference focused on Palestinian terrorism. We set it for an eight-fifteen, which keeps us in the prime slot of the evening news but just after the first commercial break—perfect timing."

"Yes, that's right," Rahav nodded.

"You will talk about your personal mission to stamp out terrorism. Israel needs a strong leader these days, someone who is not afraid to defend his people."

"A father figure."

"Exactly. You make your speech, and then we show a short interview with the Mohandas. He talks about how Israel has become impenetrable. Stronger than ever. How warriors in the holy jihad war have become frightened of Israel's might. It'll be very real, very authentic, believable—"

"And he will be saying those things because...?"

"Because I'll train him. You'll bring the Mohandas to Jerusalem, and I'll work with him. All I ask is a conference room and some time alone with him and the paratrooper."

Rahav scowled. "You can't be alone with him. He's a wanted terrorist. I'll have a couple of Shin Bet soldiers in there with you."

"No soldiers." Rosen's voice was firm. "Just me and him. And we need Uliel, the soldier. The Mohandas trusts him; he will listen to him."

Rahav leaned back in his chair, studying Rosen. "Are you sure you'll get the material you need?"

"Think about it—worse comes to worst, I don't get the interview, and we cancel the segment. It's all pre-recorded. You've got nothing to lose."

Prime Minister Rahav tried to find fault with the idea. He liked the thought of himself as the resolute leader, a protector of the land of Israel. But was the idea as foolproof as Rosen made it sound? He considered what his wife would say. Would she manage to find issues with the plan?

He wouldn't tell her. He'd figure this one out himself. Damn it, he was Prime Minister.

A minute went by in silence while Rahav pondered deeply, calculating the angles. Finally, he looked up at Rosen.

"Okay, run it again."

This time, the tiniest whisper of a sigh escaped Rosen as he began outlining the plan once more.

"We set up a special press conference tonight, focusing on Palestinian terrorism..."

Chapter 74

Roni

Roni couldn't stop shivering. They were in Rosen's van, speeding on the way back to Tel Aviv, just as they had been thirty minutes ago. Except now he wasn't driving, and Hashim wasn't seated beside him. Hashim sat slumped in the front row of seats, his hands cinched together with a thick white zip-tie, a blindfold wrapped tight over his eyes. His breath came in ragged, shallow pulls. And for the past twenty minutes—since the soldiers had opened fire on him—Roni hadn't stopped shaking.

He had heard the radio transmissions between the soldiers of the unit. They had shot to kill. It was a miracle that they had missed. That Hashim had made it.

But why? What was so important about Hashim that he was wanted dead? Wasn't it obvious to everyone that Hashim was not dangerous? He was just a kid.

Roni forced himself to look at Hashim, who was trussed up in the back seat. A medic had bandaged the shot wound on his shoulder, all the while chatting pleasantly to Hashim.

"You're lucky, eh? A few centimeters' difference, and you'd be gone. Lucky none of those shmucks know how to shoot."

Roni felt sick at the blatant hypocrisy. The pleasant medic had been one of the soldiers doing the shooting.

"Are you in pain?" the medic asked.

Hashim shook his head.

"I'm glad. The forecast is not good, though. Once the adrenaline crashes, it's going to hurt like Allah. If you can't stand it, ask me, or whoever is with you, for some Advil. It will numb the pain. Do you have Advil in Gaza?"

The van veered hard onto an off-ramp, throwing them sideways. Hashim groaned as his wounded shoulder slammed into the seat. The medic passed forward to the driver, and the two spoke in undertones. And then they were going in the opposite direction.

Roni tapped the medic's shoulder. "Why did we turn? Where are we going?"

"Change of plans. We're going to Jerusalem."

"Jerusalem?" Roni asked.

"Yeah." The medic turned to Roni with an impressed look. "We just received new orders. They want you at the Prime Minister's residence. I hope you packed something nice to wear."

It was midday by the time the van rolled into 9 Smolanski Road, Jerusalem—the official residence of the Israeli Prime Minister. The tall, graceful cedar trees lining the narrow road cast shadows that softened the blazing midday sun. Roni watched as the driver flashed an ID card at the guard, who, after scanning the occupants of the van, buzzed them in through the solid iron gate.

The chatty medic was arguing with one of the other soldiers in the van.

"I'm telling you, every morning it costs half a million shekels to transport the PM the ten-minute drive from his residence to his office."

"That's bullshit."

"No, it's true. Half a million every day. They shut down all traffic between here and the Parliament. Thirty cops, fifteen Secret Service. Bullet-proof cars. Then back in the evening. Half a million, easy."

"If that's true, then that's the dumbest thing I've ever heard."

Hashim grunted with pain as the van drove over the speed bump by the residence gates. The medic turned to him with concern.

"Shoulder hurting?"

Hashim nodded.

"I know, I know. I have something here for you, but first, I need to know what the plans are. The second I get the green light, I'll give you a shot that will make you feel as good as new. So, what do you say? Can you hold out?"

Roni stared at the medic, trying to work out what it all meant. Were they going to torture Hashim? What were they going to do to him? Why were they at the Israeli Prime Minister's residence?

The van ground to a halt, and the doors opened. There was no drama, no guns pulled—just a group of Secret Service men who had been waiting at the entrance of the residence to receive them. Roni crept out of the van, only to be grasped by his arm and marched swiftly into the house, a few steps behind Hashim, who was being dragged forward by two soldiers, his breathing heavy, his eyes still blindfolded. They were led to a small, dark room. The windows were curtained and barred. Shelves lined the walls, stacked with large plastic cases.

He was tired and apathetic. He wanted to get it over with. A swift court-marshal, jail time, and probably a dishonorable discharge.

I'm going to break my father's heart.

Was he going to be judged at the Prime Minister's home? A ruling decided by the head of state? It made no sense.

For fifteen minutes, they sat in the dark room, watched by three Secret Service guards. Suddenly, a short, soft crackle was heard coming from the men's earpieces. The three straightened to readiness as they received their orders, and then, as one, they turned and left the room, leaving the two surprised young men alone. Again.

Roni could see that Hashim was in deep pain. Sweat marks ran down his dirty face and dried snot hung stuck to his upper lip. Roni hesitated, looked around the room for cameras. Seeing none, he crossed the room and reached for the blindfold and tore it off. Hashim blinked rapidly.

"Are you ok?"

The door swung open, and a figure entered and switched on the lights. Roni squinted in the sudden glare, trying to identify the newcomer.

It was the medic. It seemed that a decision had been made. The medic crossed over to Hashim, rolled up his ragged sleeve, and expertly injected a clear liquid into his veins. Hashim stared at the syringe in terror.

"What is this?"

The medic smiled. "Don't worry, it's the good stuff. He patted Hashim's arm. "Someone up there wants you happy and energetic. You've got four hours' worth of joy in here."

On his way out, the medic stopped suddenly, and as he closed the door, he smiled at Hashim and whispered, "Good luck."

Hashim's eyes darted to Roni. "What's happening?"

"I don't know. How are you feeling?"

Hashim squeezed his eyes shut as a wave of pain coursed through him. "Hurts." He grunted.

"It should ease off." Roni said. "I think he gave you morphine. It'll kick in soon."

"It's not working." Hashim grunted.

"Give it time. Ten, fifteen minutes. Hold on."

"What's going to happ—"

Before Hashim could complete the sentence, the door flew open, and into the room strode Robert Rosen.

"Hello boys, remember me?"

Rosen hung two fresh uniforms on one of the shelves.

"Rosen?" Hashim wheezed. "We were trying to reach you."

"Well, I found you instead. God Almighty." Rosen muttered, eyeing Hashim's bandages. "What did they do to you? Are you in pain?"

Hashim could just nod. Roni answered for Hashim. "They shot him."

"I told them to give you painkillers."

"He's really hurting." Roni continued, "They just gave him morphine. He should be okay in ten, fifteen minutes."

Rosen nodded. "Good. But we don't have ten minutes to wait for it to work." He leaned in slightly, lowering his voice.

"I have a plan."

Chapter 75

Hannah

"I must confess." Yossi said, his voice thick with amusement. "You, *motek*, are the greatest surprise of my career. Hell, greatest surprise of my entire unit's career. In one week, you've done what professional agents achieve in months, even years, to accomplish."

"I don't understand. Professional agents? What agents?"

Yossi chuckled, tilting his head like he was watching a child struggle with basic math. "Come on, Hannah. I thought you'd have worked it out by now."

"We don't have agents in the brigades. We're all volunteers." Hannah was confused.

Yossi sighed theatrically. "Hannah, how do you think I knew where to find you? How do you think a silly little organization like the Brigades for Palestine could have sent you here in the first place?"

"I didn't really think about it..." the realization dawned on Hannah. "Oh God. You're Shin Bet. Intelligence."

"Well done. Ten points for the girl in the black dress."

Hannah's mind reeled. The conversations. The decisions. The meetings where Yossi had always just been there, quietly steering things in his direction.

"Of course. That's why everything we did ran through you."

"Correct."

"You made us check in with you before every protest—so you could report to your superiors."

"Well done. And most of the members in the boring little group of bleeding hearts did just that. I cannot even begin to describe what a mind-numbingly boring job it was keeping an eye on you lot. But what an incredible plot twist—from a lowly, third-tier agent, you turned me into a star, Hannah! My superiors think I'm a genius."

Hannah felt heat creeping up her neck. Humiliation. Fury. "That's how you had access to those terrible pictures from the border cameras so soon after the bombing, the pictures you forced me to see."

"You decided to go rogue. Serves you right."

Yossi was staring straight into Hannah's eyes as he said this. He was so close that she could smell coffee on his breath.

"But why? Why did you send me here?"

"You were meant to become our woman in Gaza. Once you were inserted into the strip, you would have been monitored and trained by a local agent. I mean—

think about it. A blonde, Israeli, left-wing extremist living in Gaza under Hamas protection? There is no end to the list of uses we could have made of you. And boy, did we underestimate your usefulness."

Hannah's face clouded with shame as she realized how stupid she had been. They had manipulated her, taken advantage of her simplistic activism, and turned her into nothing more than an asset.

"You son of a bitch. All of you."

But Yossi wasn't hearing her. "You have no idea how pleased my commander is. Of course he's pleased with me, not you, but still—my happiness is your happiness, right?"

"What do you want?"

Yossi stood up and paced around the room, his eyes dancing with excitement.

"And, of course, in the natural flow of achievement, now my commander is claiming my success as his, but what do I care? I am your handler, and I can claim a part of the victory and, hopefully, I will leave the pathetic members of the Brigades to start doing proper fieldwork. Isn't that great?"

"What do you want?" Hannah screamed. But Yossi continued to pace the room.

"I mean—the Lion himself! You managed to trap the Lion." He swung around to face her. "Do you have any idea how high he is on our wanted list? The Lion,

Assad Ibn Samir, in the flesh, and we just have to wait here, and he'll fall right into our hands." He turned to Hannah in wonder. "I think I'm beginning to fall in love with you myself."

Hannah felt the panic rise in her chest.

"But Assad left. He's gone."

"Oh, don't worry, he'll be back. He doesn't seem to keep himself away from you. What exactly did you do to him here?"

The comment—filthy, knowing—set something off inside her. Hannah launched herself at him in a whirlwind of punches, swinging wildly. But she was no match against a Shin Bet officer. Yossi easily parried her punches and finally shoved her with a force that sent her flying into the wall behind her.

"You really are surprising." Yossi muttered as he straightened his shirt and jacket. "It was an absolute pleasure to watch over you."

"You've been following me?" Hannah gasped, her breath beaten out of her.

Yossi let out an exasperated sigh. "Do you really think I'd send you alone with no backup? The tunnel you came through was under surveillance. You had your own personal drone following you. Not many agents get that kind of coverage—it took quite a lot of red tape to arrange that, just so you know. Imagine how furious I was when I discovered that some clown at the Air Force had ordered an air strike on the exact same evening you were coming through. The exact time! I thought you were dead. Then, one of our informants saw you on a shopping date at the market two days ago. Imagine my surprise. And imagine my even greater surprise when I found out that you had become the Lion's girlfriend in a few short days. Do you know that even though he's one of the most famous celebrities in Gaza, until recently all we had was a composite sketch of his face? We didn't even know what he looked like? The man was a ghost. Some people in the office thought he was actually a myth Hamas had conjured to rally the people.

"So, of course, I ran to my boss," Yossi continued, "And do you know what I told him? That my asset—my Hannah—was alive and well, holding hands with Gaza's most wanted terrorist. Boy, was he thrilled. Pleasant surprises are so rare in our line of work. Practically never happens."

"You don't understand…" she whispered.

"Oh, I understand. I understand full well. The question we need to ask here is: do *you* understand?" His expression darkened. "Do you understand that your boyfriend is responsible for more Israeli deaths than almost any other terrorist still breathing? Did he tell you that? Do you know that he was responsible for the attack that killed your friend Johnny Melmed, poor soul?"

Hannah stared at Yossi, stunned. She knew that Assad had been a wanted terrorist, a freedom fighter. But Yossi's words came as a shock to her.

"Yeah. I don't know what kinds of crap he fed you to get into your bed; men will say anything. But the man is a mass-murderer. And thanks to you, he will be retiring soon."

"You're going to kill him."

"Oh no. Here's the funny thing; your little love affair may have actually saved his life. You see, once we track down a high-ranking terrorist, the target is usually neutralized, which, between you and me, is just a polite way of saying taken-out-by-a-drone-as-he-leaves-his-safe-house. But because we know that he'll come back to see you, we have a unique opportunity of capturing him live, for interrogation. A high-ranking soldier such as the Lion will have many interesting tidbits to share with us. Add to that the morale boost it will give the Israeli public, the despair of the loss for the Palestinian public... having him alive is by far more valuable."

"But you don't understand. Please, Assad has changed. He's on our side now."

"On our side?"

"Yes. He's changed. He is fighting for peace by sabotaging the militants' equipment. I've been helping him. Please, you've got to understand. He's against everything he previously fought for."

"Very nice. The Lion has become a peacenik. Come on, you're not sixteen anymore. Do you honestly think that's the truth? You know what? It makes no difference either way. The only thing that matters is the optics. If Israel sees him as a dangerous terrorist, and the people here in Gaza worship him as a local hero, then that is all that matters to the decision-makers.

"Now, the reason I've come to visit you, the reason I've been telling you all this, is because I don't want you to ruin all the good things that you've done." Yossi's tone sharpened. "From this moment on, you are not to leave the house. You'll stay here until we have the Lion in our custody, and then I will personally come and get you out of here. It shouldn't take long. We estimate that the Lion will be back within twenty-four hours, but we're willing to wait longer. Even if it takes a month."

Hannah was shaking her head. "No, no."

"Yes. And just to make sure, we will have one of ours watching your door 24/7. You so much as open your door, and you will be punished severely. Are we clear?"

340

Hannah wasn't listening. The pain that engulfed her was too much to bear. Yossi's eyes softened.

"Don't worry. Think about this: you'll be back home any day now."

Home?

Home meant nothing anymore. Nothing mattered now.

Chapter 76

Assad

"Learn how to play chess."

When young fighters asked the Lion what skill was most important to a warrior, they expected talk of knife combat, explosives, or the art of ambush. Instead, they got chess.

"Chess teaches you how to place yourself in your opponent's chair, in his mind. More importantly, it teaches you to think without emotion. In a guerrilla war against an opponent who is stronger and better equipped than you, it is the strategists who will win. The Israelis withdrew unilaterally from Gaza, not because of our military might and not just by divine deliverance from Allah, but because of three important principles of war: strategy, strategy, and strategy."

It was an unorthodox view that unsettled many religious leaders, who would preach that it is faith alone that would bring victory. But with his long list of accomplishments, Command had wisely chosen to tolerate the young leader's opinions. As long as hundreds of youths idolized the Lion, dreaming of one day becoming like him, Assad was awarded far greater latitude than was usual.

And now it was time to take his own advice.

The abandoned room reeked of mildew and cigarette smoke, the cracked walls smeared with grease. A lone cockroach crawled across the rotting windowsill. He ignored it. Across the street, barely fifty meters away, was the Sheikh's house. The suicide jacket he had brought with him was lying on the floor, wrapped inside a tote bag.

What if they have found out?

Once the other fighters learned from the Sheikh that Assad had become a saboteur, his status would drop from hero to the worst possible title: *kha'en*.

Traitor.

The Sheikh would make an example of him, a warning to any other militant tempted by doubt. A bullet to the head was for soldiers. But for traitors? A slow, public death.

The latest order had come that afternoon. Deliver the suicide belt to the Sheik's residence. The previous order had been legitimate. The Lion had staked out the Sheik's home for more than an hour, seen nothing out of the ordinary, and walked in to be greeted heartily by the venerable leader.

Was tonight another real mission?

He took his time to re-run through the possibilities. Things would play out in one of three gambits. Either the Sheikh would welcome him alone, offer tea, even praise him, before the doors flew open, men poured in, and he would be overpowered and dragged away. Alternatively, the Sheikh's soldiers would wait outside in the shadows, striking before he even knocked on the door.

Or, Assad considered, the third and most likely option—this was a real summons, and he was still safe.

If it were to be option one or two, the soldiers would have to arrive early and prepare. So—he would just have to arrive earlier.

He had been scouting the residence for over ninety minutes. Listening. Waiting.

There was nothing. No movement on the Sheikh's rooftop. No hushed voices in the alley. No shifting shadows behind the broken trees that lined the street.

The hour of the meeting rolled in, and as far as he could tell, it seemed like he was still safe. Taking a deep breath, he picked the jacket up and, on his way, gave one last glimpse through the window.

A flicker of orange light appeared for a moment in the dark street.

A lit matchstick, flicked out of the doorway of an old grocery shop. A building that he knew was abandoned.

For five full seconds, he stood absolutely still, his pulse thudding against his ribs. *They had come for him.*

Then his instincts kicked in. Silently, he slipped out through the back entrance of the building and began running.

He had reached the endgame.

Chapter 77

The Sheikh

The Sheikh checked his watch for the twentieth time. The Lion was never late. Not without reason. Something had happened.

He opened the door and looked out. Though it was just past eight, the whole neighborhood seemed dead. He took another few measured steps outside and scanned the dark road from side to side. Nothing.

Then, without turning his head, he called over his shoulder. "You can come inside; he's not coming."

Four shadows appeared out of the alley; the three soldiers he had handpicked for this unpleasant job, and his grandnephew, Ahmed, who had shown a disturbing relish at capturing his former partner.

The group clustered near the doorway, eyes scanning rooftops and side streets, fingers twitching near the triggers of their rifles.

Ahmed was the first to break the uneasy silence. "Why didn't he come, Uncle? Do you think something happened to him?"

"No, I don't." answered the Sheikh.

The young fighter turned to his great-uncle. "Then what happened?"

The Sheikh exhaled, shaking his head. A ghost of a smile flickered across his lips. "He knew we were waiting. That's what's happened."

"He knew? But how?"

"I don't know how," the Sheikh admitted, "but we're talking about the Lion. He is a wise man, though I'm beginning to think that he might be part demon."

One of the three soldiers spoke up. "So, is he gone? The Lion knows his way in and out of Gaza. By now, he's probably sipping a beer in Cairo."

"More likely Tel Aviv, the son of a whore, *kha'en*." Added another soldier.

"Possible. Quite possible. But we may not have lost this game yet."

The men looked at him expectantly.

"What can we do, sir?"

"The woman," suggested young Ahmed.

"Yes." The Sheikh was pleased and surprised to discover an analytical mind in his grandnephew. "The Lion has become attached to the Jewish terrorist we liberated. He will not leave without seeing her. Go. You have very little time."

The four men moved as one, their boots pounding against the pavement as they ran to the truck.

"Allah protect you on your mission." The Sheikh called out.

The driver revved the engine, and the small vehicle kicked up a cloud of dust as it raced away into the night.

The Sheikh ambled back into the house, deep in thought. He knew that there was a chance yet. A good chance.

The Sheikh played chess, too.

Chapter 78

Prime Minister Rahav

Reports of the Mohandas' capture exploded on all channels in a flurry of news flashes, expert opinions, and enough social network content to fill a small ocean. Prime Minister Rahav's team had pushed the segment hard. The various news editors chose titles like "A War on Gaza Terror" and "Standing up to Violence." Quick designs were created in Photoshop featuring masked terrorists, a burning star of David, and portraits of Rahav imposed in the foreground. The scene was set.

Rahav was in his element. He didn't need to glance at Rosen's cue cards, spread before him on the table. He had memorized each one by heart.

There was hardly any breathing space for the team squashed into the tiny green-screen studio. It had been commissioned by Rosen's agency and constructed in a basement room of the Prime Minister's residence. Two digital cameras transmitted video feeds into the tailor-made system, the fastest communication network in the country. Rosen's technicians had built the system with simplicity in mind. With one flick of a button, you were on air, connected live to all four of the Israeli news studios, with additional plugins that could connect the little studio to any foreign network. The whirring computers, the blinking LEDs, the sweat-streaked faces of technicians—this was Rahav's battlefield. He thrived in it, and he had made sure that Rosen's team continually upgraded the equipment as broadcast technology evolved.

Apart from the high-tech gear, the studio setup was a simple green box. Two tables had been brought in—a simple metal table for the Mohandas, and an oversized desk for Prime Minister Rahav. Though they were being recorded in the same small room, on screen it would appear as if they were speaking from two different locations. The Mohandas was made to appear in a secret penitentiary, a stark, gray-walled interrogation room. Rahav sat before the default backdrop of his residence, flanked by Israeli flags, radiating calm, powerful leadership.

They were lying to the people, but it was a technical lie, and—being media savvy—Rahav knew that in this age, that's how the world turned. Anyway, it wasn't a complete lie. The Mohandas would be seeing a real cage soon enough.

Rosen had made the tactical call to lead with the Mohandas' interview before bringing in Rahav. Once again, Rosen's instincts paid off. Prime Minister Rahav had been elated with Rosen's work on the

Palestinian in the short time they'd had. The prisoner—dressed in a brown jumpsuit and dark cap, his eyes hollow with fear—sat beneath the bright lights. A news anchor read the pre-approved questions.

"How do the Palestinian people view the Israeli reaction to the bombings?" the anchor inquired.

"They are scared," the Mohandas responded, just as he'd been coached. "They say that Rahav is crazy, that he is too strong."

"What is the feeling on the streets?"

"People are uncertain about the future. No one is making any plans. They fear for tomorrow."

Then the big one: "Do you think the people are ready for peace?"

A pause. Then: "No. They will never want peace."

The Palestinian had coughed up Rosen's script almost verbatim, fear and shock giving his delivery authenticity. He had set the stage perfectly for Rahav's message. His Hebrew had been surprisingly fluent, His Hebrew had been surprisingly fluent, but Rahav had no time to dwell on it.

In the thirty-second break between the two interviews, two burly security men entered and whisked the Mohandas away. Tables were switched, and then it was Rahav's turn.

Seated behind the majestic wooden table, flags of Israel at attention behind him, Rahav was at his best.

He denounced terrorism; he quoted statistics; he promised retaliation to any who walked in the Mohandas's footsteps. And in the final minute of his interview, a light moistness filled his eyes as he spoke about future generations, about a peaceful Middle East—an economic, cultural, and above all spiritual center of the whole world in which the moderate Islamic states joined hands with Israel. It was a masterpiece of moving rhetoric.

The floor manager announced that they were offline, and the room erupted into applause. Prime Minister Rahav was pleased to see tears glistening in the eyes of some of the tech staff—always a good sign. He stood up, waited patiently until the soundman removed the two lapel microphones that had been clipped onto his jacket, thanked his staff, shook some hands heartily, and walked out. Rosen was at his heels.

"Well?" asked Rahav.

"Let's talk in a place where we can't be heard." Rosen navigated the prime minister into the same storage room where the Mohandas had been held less than twenty minutes earlier.

"What's with the secrecy? I think it went damn well, don't you?"

Rosen smiled at his boss; he seemed almost happy. "There is good news and bad news."

"Bad news?" Rahav's voice pitched up in confusion.

Rosen raised a hand. "The good news is that it went even better than I could have hoped for. You were brilliant. Your best. And coming right after the Mohandas, the connection between the two interviews made your speech even more powerful. I'd bet on a five-point bump in tomorrow's polls."

Rahav exhaled, pleased. "Good connection, good speech, good result." He clapped Rosen on the back. "So, what's the bad news?"

"It wasn't the Mohandas who was interviewed just before you."

In his jubilant mood, it took time for Rosen's words to penetrate.

"Wasn't what?"

"The Mohandas that you just spoke about," Rosen said, lowering his gaze to the floor, "the one we put on television, he wasn't really the Mohandas."

The blood drained from Rahav's face until he was almost white. It took him quite some time to speak again, and when he did, it came out in a whispery, almost comical squeak:

"So, who was it?"

Chapter 79

Hannah

It all happened so fast she didn't have time to think. Her body reacted instinctively—like a wild animal cornered and desperate.

Assad had come, just as Yossi said he would. He burst into the small apartment, breathing heavily, a worried smile on his face. He threw the bag he was holding onto the floor and ran to her, eyes filled with urgency.

"Jamillah. We must go. Come. Remember Chile? It's time, leave everything and…"

But there was no joy or relief in seeing him. She couldn't even feel the warmth of his hands gripping hers. The instant her mind registered his face, pure instinct seized control, and she screamed desperately while pushing him to the door, "It's a trap. Go away. The Israelis are here; run. The Israelis are here. RUN!"

But she knew her cries were useless. The Israelis had been waiting since Yossi left. Within seconds of the Lion's arrival, three masked commandos burst into the room, micro Tavor rifles loaded and aimed at his head. In what seemed like no time, they had Assad lying on the ground, his hands tied behind him with nylon zip-ties which they pulled tighter than necessary, the sharp plastic cutting into his flesh.

She attacked the closest soldier with a hail of fists, screaming, "Let him go! He's one of us. One of us! Let him go!"

The commando didn't hit back. Suited up in a bulletproof vest and tactical gear, he could hardly feel her attack. Calmly, he blocked her punches while the other two soldiers lifted the Lion from the ground and dragged him out.

"Get him to the van. I'll hold her for two more minutes, and then I'll join you."

And with that, Assad was gone.

All the fight drained from Hannah's body. She sank to the floor, her eyes staring blankly into emptiness.

Was this how it ends? So futile and pointless, a story with no beginning and no resolution?

Her guard stepped away, eyeing up the bag Assad had been holding. He emptied the contents onto the floor. A suicide vest fell out, explosive-filled pockets glinting ominously in the dim light.

"Good God!" he exclaimed, staring with horror at the TNT-filled pockets. "I could have just blown us both to—"

A storm of gunfire erupted outside the building. It sounded as if a battle had broken out in the street below. Hannah could hear automatic fire, the sounds overlapping and building on each other, suggesting many different weapons. Arabic and Hebrew shouts mingled in the air as the gunfire increased in intensity. The soldier spun toward the door.

"Stay here. Lie down below window level." With three bounds, he was out of the apartment, racing to back up his team. Hannah ignored him and stumbled after, heart pounding in her chest.

An eerie silence followed the initial barrage. Were they all dead?

Once outside, she saw no one, not even the soldier she had just been following. The street was mysteriously deserted; the neighborhood had turned into a ghost town. Only a nearby gate creaked in the wind. She searched up and down the dark street, her eyes slowly becoming accustomed to the darkness. Suddenly, a single, whispered voice cut through the night air.

"Jamillah."

Her heart surged. Assad! She strained her eyes until she recognized a dark shape lying in the middle of the narrow road. She started to move in his direction when a shot rang out from behind a low wall, a tracer flashing a few feet away from her. Three shots rang out in answer from a doorway to her right. A dark figure darted out of one of the doorways and dived into a gateway, his short trip covered by blazing gunfire. The contrast between the deathly silence and the roaring gunshots was unbearable.

But her heart was filled with hope. Assad was just a few meters away, alive!

"Are you okay?" she whispered to Assad. "Did anything happen to you?"

"I'm okay," Assad's voice came from the shadows. "But I can't move. My hands are tied—plastic cuffs. I can't break them."

He was unhurt. She moved forward, just a step, before his voice stopped her cold.

"Jamillah, no! Step into the street, they'll shoot you."

Hannah froze in the doorway. "I can't leave you out there."

"Stay there," he gasped. "I'll come to you."

Hannah watched as Assad began to crawl on his stomach, his strapped hands making the progress slow and frustrating. He spoke to her as he crawled in the darkness.

"Don't worry, Jamillah. My Palestinian brothers are terrible shots, praise Allah."

"I don't care about the soldiers."

"My brothers aren't aiming for the soldiers..." Assad answered wryly, as he dragged himself closer.

"Careful Assad! You're almost here."

"Now I know what it's like to be a worm," Assad grunted.

Gunfire peppered the ground near him, sharp splinters of stone flying dangerously close.

"A little more, my darling," cried Hannah, her voice on the verge of hysteria. "I'm not going to lose you."

"I'm not sure I can make it, Jamillah."

"You'll make it, Assad," tears were flowing down Hannah's face as she spoke. "We will both make it out of here, and we will spend the rest of our lives bringing peace to the world. We will. Together."

"Promise?" Although it was dark, she could hear that Assad was smiling. His voice filled her heart with hope.

"Promise," she whispered fiercely.

A low hum of an approaching helicopter became audible, growing in strength. The Palestinians began to retreat from the area, followed by shots fired at increasing speed by the Israeli commandos who, she now realized, were the shooters on her right. The sound of the helicopter grew louder until Hannah could feel the vibrations in the pit of her stomach. Suddenly, a bright point of light appeared at the end of the street and, with unbelievable speed, it crossed right past her. The missile exploded in a massive ball of flame, killing three of the Palestinian fighters instantly.

For a moment, the missile explosion illuminated everything.

In the blinding yellow light, she could see Assad lying on the ground not ten meters away. She could see the Israeli commandos on her right, rifles aimed over the broken remains of a concrete wall, their night-vision goggles raised as they squinted in the bright light.

And, out of their line of fire, she saw the young boy, Ahmed, who had not retreated with the others, and so had survived. She watched in horror as he stepped forward into the street, raised his rifle, and took aim. She screamed as the bullets hit Assad, each shot nudging his body toward her. Shot after shot, the empty casings clinked onto the ground, each metallic ping ringing in her ears.

After he had spent his last bullet, the young boy looked up at her with a victorious smile. He was still staring defiantly into her eyes when the commandos shot him down.

Chapter 80

Hashim

Hashim stared out of the bus window, a faint smile on his lips and his heart full of gratitude. It defied logic and went against everything he had been taught. Two Israelis had just sacrificed their freedom for his. He stared, still in disbelief, at the unit insignia that hung from the shoulder strap of his shirt. Paratrooper Brigade. Gaza Division. The hated emblem was now bringing him home, keeping him safe. His lucky charm. He patted the uniform pocket, checking for the painkillers. They were there, waiting for when the pain of his shot wound would return.

Rosen had thought of everything.

His mind drifted back to the astonishing meeting at the Prime Minister's residence, tucked away in a cramped, shadowy room at the back of the building.

"Hello boys, remember me?"

Hashim had struggled to focus through the haze of pain and fatigue.

"We've got very little time," Rosen said briskly, urgency sharpening his voice. "So I'll be brief. Roni, you have a choice to make, a choice that could save a life."

"Whose life?"

"His." Rosen pointed at Hashim, who was still too woozy to react.

"What do you mean?" Roni's confusion was evident.

Rosen pointed at the two uniforms he had brought with him. "I have two new uniforms here: one is a prison uniform; one is a paratrooper uniform. I want you to switch. You, Roni, wear the prison uniform, and you, Hashim, take Roni's uniform. You two are the exact same size. You even look similar. We just need to shave Hashim's head to strengthen the resemblance."

"What? Are you insane?" Roni exploded.

"The only way Hashim will ever get back to his family is if I manage to smuggle him out."

"But I'll be caught." Roni protested, panic rising. "I'm already in trouble."

"You are. Deep trouble. The Prime Minister sees you as an accomplice. Don't you realize? They weren't searching for the Mohandas alone. They were hunting *both* of you. Haven't you wondered why you were brought here with Hashim instead of being sent home? You're drowning in a heap of trouble. You deliberately disobeyed a direct order from the head of the Shin Bet. You're about to lose your stripes and become a private, spend at least half a year in military prison." Rosen let the implication hang heavily in the air.

Hashim watched Roni, a sickening feeling of guilt twisting inside him.

"But," Rosen's voice softened, "there could be a way out. Prime Minister Rahav wants to show the troops that no one messes with him. He's working the tough commander angle, that no one defies him without consequences. We can use that. I've worked out a way for all of us to come out on top. Remember his promise to send you to officer training? It can still happen. But you'll have to trust me."

"What happens when they discover we've switched?" Roni looked up at Rosen.

Rosen stepped forward, placing a reassuring hand on Roni's shoulder. "By then, it will be too late. They'll only realize after you've been interviewed as the Mohandas on all three news channels."

"What?!" Roni nearly shouted. "You want me to pretend I'm an Arab on national TV?"

"Not just any Arab," Rosen corrected, calmly. "The Mohandas himself."

"It won't work." Roni's voice edged on hysteria. "Everyone who knows me will recognize me. Strangers, too. I was on the Didi Dimor show last night."

"With these clothes, and cap, and the angle I'll have them shoot you, your own mother won't recognize you.

Roni stared at Rosen, too stunned to speak. Rosen continued, his voice earnest.

"You've reached a serious crossroads in your life, son. But if you trust me—if you pretend to be the Mohandas on television while I smuggle Hashim out—then Hashim gets to go home, and you get to have a future."

Roni shook his head slowly. "It's impossible. Won't happen."

"Look at it this way, a little fact to help you make your decision," Rosen smiled ruefully, "I will be putting my neck on the line, too. If this fails, I'll be sitting in jail right alongside you. It's not just you who has to take a giant leap of faith. I have to make it work for my sake, as well as yours."

Hashim watched Roni. The young soldier had a terrible decision to make, and it was all because of Hashim's actions. Because of those damn rocket fins he had redesigned, in what felt like a million years ago. But, unfair as it was, Hashim wanted to go home. He yearned for the peace of his house like never before. And he knew what would happen to him if he were sent to an Israeli Prison. His words came out softly—

the words of a child who, in a short span of time, had become a man:

"My brother. I know it's not fair, the situation I've put you in. But please—if you don't do it—I'm as good as dead. I've heard of what goes on in those prisons. I prefer to die rather than face a prison sentence. I ask you. Please. Make the right decision."

The room fell silent. Finally, Roni looked up at Rosen, resignation in his eyes.

"So, if this doesn't work, you're screwed, too?"

The bus shuddered to a halt, jolting Hashim from his thoughts. He ran through Rosen's instructions again.

"When you get to Sedera, you'll have to hitchhike to the Erez crossing. Once there, just wait. You'll be seen to."

The last remaining passengers stepped off, leaving Hashim alone with the driver.

"You fall asleep, soldier?"

"No. Where are we?"

"Sedera. Last stop."

"Thanks." Hashim climbed out.

"God protect you." The driver smiled at him as the bus turned into the night on its way back north.

Under the pale moonlight, he took a deep breath, steadied himself, and started down the empty road leading toward the Erez border.

He had done exactly as Rosen had instructed him. He was almost home.

Chapter 81

Hannah

"All clear. Let's move." She heard the commando team leader order his soldiers.

But one soldier stood frozen, his eyes locked on young Ahmed's inert body, sprawled less than two meters away from Assad's lifeless form.

"Did you see how that little bastard gunned down his own friend? Fucking kids with weapons."

"It's okay. You were right to get him. You did right," a second soldier answered, placing a reassuring hand on his comrade's shoulder.

"Yeah. Fucking kid."

"It was either him or us," their leader broke in firmly. "You saved us all."

"He was just a kid. Who gives a kid this age an automatic weapon?" the fighter muttered, still staring at the body.

"Arabs, man. Arabs," another voice replied bluntly. "Now, let's roll. If we rush the debrief, we could be home by breakfast."

It was as if the words were a faint buzz, coming from a million miles away. The team of commandos was clustered around young Ahmed's body, but

366

Hannah paid them no attention. She sat numbly on the cracked asphalt, cradling Assad's cold, lifeless hand. Tears traced paths down the grime on her cheeks as she swayed, lost to the world around her. The moon rose higher, its silver light reflecting off Assad's vacant eyes, creating a haunting illusion of life. Her trembling palm pressed against his shirt, desperately willing his heart to beat once more. But the shirt was cold, damp with blood.

She wished for time to stop so she could hold on to this moment forever.

"Hannah. Time to go." Yossi warned. "There'll be an entire brigade here in a few minutes."

She gave no answer. A powerful hand grasped her shoulder and shook her sharply. She spun around in a sudden panic. Yossi was standing above her.

"It's time to go home. Let's move."

Home? She had no home. There was nothing real in her life—no purpose, no one to miss or love. She was empty, and the void in her soul was black and bitter. She could not even summon hatred for Yossi.

Yossi stared at her, eyes darkening in irritation. "Have it your way. I'm out of here. You want to come, you come now. You want to stay, well… I don't think that would be a good idea. The whole Palestinian fighting force will be looking for you, the Jewish spy who brought down the Lion."

She stared at him, saying nothing. A few long seconds passed.

"Okay. Your choice."

Yossi called the soldiers, and after a quick magazine count and reload, the team began walking back to the beat-up truck that had brought them in.

"Wait!" Hannah's voice rang out hoarsely. "I need to get my bag." She scrambled to her feet and stumbled back to the apartment.

"Your what?" Yossi called out after her, incredulous. "Your bag? Now? The whole of Gaza is on its way to kill us, and you need your bag?"

But Hannah said nothing as she disappeared up the stairwell.

"*Yalla*, let's go!" she heard the driver calling impatiently from the cab of the truck.

"We'll give her one minute." Yossi answered. "If she doesn't come out in exactly sixty seconds, we're out of here."

Hannah scrambled up the stairs, slipping through the door that now, after the commandos' break-in, was swinging on one hinge. Darkness filled the apartment. The electricity had been cut. Carefully, she navigated the small living room, hands outstretched to feel her way, until her foot struck something. She bent over and touched the object. It was Assad's white bag. She picked it up and slowly left the room for the last time.

She emerged from the building just in time to see Yossi climb into the truck's cab beside the driver.

"Go."

"You don't want to wait for the girl?"

"No. Drive."

As the truck rolled forward, Hannah stepped into the harsh glare of its headlights, making the driver slam the brakes.

Yossi rolled the window down, irritation etched clearly across his face.

"I'm *so* happy you have your precious bag. Get in the back. Now!"

Chapter 82

Hashim

If the road leading to the Erez border crossing was quiet during the day, at night it was utterly deserted. The silence was so profound that Hashim could hear approaching vehicles ten minutes before their headlights broke through the darkness. He stood waiting, heart racing with each set of distant lights, but vehicle after vehicle turned away into Sedera instead of continuing west.

Finally, after three hours of waiting, a small honey delivery truck stopped for him. The driver offered to take him up to Kibbutz Yad Mordechai, a mere three kilometers away from the Erez crossing.

The surprisingly short drive was filled with anxious thoughts. Rosen had assured him that once he reached the crossing, he would be "seen to." But by whom? Would there be someone actually waiting for him? Troubled, he offered no conversation, lost deep in his own worry, a poor companion for the driver who had generously picked him up.

It was almost sunrise by the time Hashim reached the Erez crossing. A faint, ghostly gray glow illuminated the eastern horizon, although the stars still shone brightly overhead. After thanking the driver for the ride, Hashim had walked down the last stretch of road until he was reached a cluster of trees just opposite the crossing. He had come through that very crossing on his way out only a few days earlier, but he did not remember or recognize anything.

Ahead, the giant border roof cover dominated the view. Two sleepy patrolniks were guarding the single open lane, talking in a subdued tone. A third soldier guarded the outer perimeter of the crossing. Apart from the hoot of a desert owl from somewhere above him, the crossing seemed quiet. Hashim had no idea what to do.

Rosen had not led him astray yet, though. Hashim just had to trust him and hope.

Keep calm and focused.

Hashim took a deep breath and started walking toward the crossing. All three soldiers looked up in mild surprise as he approached. Hashim steeled himself and carried on walking. Then his heart leaped in his chest as he noticed that the crossing was not vacant. Far from it. Although it was still dark, a long queue had already formed on the Palestinian side—a line of dejected faces hoping to cross into the land of quality medical care, food, and thriving business. There were hundreds of people lined up. Yet still, the area was completely, unnaturally silent.

What if someone on the Palestinian side recognized him?

Keep calm and focused.

His legs felt leaden, his instincts screamed at him to flee, but he pressed on. He passed the bulletproof barrier, the military-only latrine, and the low line of office buildings.

As he approached the perimeter barrier, the guard turned to him.

"Soldier, you called Roni?"

Hashim froze, nearly blurted out "no" before his mind caught up.

"Yeah. Roni."

"Someone's waiting for you." The guard gestured with his thumb. "Go into the barracks. Big guy, he's sleeping in the TV room."

Like in a strange and impossible dream, Hashim walked past the perimeter guard, hardly daring to breathe, and entered the small, box of a building. It was impossible to think that he was actually inside the Erez Crossing military compound.

Inside the room, he could see a big-screen television, a bunch of dusty PlayStation games scattered around the low table, and a coffee table with an ashtray overflowing with cigarette butts. Sprawled on a small gray loveseat was a very large man, legs hanging off the end, snoring like a drunken sailor.

Gaza Gil.

Hashim hesitated, unsure how to proceed. Should he wait? Should he wake him up? If so, how?

He gently called out, "Gil? Gil?"

Nothing.

He stepped forward and tentatively gave Gil's shoulder a gentle shake.

"Gil?"

Nothing. A stronger shake—then stronger and stronger until the rickety loveseat threatened to fall apart. Finally, Gil let out a strangled snore, and his eyes opened, consciousness returning with a flicker like a faulty neon light. He looked about until his eyes finally found Hashim. It took a few seconds before he recognized him, and a few more to work out where he was.

"You made it," he said as he straightened and stretched his arms backward. "Son of a bitch, my foot has fallen asleep." He stood up and stamped his feet a few times while yawning. Once fully awake, he stared at Hashim. "You're very quiet."

"I don't know what to say."

"Yeah," Gil grunted, "I get you. What time is it?"

"Don't know. Early dawn."

"Already? Then we don't have much time. There is a team inside Gaza, and with that team is a buddy of mine—real bastard who would love for me to owe him a favor. They should be back by sunrise…any minute now. This buddy of mine—he'll take you a few kilometers in, and once you're out of sight of the crossing, off you go. Understand?"

Hashim nodded.

"Will you manage on your own? Will you be able to make it home?"

Hashim nodded, his throat tight. "Yes."

"Good." Gil frowned, assessing Hashim critically. But first, we have to get you out of that paratrooper uniform. I don't think that setup will get you far in Gaza."

Chapter 83

Hannah

The powerful truck bumped along the rough road out of Gaza City, slowing every few minutes to navigate deep potholes and trenches carved by decades of neglect. Hannah sat numbly on a wooden bench in the truck bed, oblivious to the commandos who were chatting energetically as the truck drove eastward. Finally, the vehicle rattled through the heavily fortified gate at the Erez border crossing and entered Israel. The soldiers dismounted and left to change out of their Gazan civilian disguises. Yossi climbed down from the cab and walked around to the back, pausing to stare at Hannah, her body shivering with shock, tears running freely.

"*Yalla*, it's over. You're going home." Yossi chuckled. "Which is more than I can say about your Palestinian boyfriend."

Hannah stared at Yossi as if stung.

"Come on, get out." Yossi signed for her to climb out of the truck. She climbed down painfully and looked around. The Erez crossing. She was back at the site of her ill-fated protest. From this angle, she could see the myriad of holes in the walls and gouges in the concrete, grim reminders of the young girl who had detonated herself here—taking Johnny and ten Israeli soldiers to their deaths.

"I've arranged a ride for you, special delivery, straight to your home. Stay at home for twenty-four hours. I'll make sure that no one bothers you. In about a week, you'll be ordered to come in for a debriefing. After that, your life is your own again. Understood?"

"I won't see you again?"

Yossi snorted. "As much as I'd love to meet you again, this is where we part."

"I need a bathroom," she whispered. "I need to change."

"Now? Don't you want to go home? Your ride is here, ready to take you home."

No answer.

"Fine," Yossi sighed, waving her off. "Use the one by the barracks. But hurry up. I want you gone in ten minutes."

When Hannah returned, the sun had begun to rise, a soft-orange disc climbing above the eastern plains. She watched as the mass of Palestinians shuffled forward along the gray concrete passage connecting Gaza and Israel. Palestinian policemen paced up and down the line, scribbling notes, names, and suspicions into their worn, black notebooks.

She began to advance upon Yossi when a tall, blonde man and an Arab approached him. She stopped a few meters away.

She needed Yossi alone.

The giant spoke first. "Yossi."

"Gil." Yossi nodded curtly. "It's quite a special honor meeting you this early. How's business?"

"Booming. Now, about that favor Rosen requested," the tall blonde spoke in an undertone. "I need you to take this kid a few clicks inside Gaza and drop him somewhere out of sight. He'll manage the rest."

Yossi eyed the young Arab standing nervously beside Gil. "Who is he? Why are we taking him in?"

Gil shook his head slightly. "Sorry, mate, can't tell you. All I can say is that this is an order straight from the Prime Minister's residence."

"Straight from the Prime Minister? That's good to know."

The giant took a giant breath. He exhaled as he watched the eastern horizon turn from gray-yellow to peach. "Look at the sky. Beautiful, eh?"

"Sure, but let's move on with our lives." Yossi answered, glancing at his watch.

"I owe you one, my brother," the giant grinned.

Yossi tapped on his watch. "I was meant to be on my way home already. I've been operational all night."

"I'll buy you breakfast," Gil smiled expansively.

"It'll take more than breakfast to pay me back on this one."

"What can I say," Gil sighed. "You always were an asshole."

"We all have our strengths." Yossi replied dryly, then he turned to the kid, who was dressed in civilian clothes that were two sizes too large for him. "Ready to go?"

The young Arab nodded. Yossi began to walk back toward the truck.

She could wait no longer.

"Yossi."

All three men turned, startled, as Hannah approached, her eyes locked fiercely on Yossi's. She stopped just opposite Yossi and shrugged off her shirt.

Deathly silence.

"Bomb!" screamed one of the soldiers on watch, plunging the silent crossing into chaos. A siren blared, gates locked with a crash. The queue of Palestinians scattered in terror as they began running back into Gaza, their panicked shouts and cries for help deafening. The soldiers at the barricade sprawled on the ground.

Yossi stood frozen, horror etched on his face. "No, Hannah, please don't…"

Strapped to her bare torso was a suicide vest. It was a hideous contraption—a jungle of electric wires connecting the various sticks of explosive, pockets bulging with deadly shrapnel. In her trembling right hand, she clasped a primitive electric switch.

Yossi's words faded away as a raw, inhuman howl escaped from Hannah's bared chest, a howl that grew louder as she vented her endless pain, leaving it all behind as she left this earth.

The three men watched with horror as her fingers closed on the trigger.

A short, almost inaudible click was heard, then—nothing.

In a daze, Hannah stared dumbly at the trigger in her hand. She tried again. Nothing. Within a split-second Yossi and the blond man lunged, pinning her arms as they slammed her down to the pavement.

Lying flat on her back, staring numbly upward at the brilliant morning sky, she suddenly understood. A giant grin crept across her face, which then became a low chuckle.

Assad.

The low chuckle turned into uncontrollable peals of laughter. Of course. She should have known. How wonderfully stupid of her. The vest was rigged with Assad's harmless TNT substitute.

"It's cornflakes!" Her laughter rang loud above the mayhem.

Assad had succeeded. In his mission to save lives, he had saved hers. And she would live to continue what he had started. She would see it through—for him and for the world they had hoped to change together.

She had promised him.

Chapter 84

Roni

Roni peeled back the Velcro flap of his watch, the sound loud against the desert's breathless silence. He had pushed hard on this last stretch, his pace relentless, and now he found himself at the waypoint a full two minutes ahead of schedule. Most of the guys in officers' training hated these solo-navigation runs, but not Roni. He thrived on them, especially out here. The grueling officers' training fieldwork took place mostly in the blistering sands surrounding the Bahad 1 officers' academy, deep in the southern wilderness. This was his territory, the desert. He had been raised in this unforgiving landscape. It was home.

He wiped the sweat from his brow with a dusty sleeve. The waypoint he had reached stood at the summit of a small hill, giving him a sweeping, three-sixty-degree view of the terrain. He took a few breaths to lower his pulse rate as he looked around.

Ahead, he could make out the course he had been required to memorize. Opening a map during navigation runs would be considered cheating, grounds for instant expulsion from the academy. They had to learn the course by heart and navigate purely from memory. A real officer didn't rely on anything he couldn't carry in his own mind.

His watch beeped. The seconds counter had reached zero, and it was time to move on. And yet he lingered at the hilltop, looking at the endless sands. Just a few more seconds.

The open desert was the only place Roni felt at peace. But even at this moment, memories flashed back through his mind like shockwaves.

"You've had it, you lying bastard. You've reached the end of your life, you hear me? You're finished! I will personally end you."

Minutes after his television interview had ended, Roni—still dressed in brown prison garb—was shoved violently into a holding room where Rosen was already waiting. Prime Minister Rahav stormed in behind him, face blotched red, veins bulging at his temples.

The plan had failed. They were both going to jail; that much was certain. Rosen just stared at his shoes as Rahav ranted about betrayals, about incompetence, about how he would make sure they both rotted.

Finally, Rosen looked up. "Oh, just shut up."

Rahav almost choked.

Rosen continued, "Shut up. Try thinking. Do you know how to think on your own, or should I call your wife to do it for you?

"You have two choices. One—own up. Tell the public how you were duped on live TV. Let the press label you as the biggest idiot in the history of Israeli politics. Or two—leave things as they are. Stay the hero. Ride the wave. Probably get re-elected without having to lift a finger."

Rahav froze. He stared at the two of them, his chest heaving.

"There are four people in the world who know what happened. You, me, this kid, and the Arab, who at this time is probably already back home in Gaza. I don't need anything more from you; the kid here only wants you to fulfill your promise to transfer him to officers' training school. That is—if you choose option two. So, what's it gonna be?"

Being Prime Minister involves growing the thickest of skins and developing the shortest of memories. Rahav knew Rosen was right. He was riding on the biggest wave of popularity since his election. Rosen was a conceited, blackmailing, lying bastard, but he had made the current administration popular again. The path to reelection was set, and this evening's interview had helped cement his political power.

Prime Minister Rahav headed for the door. Before stepping out, he glanced back at Rosen.

"Fuck you."

* * *

Two weeks later, a special request ordered the transfer of Private Roni Uliel to the Bahad 1 officers' training academy. Back home, his father beamed with pride and hugged him for a full two minutes. Within a few hours, the whole of Sedera knew about Roni's new posting. Most of the young men of Sedera were drafted into dead-end military positions—kitchen work, truck drivers, perimeter guards. As the only Paratrooper Brigade officer to ever come out of the southern township, Roni became an instant local hero.

At the academy, the days rushed by in a blur—his studies exciting and challenging, his heart bursting with joy at becoming an officer. But the nights...the nightmares made him dread sleep.

He would see soldiers shooting into an olive grove, Secret Service men pointing handguns at his face. He would see his commanding officer, Roy, spattered in cow blood.

But it is the girl who ends every dream. She is walking up to the Erez barrier, dressed in a flowing white dress. She stops, sees him, and smiles radiantly.

The next thing he knows, he is wide awake, his pulse beating loudly, sweat clinging to his neck and dampening his shirt.

The girl in white would never leave him; he knew that. The beauty and the violence would continue to haunt him for as long as he lived.

Epilogue

"Hello?"

"Hi. It's me."

"Good God! How are you? How are you calling?"

"I bought an Egyptian prepaid phone. I have about two minutes on it. I can't talk on my phone; it might be bugged."

Long pause.

"Are you okay? How did your people react to seeing you back in Gaza, just appearing like you did?"

"A lot of people are suspicious since I got back. The only reason they haven't come after me is because I was under the Lion's responsibility. He's a big celebrity here in Gaza, bigger now that he's a *shahid*. A martyr."

"How are you?"

"I'm studying. I've begun my first year at university. Engineering. But I called to ask about you. Are you safe?"

"Yes. Rosen managed to pull it off. We're all in the clear."

Hashim released a sigh of relief. "Praise Allah. I have been thinking of almost nothing else. I had to call you; I had to know what happened to you. And Rosen?"

"He quit his job with the Prime Minister, and he's started a new company. Crop dusting. You wouldn't recognize him. All he wants to do is fly."

"That's crazy."

"I know. I wish you could come and see him in the air. He's nuts."

"There is nothing I would want more than to thank both of you face to face."

"I wish we could meet again. I wonder if it can ever happen?"

There was no answer. The two minutes ended with a soft click. Roni was left listening to a faint digital crackle.

Yaron Levite is a former actor, director and business entrepreneur. The Mohandas is his first foray into writing fiction, and although the book is purely fiction, the characters, places and events are all faithfully reproduced from his experience as a first Sergeant in the Israeli Army, and current fly-on-the-wall status as script writer and artistic director for large scale national ceremonies and televised events.

Yaron can be contacted at office@levite.co.il